Winter on the P Bar J Ranch

Also by Patrick H. Boles:

Fiction:

Summer on the P Bar J Ranch (2012)

Non-fiction:

Gone to Fetch a Bucket of Water: My Mother's Story (2014)

The Trails of John Lovelace: Roaming His Burro Creek Country (2014)

Rangelands, Ranches, and Ranchers: Volume One (draft)

Additional copies of this book, as well as others by Patrick H. Boles are available for purchase at Amazon.com or they may be ordered through local booksellers/bookstores.

Winter on the P Bar J Ranch

By

Patrick H. Boles

This book is a work of fiction. Any references to real people, historical events, or actual locations are made fictitiously. The characters, locales, incidents, etc. are either the products of the author's imagination or are used fictitiously, and any resemblance to actual events, persons, or locations is completely coincidental.

Winter on the P Bar J Ranch
Copyright © 2013 by Patrick H. Boles
Revised edition July 2016

Fiction: Adult general fiction, Southwestern U.S., Arizona, cattle ranching, 1950s ranch life, Route 66, cowboy lore

All Rights Reserved. No part of this book may be reproduced, stored in a retrieval system, or transmitted in any form by any means including: mechanical, electronic, photocopying, recording, or other, without the written prior permission of the publisher, except by a reviewer who may quote brief passages for a review to be published in a newspaper, journal, or magazine.

ISBN-13: 978-1478160557

ISBN-10: 1478160551

Dedication

In memory of my brother Jimmie K. Boles
1945-2003

Acknowledgements

In order to reach the final stage this book has gone through a number of drafts and revisions that were reviewed and commented on by a number of people. The final version of this book was edited by Esty H. Geissmann. My reviewers and editor were helpful in finding typos that I had overlooked, grammatical errors, and providing feedback on the story, its setting, etc. However, the author is responsible for any errors that survived the review process to find their way into the published work.

Table of Contents

Chapter	Title	Page
1	Cold December Days	9
2	Out Chopping Ice	30
3	Christmas Trees and Sledding	40
4	Riding the Pipeline	51
5	Road Trip	63
6	The Horse Wreck	79
7	Pushing Cattle	91
8	New Ranch Hand	113
9	Parker and the Owsleys	121
10	The Turkey Delivery	129
11	Christmas Morning!	136
12	The Big Snow	147
13	Pasturage Cattle	166
14	Shootout on Broken Wheel Mesa	188
15	A Night on the Mesa	212
16	The Buzzards Return	226

Chapter 1
Cold December Days

Summer or winter, hell, it really didn't affect the time I got up in the mornings. My schedule didn't vary much with the seasons. Sure there were some times in the hottest part of the summer when I was going to be on horseback all day that I might get up an hour or two earlier in order to get a good start on the day's work before the sun got too brutal. But that was about the extent of it.

On a southwestern cattle ranch there was always more than enough work to fill long days, so I sure as hell couldn't afford the luxury of sleeping in ... even in the winter. There was work that needed doing. So as usual on this December day I awoke when the alarm clock sounded at 5:00 a.m.

Reaching over to the night stand to turn it off I muttered "Ahhh, hell. The damn morning sure got here soon enough." As usual I made sure I made my early morning complaints low enough so I wouldn't wake my wife even though on this particular morning she wasn't home. She had left a few days earlier to visit relatives.

My thinking was that I might have to get up early but I sure didn't have to like it. Back when I was young and had to get up early for school or chores and complained about how hard it was I would be told by my parents and grandparents how eventually I would get used to it and just get up at that time out of habit. And as a matter of fact I knew some city folks who once they retired would tell me how they still woke up automatically at the time they used to have to get up for work. But I am here to tell you that it sure as hell hadn't happened to me. Not yet anyway. I couldn't help but wonder if my internal clock was broken, or at least running a little slow.

Speaking of clocks, sort of, I hadn't ever gotten a fancy alarm clock or clock radio with a snooze button because I figured that would just be prolonging the agony. I could see myself waking up several times through a series of nine-minute snoozes. No ... better to just wake up once per morning and get it over with I told myself.

So I had kept my old wind up Westclox Big Ben that my wife said was loud enough to wake the chickens down at their coop. The luminous dial of the clock made it easier to find it when I reached out for it in the dark. I always shut it off first thing before turning on a light.

Searching blind for the switch on my bedside lamp I thought that a man shouldn't have to be getting up when it was still dark outside. Just getting out of a nice warm bed on a cold winter morning takes a lot of will-power. I knew my bedroom would be cold since we always turned the heat off at night rather than just turning it down. I had always preferred sleeping in a cold room rather than an overheated one where a person couldn't even enjoy snuggling down under a couple of heavy quilts. That was one of the few pleasures that I found in winters ... except, of course, when it came time to get out from under those same warm quilts.

After turning the alarm off and the light on I spent a few minutes just lying there under the warm covers thinking about getting dressed on this cold winter morning and how bone-chilling the heavy canvas-like material of my old Brush Popper shirt was going to feel when I first put it on. But I knew the momentary discomfort was sort of off-set by how warm the shirt would feel after I had had it on a while and how good the heavy material was at cutting a cold wind or turning the thorns of brush. It was old and patched in a few places and the cuffs were frayed but I liked that brand ... once I got them on and the canvas warmed up. Of course some of the Brush Poppers had colors a little gaudier than I liked, but during the winter I usually had a coat or jacket, or two, over them anyway.

That's when the especially bright-colored shirts would get worn.

It seemed that every winter it was taking me just a little longer to leave the bed in the mornings, but that morning like all the others I finally managed to do it. I was thinking that maybe I should look for a clock radio the next time I had to go into town. It wouldn't hurt to try a snooze button I guess. But I knew when I did get to town a clock radio would be the last thing that I would be thinking of buying.

I had had a pretty good night's rest but I still hadn't wanted to get up. I hadn't had any dreams that I remembered, unlike one morning a week or so earlier when I had actually been happy, or I guess relieved might be a better word, to hear the alarm clock clanging away. There had been a number of things on my mind when I had gone to bed the previous night. I had managed to finally fall asleep but it wasn't exactly a restful night.

The newer windmill towers on the ranch had hinged bases. When we needed to work on the motors instead of climbing up on the tower with all of the necessary tools and trying to fix it while also trying our best not to fall off we would simply unbolt one side of the base and with a winch mounted on a boom on the back of an old flatbed International truck we would lay it down on the ground. Yeah, it was still a hell of lot of work but it was at least safer than the old way. It seemed that the periods between having to work on the windmill motors were getting shorter all the time. Old-timers will tell you that's because everything is made cheaper nowadays.

But that particular night as soon as I got to sleep I started dreaming that a couple of my cowboys and I were working on an old Dempster windmill motor and it was turning out to be a real bitch. We would lower the tower, make the repairs, set it back upright, and try it out. The water would flow for a minute of two and then it would break down again. We would then go through the whole damn blasted process again. Before I was awakened by the alarm I figured we must have raised and lowered that goddamn windmill's tower five or six times. In the dream I was even getting busted up knuckles working on the motor. Not only did I have to get up early on a cold morning but I had to spend the night working on a windmill! Why couldn't I have a dream that time of year that it was a childhood summer day spent bike riding with Lenny, or horseback riding with Lynda?

Well, enough of that blasted dream ... now back to the present morning. As fast as possible I slipped on my cold shirt and pulled on my equally cold blue jeans and then headed into the kitchen to fix a quick breakfast before getting going on the day's work that I had planned ... I was going out looking for a lost, or perhaps missing or stolen, bull. After getting the coffee started I went back to the bedroom and grabbed a fresh pair of socks and my insulated work boots.

It was getting on toward the middle of December and most of the days were windy and cold. I was wondering where another summer and fall had gone as I looked out the kitchen window at the leafless, swaying cottonwood branches when I placed the dirty breakfast dishes in the sink. Since I wasn't looking forward to going outside in the cold I had taken my sweet time with breakfast, even having an extra bowl of cereal while I finished the pot of coffee. But I knew that I could only put it off for so long.

There wasn't even anything worth reading on the back of cereal boxes anymore. That would have killed a few more minutes in the warm kitchen.

Although it seemed like summer and even fall went by faster every year, the winters always seemed to last long enough. I was already tired of it this year and really, according to the calendar, it hadn't even officially started yet. Damn! Spring couldn't arrive fast enough to suit me.

Folks talk about dog years being seven times longer than people years. I always thought that comparison would be about right for a cold winter day versus a sunny summer day. Especially when I was a kid, and even now I still much preferred summer to the other seasons. Spring and fall were mostly tolerable, but I could get along fine without winter weather at all. Of course I knew that folks in some other parts of the country had to deal with a lot harder winters than we had to put up with in northern Arizona.

Going out the door I was thinking that at least there wasn't much snow on the ground to have to walk or drive through. There were just a few patches left in shaded areas from the last storm. Good. At least I wouldn't be needing to bother with my overshoes.

As I started out from the headquarters in the early morning, after scraping ice from the pickup's windshield, I was figuring that old outlaw bull had to be out in the big pasture in the northeast corner of the ranch somewhere. My cowboys hadn't been able to move it the past fall when the cows were moved off that pasture. Since then the bull hadn't been earning its keep. No one had even seen it for a while.

Now I just had to figure out exactly where the damn thing had gotten off to among all the draws and junipers. Evidently that old bull knew all the tricks.

Bulls that had been on a particular ranch for a long time like that one usually knew all of the good hiding places to hole up so as not to be bothered by cowboys that wanted to move them someplace they didn't particularly care about going. The bull had most likely found a nice secluded draw with enough trees to cut the wind and to keep him hidden.

Since I was in my truck I wasn't expecting to actually see the bull in the flesh that day, but thought that at least I could figure out where he had been watering.

With the cold wind blowing it hadn't taken much to talk myself into doing my searching for the bull from my pickup that morning rather than horseback. I had always hated having to be out in a cold wind for any length of time, and I figured that I would probably have just as much luck doing my searching with the truck as on horseback since I would be able to cover a larger area. However, with the truck I wouldn't be able to check the remote draws and other rough country, but that was okay since mostly I just needed to stop and look around at the corrals and water lots to see if there were any fresh signs of the bull. For that the truck and its nice warm cab would do just fine.

Since the dirt tanks at the water lots required regular cleaning with dozers that had to be trucked in, there were established roads to all of them. Several of the water lots at the tanks had loading chutes for shipping cattle, which also made good roads that would accommodate large trucks a necessity. So checking waters with a pickup was a far more efficient use of time than doing it from horseback.

My plan was that once I found out where the bull was watering I would shut the gates to that water lot and set the triggers. Then later when he used a trigger to enter the water lot he would find himself trapped.

So once the gate was shut and the triggers set it would just be a matter of checking the water lot a few times a day until he showed up. Then I would either have a couple of the hired hands on horseback push him, or just bring a truck and trailer out here and get him loaded up and take him over to the pasture where the cows were waiting for him. The truck and trailer might be the easiest on the cowboys and their horses depending on how agreeable the bull was to being pushed, or herded, across the ranch to that other pasture.

Back a few years ago on a neighboring ranch an old bull had turned on a mounted cowboy who was pushing him and rammed the side of his horse. He managed to knock the horse down and the cowboy ended up with a broken leg and stove-up ribs.

I didn't want to just shut the water lot gates on all of the stock tanks in the pasture, even though the cows had been moved out of it, since that would prevent some of the wildlife that depended on the waters from getting to them. Deer, pronghorn antelope, javelina, and the recently arrived elk wouldn't last long in this country without the waters that ranchers had put in for their livestock. Of course a closed gate wouldn't deter the elk.

Even if the gates were wide open the elk would still be likely to flatten a fence going and coming from watering. Whenever I saw the damage elk continually caused to my fences I thought about how the damn things hadn't even been in this country back when I was a kid.

During my search for any sign of the bull I made notes on the small pad that I always carried in a shirt pocket on a couple water lots where elk had knocked down sections of fence. It seemed to me that elk always hit the fences along the south side of the water lots.

I would need to send a cowboy or two out to make repairs. I sure didn't need more maintenance costs but with elk present it was one of the constants that I had to deal with nowadays. And my long experience with the sorry ass game department told me that it was only going to get worse.

At one of the water lots I noticed that a creep feeder had been badly mangled by elk trying to get to the feed that had been in it. A creep feeder is a little fenced off area about ten feet by ten feet for feeding calves. They don't have a gate, and instead there is a small opening through which calves can "creep" or crawl inside in order to reach the feed that is placed within it. This allows the calves to eat the feed without having to try and compete with adult cows for it.

Looking at the damaged feeder I mumbled a "damn it' directed at the elk along with the agency that was supposed to manage them and pulled out my pad and scribbled out another note to myself. Something else that would need to be repaired and more time and money chalked up to the elk.

Elk are large enough to go pretty much where they want to without regard to fences whether they are around a water lot, a pasture, or along a ranch boundary. It had become pretty much part of the routine to check all fences more often to see where the elk had flattened or broken them.

If a pasture fence had been knocked down then cattle had probably moved into the adjacent pasture so then we had to spend time and move them back to where they belonged. The same work was required when a boundary fence was down and cattle got off their home range. The presence of the elk and the damage they caused really added to the labor and materials costs of operating a cattle ranch in northern Arizona.

With the explosion in the elk populations some ranchers I knew had just given up and had sold out to sub-dividers. They found that the elk were preventing them from managing their ranches, as well as breaking them on maintenance costs. Some ranchers weren't even able to count on a rested pasture being available for their cattle when it was needed. The elk, with their movements not restricted by fences would go into the rested pastures and leave them looking mowed off by the time the ranch's pasture rotation schedule called for moving cattle into them.

The presence and artificially high numbers of elk had also removed the ranch management practice of holding the forage in a particular pasture in reserve for drought as an option for cattle ranchers in northern Arizona. The elk would have mowed the grass down long before the cattle ever reached it in times of need during drought conditions. Then the rancher would be forced to buy supplemental feed to carry the cattle through a period of drought. Of course, the elk would also consume any of the supplemental feed that they could get to.

What I found at the fourth water lot that I checked that morning gave me a nagging feeling in my gut that the bull had been rustled. I saw tire tracks going up to the loading chute and fresh cowpies and hoof prints from the bull in the corral. The corral wasn't very far from the north boundary, so it wouldn't have been too difficult to get a truck in, load up the bull and be gone without anyone seeing anything.

I figured that the rustlers had also seen where the bull was watering and had set the triggers in that water lot just like I had planned to do. Then they had kept close watch and as soon as the bull was trapped they moved a truck in and hauled him off.

After the discovery of the tire tracks and the other signs I wasn't really expecting any longer to find the bull, but at the very least I had to make a good search before contacting the sheriff's office. It would be the first thing the doofus deputy would ask me. So I kept searching just to make sure the bull was gone before heading back into the headquarters and making a call.

We had had several relatives visit us for Thanksgiving a few weeks earlier. My wife had cooked a couple turkeys along with a ham for those who preferred it to yard bird and we had ended up with a lot of leftovers that had gone into the freezer.

When I was getting ready to leave the house that morning, knowing that the search for the bull could take a while, I had grabbed a leftover turkey leg out of the fridge and wrapped it in aluminum foil. Before I wrapped it I had sprinkled a little extra garlic on it to add to what had been applied when it was cooked. I had moved it from the freezer to the fridge the night before so it would have a chance to thaw out. This morning as I started out from the headquarters I had stuck it on the floorboard of the truck directly below the heater vent. The heater was on full blast and before long the cab was filled with the smell of that roasted turkey seasoned with garlic. I sure do love that smell.

Bumping along the rocky two-tracker ranch road in low gear, enjoying the smell of the warmed up turkey leg, I continued to scan the adjacent range for the missing bull. I had the radio on and it was tuned to a station playing Christmas music. There was a news story about the hot toy that parents were buying for their kids that Christmas and how the supply hadn't kept up with the demand. The toy was a talking doll of some sort based on a character from a kid's television program. As I slowly chugged along a rutted ranch road in first gear I listened to the announcer talk about how parents were out frantically searching for stores that still had the doll in stock. That and the smell of the turkey got me thinking about a search I had made one year. I was looking for just the right Christmas present for Lynda in 1952.

***

It would be my first Christmas on the P Bar J Ranch. My twelfth birthday had come and gone that November as had a lot of the time I had been able to devote to riding Bucky, my prized Schwinn Black Phantom bicycle, reading the latest Roy Rogers novel or comic book, and just goofing off with my best friend Lenny. My parents, yes, parents, had told me that I would be expected to help out more on the ranch since I was growing up and could handle more responsibilities. They had been back together since the end of summer. So no longer was it just Mom or just Dad, but parents!

The Howards' twins, Lenny and Lynda, had also turned twelve since the summer. Lenny's parents had given him the same news about having to take on more responsibilities on the ranch. In addition to the chores she was already doing, Lynda was helping her mother more with the housework. At her request, or rather insistence, her parents promised Lynda that she would also be able to do some of the cowboy work from horseback like Lenny and me. She was definitely a cowgirl at heart.

Unlike me, Lynda actually liked horses. Every time I rode one I couldn't help thinking about the time I had been bucked off a ranch horse down by Tucson. I had gotten a concussion and a couple of broken bones and as a result missed out on being able to play much that summer while I was mending.

Although I had crashed my Black Phantom late last summer while showing off for Lynda, I hadn't gotten any broken bones. Instead I ended up with just a few abrasions, bruised ribs, and a cut over one eye that had required several stitches. Bucky hadn't been so lucky. I'd had to replace some broken parts on the front springer fork and there were dents and scrapes here and there on my bike. Looking at my prized bike after the accident I felt worst for it than I did for the injuries that I had received.

Lynda had taken the loss of her favorite ranch horse, Smokey, last summer pretty hard. The horse had been shot while it was being used on a posse that was chasing down members of the Owsley gang. To help her get over the loss, Lynda's parents had given her a new horse, a paint mare, for her birthday. She had named her Trixie after the main character in a series of books she enjoyed reading.

At the end of the summer Mom had intended to try and get hired on as a schoolteacher in Seligman, Peach Springs, or Valentine. However, about the time she had gotten all settled in at the P Bar J Ranch and had started making the rounds of the schools she realized that she was expecting. There had been a side effect to when Mom and Dad had gotten back together in August.

So Mom had to put her teaching career, and the paychecks that went along with it, on hold for a while. Since at the time Mom and Dad had made the agreement with the Howards to lease the P Bar J, with an option to eventually buy it, they had figured on Mom's income from an outside teaching job, money was going to be tight for a while. For now Mom was helping Mrs. Howard home school us.

My mother had dark brown shoulder-length hair that she usually wore in a ponytail. She was shorter than Dad, but taller than the average woman. Mrs. Howard, Abby, was a pretty woman with long reddish brown hair and I figure that she was probably in her mid-thirties at the time. She was a few years older than my mom. While working in her house Abby normally wore a faded red apron that, I seem to remember, had once belonged to one of her grandmothers. I think I had heard that from Lynda.

I only knew that Abby was slightly older than my Mom because I had overheard them talking about how their fortieth birthdays weren't all that far off. Mom had joked that Abby would get there first. They were both saying how they had started noticing a few gray hairs here and there. Of course no one could have guessed it at the time, but Abby Howard would never see her fortieth birthday.

Even with the financial pinch it was causing Mom and Dad, they were both happy about the prospect of another child. They had even picked out names for the new baby. If it was a girl they were going to name her Emma Jean after Mom's mother. A boy would be named John Harold after both of the grandfathers.

Dad had celebrated his first anniversary on the P Bar J a few weeks earlier in November. The Howards had surprised him by presenting him with a new Remington .30-06 hunting rifle. They had also invited us over to have a fancy dinner to mark the occasion.

As I remember during the dinner the adults at the table had been discussing the results of the recent presidential election. The Howards and my parents were all happy that Eisenhower had won instead of the "stinking lawyer" as Dad referred to Stevenson and others of his kind. Dad was a big fan of Ike primarily due to his service in World War II. He respected the job that the old general had done.

My dad looked and dressed like a working cowboy. It was a look that I would emulate in the coming years. He stood about six feet tall and had a lanky build. Most of his Levi's had the usual holes from getting snagged by barbed wire or burned from sparks from a welder while repairing ranch equipment. He would usually keep a pair or two of nice jeans for times when he would be going to town or visiting friends and family. A well-worn brown leather belt with DEAN stenciled on the back and a silver buckle he had won roping at a high school rodeo held up his Levis. Sometimes during hot weather he would have a bandana around his neck to soak up sweat and to protect him from the sun. At other times he would have a bandana sticking out of a back pocket of his jeans.

The bandana was a handy tool for a cowboy. It protected his neck from the sun, was used to wipe sweat from his brow, used to clean his hands after doing an unexpected repair job on a windmill motor, or to dry his face and hands after freshening up at a water trough while taking a break out on the range. They were also handy should a tourniquet be needed. A cowboy did a lot of things that could go wrong and result in bleeding.

His scuffed-up brown cowboy boots had high heels and pointed toes for the days spent on horseback. If he wasn't planning on doing any riding he would wear lace-up work boots since they were more comfortable for walking.

Dad's hat that he wore year around was a battered and dusty black Stetson with a flat brim that drooped down in the front and back. He preferred that style of brim over the hats with rolled-up edges that most other cowboys wore, since the low, flattened hat brim was a lot better at protecting him from the sun and for shedding rain.

Normally Dad was clean-shaven however he would occasionally grow a mustache. But Mom didn't like them so presently he was clean-shaven. Dad and I shared blond hair and blue eyes. He had served in World War II and had lost the tip of his ring finger on his left hand in combat.

Over the past few months Lenny and I had had to take on more of the day-to-day type ranch chores in order to free up the hired hands, Jay Kirby and Clay Jarrett, for the harder jobs. Clay's full first name was Clayton, but he preferred going by the shortened version.

Dad had recently told me that once Lenny and I had grown a little more and had acquired the necessary experience handling cowboy tasks, he was going to expect us to take the place of the two full-time hands. He figured that Jay would be retiring after a few more years, but was counting on him especially to make good cowboys out of Lenny and me before then. Dad expected Clay to drift on to another ranch at some point since cowboys, as a rule, seemed to like to move around from place to place. That wandering habit led to cowboys often times being referred to as "fiddle-footed."

A move for Clay in the future would be likely if he got an offer from another ranch for more pay and perhaps a foreman's job. Clay had told Dad that his goal was to run a ranch someday. Since Clay was paying child support to an ex-wife in Cheyenne, Dad understood that if an opportunity to make more money presented itself, his cowboy would take it and there would be no hard feelings. He had been in that position himself.

Clay had been hired from a ranch in Wyoming at the end of last summer to replace Michael T who had died in an accident during a roundup on the R_X Ranch which bordered the P Bar J to the east. Clay was in his mid-forties and walked with a limp that I learned was from injuries he had received as a bull rider while following the rodeo circuits when he was younger. He had done his cowboying mostly on various Wyoming ranches. When he had first came to the P Bar J he was clean-shaven except for a drooping mustache, but since the fall he had started growing a full beard. He referred to it as his winter pelt.

There was a pretty nasty-looking scar around the base of the thumb on Clay's right hand. The digit had almost been torn off when a half-wild horse he had been in the process of tying to a hitching post chose the wrong moment to jerk back on the rope. The thumb and other parts of his body injured during his rodeo career and as a working cowboy had developed arthritis and Clay had accepted the Arizona job thinking the warmer weather would ease the pain a little. I noticed that he would usually be limping more on cold winter mornings.

I knew boys on other ranches that had taken on cowboy duties a lot earlier than at age twelve. Dad had wanted me to enjoy being a kid for as long as possible. He told me about how a friend of his had put his boy on a horse at ten doing cowboy work and a year later had expected him to be riding as much as one of the hired hands.

Between our home schooling, the regular chores, and helping Dad and his cowboys, there wasn't a whole lot of time for playing. However, with Christmas a little more than three weeks away, Mom and Mrs. Howard had let us have some time off from our schoolwork like the kids in town. Actually we got a little extra compared to the city kids since we had gotten ahead in the lesson plans. At the same time as our schooling break our mothers were getting a little time off from teaching that they could spend on planning for Christmas and other things that required their attention.

With schoolwork out of the way all I had to do besides the ranch work was to take care of getting presents for my family and friends. Both sets of grandparents had given me fairly generous amounts of cash for my birthday, plus I had gotten paid for some work that Lenny and I had done for Doc Thorpe over on the R_X Ranch the past fall. I had saved most of the money, figuring that I would need it for

Christmas presents. Especially since gift buying this year was going to include something new and very different. In addition to getting Mom and Dad presents I was also going to buy a gift for a girl.

I had decided that Lynda was going to get something special from me. That was if I could find the right present and afford to buy it. At the time I was stumped on what to get her. I knew that adults sometimes found Christmas a stressful time, but this was the first year that it was so for me. Then there were also Lenny and Mick. I thought that if I gave Lynda a present I should also get something for her brothers.

I was still pretty much trying to hide my growing liking of Lynda and how much I enjoyed getting to spend time with her. Since our horseback ride to Heckler Tank the previous summer we had taken a few more horseback rides together. The frequency of the horseback rides had increased since she'd got Trixie. I had even gotten her to go on a couple bike rides with me.

On the first bike ride we took together after I had gotten Bucky repaired Lynda had jokingly asked me, "Jeff, you aren't going to crash again, are you?" My answer was a short, "I sure hope not."

I wondered then if Lynda realized that the reason I had been going so fast on that downhill course that Lenny and I had set up at an old borrow pit was that I was showing off for her. I decided that I would try and control that urge in the future, but at the same time figured that it would probably be impossible to actually do so.

Bucky had been a 1951 Christmas present from my Grandpa Harold. I had given the bike the name Bucky because of the big spring on the front fork. Of course after the big wreck and subsequent repairs that were needed, parts of the springer fork were no longer original. While I was replacing the broken parts on the fork assembly I had also removed some of the unnecessary accessories on the bike to make it lighter and a little easier pedaling out on the ranch roads. I had removed both of the heavy chrome fenders, the headlight and taillight, and the tank with the built-in horn. The tank and the front fender had gotten dented in the crash. The lens of the headlight had also been broken. The parts were all safely stored in a box on a shelf in the barn. Year later I would be really happy that I hadn't just thrown them away.

This particular morning Mom and Dad had left early to drive into Seligman to pick up a few things that Mom needed. I waited next to my house until I saw Lynda and her little brother Mick start down to the chicken coop, barn, and corral from the main house to do their morning chores. I then started down that way myself ... by sheer coincidence, or so I hoped she would believe was the case anyway.

My blond hair that I had gotten from my Dad, rather than my mother's dark brown hair, was a little longer than it would have been during the school year when we lived in Winslow. My mom usually kept my hair cropped fairly close when I was in school. However, she did let me grow it out during the summers. Since I was being home schooled my mother didn't mind me going a little longer between haircuts. She probably felt having my hair covering my ears and neck a little would provide my head with a little extra shade from the sun while I was outside playing or doing chores.

My summer straw hat had been replaced by a black felt cowboy hat like Dad's. I had a canvas work coat on over a long-sleeve plaid shirt. My blue jeans were rolled up at the cuffs and of course they had a few patches. Instead of the high-topped canvas tennis shoes I wore in the summers I had on a pair of lace-up work boots that hadn't seen any polish for a while. I seem to remember that they had been black at one time.

I noticed that the puddles in the low places on the roads between the houses and barn were covered with a thick layer of ice. The night had been clear and it had gotten down well below freezing. I knew that Lenny and I would have a chore chopping ice that morning.

Lynda saw me and as I walked up she waved and said, "Mornin', Jeff." She gave me a big smile right back. Suddenly it didn't seem as cold.

"Morning, Lynda" I responded and then quickly added, "Hey, Mick. How are you doing?" He just gave me a little grunt in return and continued on his way ahead of us. I fell in beside Lynda and we talked as we were walking on down to the barn.

Lynda's hair was even longer than it had been when I had first met her at the beginning of the previous summer when I had arrived on the P Bar J. Her hair was reddish brown like her mother's and she usually kept it pulled back in a ponytail. The ponytail showed under the red knit hat she was wearing. Her coat had a fur collar which was turned up. For chores Lynda favored wearing bib-styled overalls.

Thinking that maybe I could get some clues from Lynda as to what she would like for Christmas I volunteered to help her and her little brother gather eggs. But I still hadn't decided exactly how to go about it. This was new territory for me. I even found myself stuttering once in a while when I couldn't come up with something clever to say when she was around.

I mentioned to Lynda that after a while Lenny and I would be heading out on horseback to check stock tanks and troughs for ice and to make sure the floats in the troughs were working. Normally we would already have been saddled up and on our way out but Lenny had gotten into trouble with his BB rifle again and was getting another lecture from his mother. I figured that it would be quite a while before that Red Ryder gun saw the light of day again.

It seemed to spend most of its time put away in his parents' bedroom closet.

Down at the barn I had a few things I needed to do before helping Lynda and Mick gather eggs. First I went into the tack room and carried outside the saddles and blankets that Lenny and I would be using that day. Since it was cold that morning there was a light coating of frost on the ground but the sun was up enough to start feeling warm. The frost would be gone before long.

I draped the blankets over the top of the corral fence where the sun would soon be on them and tipped the saddles up on their ends so the sun would be hitting their undersides. This was so the blankets and saddles would be warmed up a little before Lenny and I saddled the horses.

I had learned that horses had a tendency to buck when a cowboy immediately mounts up after cold blankets and saddles are put on them. I had done that once and as soon as I swung up into the saddle the horse started to crow hop before my right foot had reached the stirrup. I don't think I even stopped moving when I felt that, instead I instantly reversed my motion and jumped back down. Crow hops are usually a warm up act for full-fledged bucking and I wanted no part of it.

It makes the horses a lot more comfortable if the blankets and saddles are warm when they are first put on their backs. The blankets and saddles aren't the only things that need to be warmed up. The horses have less of a tendency to buck if they are warmed up, too on a cold morning. Knowing that, once I got my horse saddled during cold weather I would always lead him around a little with a halter to sort of get him warmed up. It was kind of like an adult having a cup or two of coffee and reading the paper before starting their workday.

Once the blankets and saddles were out in the sun, I grabbed an ax and broke up the ice in the troughs and then used my Roy Rogers pocketknife to cut the twine on a couple bales of hay. I kept a sharp edge on the knife's blades using the grinding wheel in the workshop. Dad had shown me how to properly sharpen knife blades along with the edges on axes using the grinding wheel, files, or whetstones. As a result it easily cut right through the heavy twine.

Then I tossed flakes of the hay on the ground out in the corrals for the horses. Lynda helped me and threw out a couple flakes. Grabbing the ax again I broke the ice on the surface of the drinker out in the corral so the horses could drink.

Earlier when I had told Lynda the plans Lenny and I had for the day she had said, "I sure do wish I was saddling up Trixie and riding out with you guys this morning, instead of having to help my Mom with the house work."

While trying not to sound overly enthusiastic I agreed that it would be nice to have her join us. I then told her, "Maybe you can go with us next time."

With the cold spell of the past few days it had become a regular job for us checking to make sure that the dirt tanks and drinkers had at least a small area free of ice where the cows could get a drink.

I felt that it was unfair that Lynda had to spend so much of her time doing housework and other chores in the house to help her Mom simply because she was a girl. Lynda was able to handle anything on the ranch that needed doing as well as Lenny and I. She was definitely better with horses than either of us. I hadn't seen her handle an ax to break up ice but I figured she could do that, too as well as Lenny and me.

Lynda and I only managed to talk a little, while we did the rest of the chores, and soon she and her little brother were headed back up to their house. They had also helped me with the chores that Lenny and I normally did since he was getting a lecture. I wanted to have the chores out of the way when he arrived so we could saddle up and get going without any delays. I wanted to get the ice-chopping over with.

As I watched Lynda and Mick walking toward their house they met Lenny who was on his way to the barn. He pretty much ignored them as he passed by them. I noticed that he was walking with his head down. I figured that wasn't a particularly good sign.

Chapter 2
Out Chopping Ice

Seeing Lenny coming I grabbed two halters down from their pegs and a bucket that I had already filled with oats, and walked out to the corrals. Using the oats for bait I quickly caught the two horses we would be riding. While the horses tended to shy away from someone on foot carrying halters or bridles, the bucket of oats made them come to me. After slipping the halters on them I led them up to the side of the barn closest to where I had earlier set the saddles in the sun and tied them to one of the rails of the corral.

Once the horses were tied I dumped the bucket of oats into a wooden feed trough that was attached to the middle rail of the corral. Both horses immediately stuck their muzzles into the trough and went to work on the oats. Knowing it was going to be a long, cold ride for them today and that they would be needing some extra energy I refilled the bucket from a large storage bin and added those oats to the feed trough.

I then started in brushing the back of the horse that I would be riding that day. That's what I was doing when Lenny finally walked up. I thought that he had certainly taken his time walking down from his house. He had probably kicked every rock along the way. I returned his nod and then looking over at the nearby workbench I said, "Hey, mornin', Lenny. There's another brush over there."

Lenny didn't say much while we brushed the horses and got them saddled. I could only guess how the lecture he had received from his mother had gone. Lenny had also inherited his mother's reddish brown hair and so had his little brother Mick. During the summer they had both had butch-style haircuts, but Lenny was now wearing his a little longer like me.

It was important to give the horses a good brushing before saddling them in order to remove any burs or anything else stuck in their hair that might irritate them once they had the combined weight of the saddle and rider pressing down on their backs. If a bur, sharp sticker, or anything similar wound up between the horse and the saddle blanket it could lead to a sore developing on the horse's back. It could also lead to a round of bucking. As far as I was concerned that was by far the greater potential problem. Once they were saddled we spent a few minutes leading the two horses around the corral to get them warmed up a little.

Soon we were headed up towards Dead Car Tank. While I had been waiting for Lynda earlier I had seen Jay and Clay saddle up and head out toward the west. They had taken the dogs, Skipper and Jenny, with them. Both of the dogs were border collies.

Jay Kirby was the older of Dad's two cowboys and the one he relied on the most. He wore a well-used dusty black cowboy hat winter and summer that covered his mostly gray hair. He would have been only in his late-fifties at the time, but he seemed older. When I had first met him I had thought he must have been well into his sixties or even seventies. Of course when you are a kid even fifty seems pretty ancient. Jay's faded blue jeans were held up with a brown belt that was trimmed with what had looked like it had once been white stitching and was cinched tight below his potbelly. Jay's belt was fastened by a silver buckle that had pieces of turquoise on both sides with a capital J in the middle. Like a lot of other Arizona cowboys he was originally from west Texas and had worked with cattle all of his life, except for a hitch in the army during World War I.

Shortly before the 1930s drought had hit the Southwest Jay had taken over his family's cattle ranch in Texas. The drought wiped out his herd and his finances. The bank ended up with the ranch. Since the majority of the other ranchers and farmers were also ruined by the drought he had lots of company. He had worked on a few ranches in New Mexico before drifting on into Arizona in the late 1930s. Jay had been on the P Bar J when Dad was hired to run it and had been more than happy to show the new boss around. Dad had told me that the Howards had offered the ranch manager's job to Jay but he had declined it. He preferred to remain just a working cowboy without the worries of the top job.

Jay was clean shaven. After Clay had started growing a beard to protect his face in cold weather I had asked Jay one day while we were out riding if he ever thought about growing one. He grinned and said, "Well, a thick, bushy beard might feel good when the cold wind is blowing, but then again my lady friends in Seligman don't seem to take too kindly to them. So all things being equal I sort of believe my winters might be a tad colder overall if I grew one of them scratchy things." Being a kid there were a lot of Jay's stories that I didn't fully understand at the time they were told to me. It was often years later when I would recall one and break out in a grin. That was one of them.

Lenny and I were going to be riding over to the northeast part of the ranch. Dead Car Tank would be our first stop. It had a leaky bottom and didn't hold water very well. At the time it was down to a shallow pool and Dad figured the small surface area would be completely frozen over. The high berm around the tank kept the bottom in the shade most of the time during the winter so the ice didn't have a chance to melt during the day even when it was sunny. I had an ax shoved in a rifle scabbard on my saddle. Hardly anyone on the ranch ever carried a rifle in the scabbards but they were pretty handy for carrying long-handled tools. It took us the better part of an hour to get to that first tank.

The ground on the flats was mostly free of snow with only patches from the last storm a week earlier still remaining on the north facing slopes on the hills and shaded areas. More of the snow remained up on the higher mountains off to the west.

A small bunch of cows were bedded down in the sun near Dead Car Tank just below the berm. The tall berm or dam served to block the cool breeze for the cows. I had learned that cows always seemed to know the most comfortable places to loiter in the different seasons. In the summer they shaded up in areas where there would be a breeze to help keep the flies away. In the winter they preferred more open, sunny areas that had some feature that protected them from the cold winds. In this case it was the berm, in other areas it could be a stand of trees, a hill, or the cut bank of a gully.

Sure enough the small pool at the bottom of the tank was completely frozen over. We rode up near the tank on the side opposite of the cows so as not to scare them off. We tied the reins of our horses to the limbs of a bushy juniper. Then we took turns chopping at the ice with the ax until we had an area of water opened up that was several feet long along the bank.

During one of my turns with the ax I had managed to slip and get my feet wet and they were feeling pretty cold by the time we finished our work at the tank and had mounted up. Once in our saddles we moved off a little ways to make sure the cattle would make use of our hole in the ice before it froze back over. Sure enough they had started heading for it before we had gotten very far.

Once we had seen that all of the cattle were taking advantage of our efforts I suggested to Lenny that we head back to the headquarters so I could get my feet warmed up and change into some dry socks and boots before we checked any more waters. Although Lenny hadn't gotten his boots wet he was more than ready to take a break from the cold. Riding back toward the headquarters we talked about how we hoped that when we were ready to head back out it would have warmed up a little more.

By the time we got back to my house and I had changed into dry socks and an old pair of boots, after letting my feet warm up by the cook stove in the kitchen, it was getting pretty close to being time for lunch. Mrs. Howard had seen us ride in and had sent Lynda over to have us come over and eat before we headed back out. She knew that my parents were still gone to town.

The boots that I had changed into were an old pair that was just a tad bit too small for me. My mom had made me save them for a spare when she had gotten me a newer pair in a slightly larger size. Walking over to the Howard's house for lunch they were pinching my toes and I hoped I didn't have to spend much time walking today. Just getting off the horse and chopping ice shouldn't hurt my feet too much. At least they would be warm and dry.

Mrs. Howard had lunch ready so it didn't take long before we had eaten and were heading back out on the horses. We had given them some more oats while we were warming up and having lunch so they were ready to go.

Lenny and I had both had seconds on the cherry pie that his mother had baked for dessert. Horses weren't the only ones who needed extra energy on a day like this I thought as I finished the second slice.

We hadn't gotten very far from the headquarters before Lenny, looking down at my boots said, "So, Jeff you think you can keep from falling into the water again? Maybe I ought to put a rope on you when you are chopping ice. Then I could just flip you over on your back and pull you out just like a cow that gets stuck in the mud."

I knew what he was talking about. I had watched Jay do that with a cow that had gotten stuck in the mud of a mostly dried up stock tank the previous summer. I guessed that Lenny had seen Jay or another cowboy do it too. However, I didn't appreciate the comparison.

Lightly touching the heels of my boots to the horse's flanks I started past Lenny and said, "I don't know. Think your Mom is going to find any more BB-shot birds in the yard?"

His response was something that I won't repeat here, but if his mother had heard him say it he probably would have gotten something a little more attention-getting than another lecture. But our comments back and forth were all in fun. There was no mean-spiritedness associated with them.

Cowboys liked to joke with their friends and Lenny and I had certainly picked up the habit. We were still ribbing each other when we got to another stock tank that wasn't very far from the north boundary gate. Looking north we could see the top of Indian Hill off in the distance above the thick canopy of junipers. Seeing the rocky peak got us to talking about the Owsley family whose old, abandoned homestead was located near the base of the small mountain.

The law had not wasted any time putting Garland Owsley, the surviving male member of the gang, on trial. He had been tried and convicted of murder and bank robbery in November and was at the time on death row. The articles in the newspapers during the trail sort of played up the fact that the money from the Kingman bank robbery hadn't been found. None of the gang had any significant amount of money on them when they had been killed or captured. Most everyone figured that they must have stashed it somewhere.

One newspaper article even gave directions on how to find the old Owsley homestead next to Indian Hill that the gang had used for a hideout. Dad was pretty mad when he saw that article. I heard him telling Mom that it would lead to more trespass problems for them with city people out trying to find the missing money.

Sure enough, soon after the article appeared Dad and his cowboys had to pull a couple of cars belonging to would-be treasure hunters out of mud holes on the main access road off Route 66. He had also come across some folks wandering around on the P Bar J Ranch looking for the Owsley place. They had missed the turnoff to the old homestead and had continued driving south, passed through the gate on our north boundary fence, and just kept on going. People that had most likely been driving around hoping to stumble upon the bank loot had also cut the north boundary fence a few times in the past month.

A few weeks earlier I had overheard Dad talking to Jay and Clay about the missing bank money and the treasure hunters it was drawing back into our country. Dad told them that in his opinion if the Owsleys had hidden any money from their robberies it most likely was burned up when someone had torched the old house and the out buildings at the Owsley homestead.

No one knew for sure who had done it, but Dad always figured that it was Deputy Parker who had lit them up. Parker had reason enough to wipe out all traces of that family in the area. He had lost a cousin, who was a state trooper, in the Owsleys' robbing and killing spree. No one knew at the time that there were still several more members of the Owsley family living in Oklahoma and they, too were wondering about the missing money. Although we didn't know it at the time, revenge was also on their minds.

It was late afternoon by the time we came riding back into the P Bar J's headquarters just before it started getting dark. That was another thing I didn't like about winters. It sure did get dark early. There never seemed to be enough daylight to get everything done.

Even with the lunch break, which had included the hot pie fresh from the oven, it had been a long, cold day in the saddle. Our hope that morning of a warmer afternoon hadn't panned out. A cold breeze out of the north had kicked up in the early afternoon that had made being out on horseback pretty miserable. Our ears felt frozen and our noses had been running all day.

Lenny and I unsaddled the horses, rubbed them down, and then turned them out into the corral next to the barn. We gave them each some more oats, plus we tossed out a few flakes of hay for them. I was happy to see Dad's pickup parked in front of our house. They had made it back from Seligman.

I sure hoped that Mom would have a hot supper ready. Being out in the cold always made me extra hungry. However, before heading up to the house I checked to make sure the trough in the corral was free of ice. Even as cold as it was I knew the horses would be wanting a good drink of water. Dad and Jay had taught me one of the main rules of a cowboy ... see to your horse before you see to yourself.

My feet were hurting from wearing the tight boots most of the day. I was limping a little walking up to our house from the barn. It sure did feel good to take them off and put on a pair of old tennis shoes.

During the ride that day and even while I was chopping ice and trading good-natured ribbing with Lenny I had been thinking about what I should get Lynda for Christmas. I hadn't had any luck coming up with anything yet. I had even thought about asking Lenny about what his sister might like for Christmas, but didn't want to give him any more ammunition for kidding me.

Mick had been talking recently about an advertisement for a toy called Mr. Potato Head that he had seen on television when he was staying in Flagstaff. He had been asking for one for Christmas. It didn't sound like anything Lenny or I would want to receive as a present.

Much later I learned that it had been the first kid's toy advertised on television and as a result it was the must-have toy for the Christmas of 1952. But I sure knew that I didn't have any interest in having one of them, and I didn't think that Lynda would really want one either. From what I had seen she wasn't really much interested in toys of any kind. But I did know that she liked to read, so books were a possibility I had to consider.

I would just need to figure out which one she wanted and make sure no one else was getting it for her. I was already thinking I would need to talk with Mrs. Howard when no one else was around. But then that would also require me letting her know that I was getting a gift for Lynda. Like I said earlier, that Christmas season of 1952 was extremely stressful for me.

After supper was over and I had helped clear the table and had dried the dishes for Mom, I went over to the Howards. Lenny and I would usually listen to westerns on the Howard's big floor-model radio in the evenings.

I knocked at the door that led into the kitchen and Mrs. Howard who was sitting at the table reading a magazine looked up and yelled "Come on in, Jeff." As I closed the door behind me I heard Gene Autry singing "Rudolph the Red-Nosed Reindeer." The sound was coming from Lenny's and Mick's bedroom. Mick had a copy of the record and had been playing it almost constantly over the past couple of weeks.

Lenny and I had both gotten tired of listening to the song. Mick also played the flip side once in a while. It was a song called "If it Doesn't Snow on Christmas."

I actually didn't think that prospect sounded too bad. Personally, I would rather it be nice and sunny on Christmas. I never cared much for snow unless there was enough to cause classes to be canceled when I was going to school in Winslow.

The previous Christmas had been spent in Winslow. I had received Bucky as a present and I was sure glad at the time that it hadn't been a white Christmas. Instead it had been sunny and by the afternoon had gotten up past 60° F. I had spent most of the day riding my new bike around town and showing it off to my friends. I couldn't have done that in the snow. Well, at that age and with a new bike to show off I might have but I wouldn't have enjoyed it as much.

Out on the ranch the chores still needed doing even after a big snow. In fact there was usually more to do, what with checking on the cattle and other livestock to make sure they were weathering the storm okay and had enough feed and water to see them through it. Waters had to be checked and ice chopped.

Yeah, thanks anyway Gene, but I could do without a white Christmas just fine.

Although the day had been clear I noticed that clouds had moved in after dark when I walked back to my house late that evening from the Howards'. If the clouds stayed around all night I knew it most likely wouldn't get as cold, and Lenny and I might be able to skip going out chopping ice on the livestock waters in the morning.

Remembering my cold, wet feet and the day spent on horseback in the wind I sure hoped the clouds would stick around. Chopping ice had quickly become one of my least favorite things to do.

Chapter 3
Christmas Trees and Sledding

The following morning I went outside before breakfast to check the big dish near the porch that was kept full of water for the dogs and cats. I was happy to see that it was ice free. Looking up at the sky, I could see there was still an almost complete cloud cover, but it didn't look like the clouds were carrying snow or even rain.

Actually, I could tell that the clouds were already starting to break up. They looked like they would probably burn off once the sun was up a ways.

Back inside our house I went into the kitchen where Mom had breakfast just about ready. Dad was sitting at the table with a cup of coffee going over the small notebook that he always kept in a shirt pocket to help him decide on what needed doing that day.

Dad looked up at me as I entered the kitchen and said, "Well, Jeff, it looks like you and Lenny won't have to go out and chop ice this morning. I think maybe our cold spell is over, at least for a while until the next one comes through."

I couldn't help smiling when I replied, "Yeah, Dad, I guess we won't have to. I checked the water dish by the porch and there's no ice." He had already noticed the lack of ice this morning too. I hoped the next cold spell took its time in reaching our area.

"I know that chopping ice is a tough job and that's why I gave it to my top hands," Dad said with a grin. I thought about saying "Gee, thanks!" but decided it would be best not to make a smart aleck remark. Instead I just gave Dad a grin back as I sat down at the table.

Mom put the platters of pancakes, scrambled eggs, and bacon on the table and said, "You boys go on ahead and dig in." She didn't have to say it twice.

As Dad and I were loading up our plates he asked me, "Since there's no need to check waters this morning I was wondering if you would want to take a little trip out to the hills to look for Christmas trees?"

"Sure," I quickly replied.

"Okay, before you head down to the barn to do your other chores, go on over to the Howards' and invite Lenny, Lynda, and Mick to go with us to get Christmas trees," Dad said. He told me that we would head out as soon as the chores down at the barn were all taken care of.

I hurried up and finished breakfast and then headed over to the Howards. Lynda, Lenny, and Mick had just finished their breakfasts when I arrived and were putting on coats and getting ready to head down to the barn. Lenny had also figured out already that we wouldn't need to ride out to check for ice on the waters that morning. When I told them what my dad had in mind for later after we finished the chores of course they all wanted to go.

Mrs. Howard said that it sounded like a good idea and that it would be a fun outing for us. Before we headed out the door she told us to be sure to get two trees for them so they would have an extra one for their place in Flagstaff. I told her I would let my dad know.

Then we all hurried down to the barn to do the chores. After the horses were fed, the stalls cleaned and fresh straw spread, the eggs gathered, and the troughs filled with fresh water we were ready to go. We were all moving pretty fast that morning, even Mick.

Although I was excited about the day ahead there was something that had been on my mind since Dad had first mentioned all of us going out to get Christmas trees together. Even with the temperature being above freezing it was still too cold for anyone to ride in the back all day so I knew we would be crowded together in the front seat of Dad's pickup. I couldn't help wondering how that would work out.

While this was sort of a rare morning off for Dad he was going to manage to squeeze in some work. He would be checking for signs of stray cattle, and any broken fences or gates in need of repair. He always carried some wire, a few fence posts, and the necessary tools in the bed of the truck for just such maintenance work. At times there would even be welding equipment rattling around back there.

I jumped in first and Lenny started to get in next when Lynda stopped him and said, "Lenny, why don't you sit next to the door? That way you can open and close the gates for Mr. Dean. I would, but some of those wire loops are stretched pretty tight." Lenny just nodded in agreement with his twin and stepped aside and let her get in next to me. Mick had to sit on Lenny's lap in order for all of us to fit.

With four of us sitting on the pickup's bench seat we were squeezed in close, but I sure wasn't complaining. It had worked out a lot better than I could have dreamed. Okay, maybe not dreamed. In a dream I think I would have had Lynda sitting on my lap. Of course the reality of that would have been pretty scary at twelve. But that didn't stop me from thinking about it.

Skipper and Jenny had seen everyone getting into the truck and they knew that meant we were going somewhere. They ran up to the truck yipping and barking just about the time Dad was letting out the clutch, which must have been their way of asking to come along. It worked because Dad rolled down his window and shouted "Load Up!" The two border collies jumped into the truck's bed over the closed tailgate.

After we had all gotten situated we headed back into the west side of the ranch. I had to keep my legs away from the floor shift so as not to interfere with Dad's shifting. On the rough ranch roads where speeds were slow he normally just used first and second gears.

Before heading out, Dad had tossed a couple handsaws in the bed of the pickup for us to use. I noticed he had picked up an ax in the tool shed and then apparently changed his mind and set it back down. Most likely he had decided that with four kids along, axes wouldn't be a good idea. He was probably right.

The clouds were breaking up by the time we left the headquarters and headed out on our Christmas tree hunt. It was going to turn into a sunny day by mid-morning.

At the gates Mick would hop out with Lenny. During those stops I couldn't help but notice that Lynda didn't scoot over during the periods when her brothers were outside and she had extra room on her right. Had Lynda made the suggestion to Lenny about the gates just so she could sit next to me?

During a few of the stops Dad had noticed a broken post or wire and had gotten out to make a quick repair on the gate or adjacent fence. At a few places he stopped the truck and got out to look at tracks ... from both livestock and wildlife. After one such stop when he got back into the truck he said, "Looks like a mountain lion came through here not long ago." He also saw bear tracks that day and pointed them out to us. At every stop the dogs would jump out of the bed and run around a little, sniff here and there, and then hop back in once we started moving again.

We were following a narrow two-tracker ranch road or jeep trail as they were sometimes labeled on maps, with junipers and other trees along the edges on both sides. The trees branches often overhung the roads. They served to scratch up the sides of the ranch trucks pretty regularly.

Skipper and Jenny had noticed the overhanging juniper branches and were making a game of grabbing onto them every time the opportunity arose. They were running back and forth across the truck's bed looking for the ends of branches that were close enough to get a good grip on with their teeth. Then they would usually tear off the ends of the branch, shake it a few times before dropping it onto the floor of the bed, and then start looking for the next one.

Dad was watching the dogs in the rearview mirrors and laughed and told us that sometimes, when the branches they grabbed didn't break off the dogs would be pulled almost out of the truck before letting go. The floor of the truck bed was covered with small twigs, branches, and juniper berries by the time we got to where we would be cutting our Christmas trees.

Unfortunately there weren't any ponderosa pines, spruces, or firs on the ranch, so we didn't have much of a choice in the type of conifer to choose for our Christmas trees. We were going out to an area in the mountains where there was a fairly large stand of pinyon pines. The only other kind of evergreens on the ranch were junipers and we had three different species of them. Even though we had an abundance of one-seed, Utah, and alligator junipers, no one thought they made a very good Christmas tree, unless there were no pines at all to choose from.

The one-seed junipers were bushy while Utah and alligators became trees, sometimes with trunks several feet thick. While they didn't get very tall some of the old ones, especially the alligators, were pretty impressive trees.

We continued past Catfish Tank back to the area where the pinyon pines were common. We were climbing in elevation and as a result there was an increasing amount of snow on the ground between the trees.

Dad parked the pickup near the base of a hillside that had a good stand of pinyons in a range of sizes from seedlings to large mature trees. All of us kids were raring to get on the hunt for Christmas trees. I think we all probably had the idea we were going to find the best tree before anyone else could get to it.

As we started to get out Dad said, "Jeff, you go ahead and pick out a nice tree for our house," and turning to Lenny, Lynda, and Mick continued, "Now the three of you be sure to pick out trees for the ranch house and your place in Flagstaff. Then I would appreciate it if all of you could pitch in and help look for a couple of nice trees for Jeff's grandparents." He ended with a reminder for us to be careful with the saws, although we all knew that their blades would be sharp.

Tools were carefully maintained on the ranch so they would do their intended jobs as efficiently as possible. It was a waste of a cowboy's time to expect him to do a job, such as trying to cut a new fence post from a juniper trunk or limb, with tools that weren't up to the task. The saws were kept sharp and we all knew to keep our fingers away from their blades. But to be fair to my dad it never hurt to remind kids.

One of the things Dad had said on the drive out was for us to not get really big trees. He said that trees just a foot or so taller than an adult man would be perfect. I quickly picked out a tree for our house and the Howards' kids did the same for both of theirs. After those three trees were placed in the back of the pickup we selected trees for my grandparents.

There was still a lot of snow on the mountains and after we had gotten all the Christmas trees cut and piled in the truck's bed, a snowball fight soon began. I was not sure who threw the first one, but Lynda was the closest to me when I felt the snowball smack against the back of my head. As I turned to see who the culprit was I could feel chunks of snow falling down my back inside my shirt and coat.

Before I had completed my turn I had reached down and scooped up a handful of snow and was packing it into a ball as I chose my target. Lynda was looking at me laughing, but I wasn't entirely sure if she was the thrower. Lenny, standing a little father back and off to Lynda's left a little was also laughing. I decided that I could hit Lenny with a snowball and wouldn't feel bad about it even if he wasn't the one who had thrown first. So Lenny was my first target.

He saw what I was going to do and just as I threw my snowball he bent over to grab a handful of snow. My snowball bopped him on the forehead. He yelled as the snowball hit him and spattered. I couldn't have planned it any better.

That was a pretty good lucky shot I thought as I reached with both hands into the snow for more ammo. At the same time I noticed Lynda reaching into the snow.

Up to that point Dad had been sitting on one of the trucks' front fenders watching us. But seeing that a war had started he hopped into the cab of the truck and rolled up his window. He told me later that it seemed too cold to him to risk getting snow down his shirt, so he had just removed himself from the battle.

His timing was good because just about the time that I heard the truck door slam several snowballs were flying back and forth. Even Mick was getting into it. I got Lenny good a few more times and threw a few snowballs at Lynda, but with a little less force. While I was being careful not to hurt her she didn't seem to be holding back. During the course of the snowball fight she landed a few on me that stung more than the ones Lenny hit me with.

Dad enjoyed watching us playing and allowed the snowball fight to go on for as long as we wanted, while he waited patiently in the safety of the truck's cab. However, soon we were all back in the truck, somewhat wet from the melting snow on and inside our clothes, and headed back to the headquarters. The truck's heater felt good. Since the bed was full of trees the dogs ran alongside as we made our way slowly back down the two-tracker to the headquarters. It was a fun outing and there had been no injuries from either the saws or the snowballs.

Mom was going to drop the trees off for the grandparents in Winslow the next day when she went to buy some supplies for Christmas dinner. She was also going to pick up presents from the grandparents so they would get put under our tree in time for me to be able to do a little shaking of the ones that were for me. Another reason Mom had for going to Winslow was to see some of her friends and exchange Christmas presents with them. She also needed to pick up a few boxes of Christmas decoration that she has left stored at her parents' house. Mom had an impressive collection of Santa figures that she would always put out during the Christmas season.

Down at the barn the morning after our Christmas tree hunt, Lynda asked me if I had ever gone ice-skating. I told her, "No, at least not with real skates anyway."

My friends and I had liked to go out on the Little Colorado River near Winslow in the winter and find an ice-covered pool along the channel (there usually wasn't a continuous flow of water) and play on the ice. We would run and slide across the frozen surface wearing our tennis shoes. But we never thought about it as actually skating. I didn't tell Lynda my feelings about the subject then, but I had always thought of actual ice skating as something more for girls than boys.

Lynda suggested that after our chores were finished that morning we could all hike up Heckler Creek to the tank and play on the ice. She had talked to her brothers earlier that morning and they liked the idea. As it turned out Lynda actually had a pair of skates to use. I guess I wasn't really surprised.

With the warm spell continuing this would be another day we wouldn't need to ride out to break ice at the waters. However, before giving Lynda a definite yes, I checked with Dad to make sure he didn't have anything that he needed Lenny and me for that day. Even though I was beginning to enjoy the cowboy work a little more I was happy when he told me to go have fun.

Mrs. Howard filled a thermos full of hot chocolate for us to take with us, along with some beef jerky, dried apples, and cookies. I got my Dad's rucksack to carry our snacks in. Lynda had tied the laces of her skates together and just draped them over her shoulder to carry them. The skates were white with pink laces. Again, I wasn't surprised.

Lenny suggested to me that we should take along a couple large pieces of cardboard. He told me that he had learned that cardboard made pretty good makeshift sleds during the winter days he had spent in Flagstaff. So we looked around and found two large cardboard boxes in the Howard's garage and broke them down and carried the flat pieces with us on the hike up to the tank.

With Mick along the going was a little slower than the times Lenny and I had hiked up the canyon and over the numerous boulders in the channel on our own. However, Lynda sure didn't slow us down any. If anything, she was usually out ahead of the rest of us.

We had a lot of fun once we reached Heckler Tank. It was completely frozen over and the surface was mostly free of snow. There weren't any cattle in that pasture at the time so the water being ice-covered wasn't a concern. Since the canyon was fairly narrow and deep the sun didn't hit the surface of the tank much in the winter so the ice got pretty thick. The tank stayed frozen over most of the winter months.

Lenny and I noticed that the canyon slopes adjacent to the tank had a good covering of snow. After doing some walking around up on the slopes we quickly decided on what looked like it would make a good downhill route for sledding with only a few alterations.

We then started in on the work of removing a few rocks and pieces of wood from dead, fallen junipers and then packed down the snow on a route down one of the slopes for the cardboard "sleds." We decided to use one piece of cardboard at a time and take turns, since it would be best if one of us was able to give a little push to the other. Plus, when that first piece got all torn up or wet we would still have the second one in reserve to use.

We carried the cardboard to the top of the slope, pulled up the leading edge and then one of us sat down on it while the other one gave a push to get it started down the hill. The cardboard worked like a toboggan. We would go flying down the slope and then out across the ice covered tank.

Lynda had to keep a wary eye out for us while she was skating since we would come tearing down the slope and across her skating rink pretty much out of control. Sometimes we would go all the way across and have to avoid a couple large boulders at the opposite edge of the tank. On a few especially fast descents we weren't entirely successful in missing the big rocks.

We quickly found out that it was close to impossible to steer a piece of cardboard. However, aside from rips in the cardboard even the crashes didn't cause much damage to us, other than some scratches on our hands and knees. When the first piece of cardboard started falling apart we switched to the other one and continued playing.

While Lenny and I were sledding and Lynda was skating Mick built a couple snowmen near the base of the hill. We even got Lynda to try the cardboard sled a few times and Lenny went down the slope a few times with his little brother. I was tempted to suggest that Lynda and I ride down the hill together but I chickened out.

It was a fun day and we all made it back to the headquarters without any major injuries and only the few minor ones. The sledding and the hiking to and from the tank had helped take my mind off trying to figure out what to get Lynda for Christmas, but I still had that problem ahead of me.

Soon after Mom had gotten back from the trip to deliver the Christmas trees and pick up presents, our tree was up, the presents from the grandparents were under it, and I was checking them out. I noticed that the box from my Grandfather Harold seemed real heavy. The box was about the size of a set of cap guns and holsters, but the weight was a lot more. That present had me completely puzzled. I would usually pick it up and shake it whenever I walked by our Christmas tree. There were even a few rattles in the box when I would shake it, which added to the mystery.

Chapter 4
Riding the Pipeline

The large pasture to the southeast of the P Bar J's headquarters was fairly flat country except for a few little rocky hills that stuck up here and there. It had the rather unimaginative name of South Pasture. Although the pasture only had one fairly dependable stock tank, there was a pipeline that had drinkers along it at regular intervals. The pipeline and drinkers provided a reliable supply of water to both livestock and wildlife from a well. The water was pumped by a large hit-and-miss motor that was mounted with bolts onto a thick concrete base.

The well, drinkers, and pipeline had been installed by Civilian Conservation Corps crews during the drought of the 1930s and were still holding up pretty good. The only exception was the old hit-and-miss motor, which was beginning to require a lot of maintenance to keep it going after twenty or so years of use. Dad had told me that as soon as he could afford it he planned on replacing the cantankerous old motor with a diesel engine.

The motor was only run enough to fill the drinkers when cattle were in the pasture. Usually a couple of hours a day did the job. Since cattle hadn't been in that particular pasture during the time that I had been on the ranch I wasn't very familiar with the pasture, pipeline, or the old motor. I had picked up my knowledge of that area of the ranch mostly by listening to my dad. I had also overheard him and Jay discussing, and cussing, the hit-and-miss motor.

The previous summer Lenny and I had helped Jay go down into the Holden Ranch to the south of the P Bar J and gather some strays that had gotten through a break in the boundary fence. But on those rides we had gone basically due south from the headquarters and skirted the western division fence of that pasture. To get into the South Pasture you needed to angle off a little toward the southeast from the headquarters.

Dad had been looking at various ways to earn extra money that was needed for meeting the lease payments to the Howards and for medical bills for Mom and the new baby that was on the way. One method that Dad was considering to generate additional income was pasturing some cattle for others who had run short of forage on their own ranches.

With the P Bar J Ranch running low numbers there was available forage for additional cows. Dad had even had a county agent out to look at the range with him and give him some numbers on the amount of cattle and the time period they could be grazed in the South Pasture without harming anything. Dad had seen his share of overgrazed land and didn't want it to occur on the P Bar J Ranch even if it meant some extra money coming in.

The county agent had conducted a study of the plants in that pasture and had clipped and weighed a number of small plots of vegetation. From those samples he had run calculations based on the acreage of the pasture to determine how many cows the forage would support for a given number of days.

Before making a decision one way or the other Dad had talked it over with the Howards. They had agreed that it would be okay with them for him to seek some pasture cattle in order to generate additional income. They had complete faith in his management of the ranch.

Dad told me at breakfast a couple days after our outing to cut Christmas trees, "Jeff, I was thinking that I need to take a drive down to the South Pasture Well and fire up the pump motor. Before I go ahead with my plan of looking for some cattle to pasture I need to make darn sure that old motor will pump enough water to keep all of the drinkers along the pipeline filled. I also want to make sure that the float valves in all of the drinkers are working."

Dad paused about there long enough to take a couple bites of bacon and eggs and then wash it down with a gulp or two of coffee. He made a face after the coffee and said to Mom, "Betsy, hon, is there any more coffee in the pot? I have gone and let what I have in my cup get cold."

Mom nodded yes and turned to pick up his cup. She then dumped out the cold coffee into the sink and refilled it from the pot on the back burner of the stove. Dad must have known that there was coffee on the stove but the question was a way of getting Mom to refill the cup for him while he worked a little more on his bacon and eggs.

After Mom set the full cup of steaming coffee on the table next to his plate Dad thanked her and immediately took a sip. He then resumed telling me about his planned trip down to the South Pasture and what he wanted me to do to help out.

"So I thought that you could ride along with me and once we get the engine up and running you could stay there and watch it and I would come back in a couple hours after the drinkers have had time to fill and then we could drive around and check them," Dad explained.

Since the whole purpose of going after a contract for some pasture cattle was to make extra money, he needed to make sure the old pump was up to its job. It wouldn't make much sense financially to do a pasture agreement if he first had to spend a lot of money on a new motor, or any other major maintenance work on the pipeline and drinkers.

The day was sunny and the wind was fairly light so I had an idea. "Dad, I was just wondering … if it's okay I could put my bike in the back of the truck and take it with us. Then after the pump had run a couple hours I could shut it off and then use Bucky to ride the pipeline and check the drinkers for you."

I knew Dad was pretty busy and I thought that this was a way that I could help him plus at the same time be able to get out and ride my Schwinn. It would be easy to check the drinkers with my bike since I knew from what Dad had told me they were arranged along the pipeline which had a two-tracker ranch road along it. I could pretty much make a loop along the route and then head back to the headquarters. The ground was mostly flat so it would be easy pedaling.

Dad smiled at my offer and said, "That sounds like a real good idea, son. It would sure help me if you did the checking and then just let me know if you see any floats or anything else that is going to need work." He slapped me on the back as he got up and told me that it sure was nice having a good hand on the ranch to help him with the work.

When we finished breakfast Dad told me to go ahead on down to the barn and corral and get my chores finished. He glanced at his pocket watch and said, "Lenny and his sister and little brother are most likely already down there. I got a few things to take care of and then I will be down to help get your bike loaded in the back of the truck."

Sure enough when I got to the barn Lynda, Lenny, and Mick were already there working. Lenny looked up and said, "Morning, Jeff. Looks like we beat you down here. You city boys sure do like to sleep in."

Before I could respond he continued, "Mom is taking us to Flagstaff today. We are taking the Christmas tree we got for our place there and Dad is going to take the afternoon off from the bank and we are going to decorate it. We are also going to do some Christmas shopping."

They had gotten an early start on their chores and were going to leave for Flagstaff as soon as they were finished with them. They were just going for the day and would drive back to the ranch in the evening. Working together we quickly finished the chores.

I looked up at our house and saw that Dad was on his way down to the barn. Mrs. Howard stepped out of her house and called to him and he walked over to see what she needed. A few minutes later when he got down to the barn Dad went into the tool room and got a spool of heavy twine. As he started back up toward the Howards' house, Dad paused to tell me there would be a slight delay in our plans. He told me that he was going to tie down a Christmas tree onto the roof of Abby's station wagon.

Of course, while my dad could easily have gotten Jay or Clay to do the menial task he didn't pass things off just because he could. Just before leaving with the twine he turned and said, "Jeff, this won't take but a few minutes and then I will be back to help load your bike."

While I waited for Dad to take care of that little chore I rolled my bike outside the barn where I had been keeping it stored for the winter in an out-of-the-way corner and checked the tires. They were both a little soft so I got a hand pump out of the tool room and aired them up.

Just as he had said it didn't take him long to secure the tree to the roof of the station wagon and five minutes or so later Dad was back at the barn. He opened a drawer in a work bench and pulled out a small notebook, the kind that fits into a shirt pocket, along with a short pencil and handed them to me. I noted that the pad and pencil were like the ones he always carried in his shirt pocket to keep track of everything from moving cattle to rains. In the evenings after supper, he would go over the entries in his notepad, while planning cattle moves, scheduling any repair work, the ordering of supplies, or any number of other things.

As he turned and handed the notepad and pencil to me, Dad said, "Jeff, this little tally book will help you keep track of anything that is going to need my attention. The drinkers all have numbers on them so all you will need to do if you see a problem at one of them is to write down the number and then anything you see that looks like it needs fixing."

It may seem like a small thing but Dad giving me that notepad made me feel pretty grown up and indicated that he was going to trust my judgment regarding the functioning of the pipeline and drinkers. That notepad in my pocket was a big step that Dad had made seem natural. I felt pretty big that morning when we left the headquarters in his truck. I would fill up a lot of those notepads in the coming years.

I dropped the truck's tailgate and Dad laid my bike in the bed on top of a spare truck tire and a few fence posts. The Howards were pulling out on their trip the same time as us. I noticed Lynda waving and I waved back.

Once at the well it didn't take Dad long to get the hit-and-miss engine running. As I remember it was a Fairbanks-Morse engine. He used a crank to start it, and once he had it going he adjusted the spark control lever to advance the spark. As it chugged along Dad explained to me how to shut it off after two hours had passed by moving the spark control level all the way back in the opposite direction. He also showed me how to be sure the gas was shut off and the oiler was closed tight.

After Dad had given me the instructions on the engine and warned me to be careful around the flywheel he jumped up in the bed of the truck and handed my bike down to me. I rolled the black-and-red Schwinn over to where it would be out of the way and put down the kickstand.

Dad said that since I had the bike with me I could ride down to the first drinker and check to make sure that it was full before shutting the motor off. Before he left to attend to his work he gave me his pocket watch so I could keep track of the time.

As he was starting off Dad laughed and said, through the open window of the truck, "Now, Jeff, don't you be late getting back for supper or your Mom will blame me." It was sure my intention to get back before the sun got low enough for the temperature to start cooling off.

Before we had left our house I had filled a paper sack with a peanut butter and jelly sandwich, a couple cookies, and a handful of hard candy and stuffed it in one of the large patch pockets of my coat. For water I was going to just use what was in the well. I figured it wouldn't be any different from what I was used to drinking from the well that supplied our drinking water at the headquarters. At the drinkers if I needed a drink I would just cup my hands and collect it as it flowed out of the pipe.

Watching Dad drive away I was thinking that I should find a spot to sit and eat my sandwich as the first order of business. I knew the sandwich wouldn't keep very well in my pocket so the sooner I ate it the better it would taste. I walked out a little ways from the well in order to get at least a short distance away from the popping and whooshing of the hit-and-miss motor. I was glad that there wasn't one of those old engines powering anything at the headquarters. It was the first time I had heard one and afterwards I never thought a diesel engine on a pump or generator sounded very loud.

Fishing the sandwich out of the patch pocket I was happy to see it hadn't gotten all smashed up. I found a rock to sit on and started working on the sandwich. One of the smaller chest pockets of my coat closed with a zipper. I thought that would be a safe place to carry Dad's pocket watch so there wouldn't be any chance of it falling out while I was riding my bike or when I was just walking around.

Unzipping the pocket I started to drop the watch into it and then thought that I had better make sure there was nothing in it already that might scratch up the crystal face of Dad's watch. That turned out to be a good thing. Reaching into the pocket I discovered a couple arrowheads and a piece of quartz that I had picked up a month or so back and had completely forgotten about.

The sharp edges of the stone arrowheads and the quartz which had been chipped on all sides by an Indian trying to make a tool of some sort would have made a mess of the face of Dad's watch. The same pocket also yielded a square nail that I had picked up somewhere, a couple valve caps, a gum wrapper, and a piece of lint-covered hard candy.

After transferring the contents of the zippered pocket, except for the candy, to the patch pocket that had previously held my lunch sack I dropped the watch in and closed the zipper. I had just tossed the piece of candy away. It had been way beyond saving. Sitting on the rock and working on my lunch I unzipped the pocket and pulled the watch out once in a while to keep track of the time.

I planned on taking a ride down to the first drinker after an hour had passed just to check on the progress. By then if everything was working right the drinker should be about half full at least. I was going to do it more to past the time than anything else. I could see the first drinker along the pipeline about a quarter mile or so to the east and knew I could be there in only a few minutes on my bike. The pipeline ran east from the well to the first drinker and then turned south and finally headed west. After I had checked the last drinker on the route I would take ranch roads northwest back to the headquarters.

Seeing a few rocks piled up off to the south a short distance from the well I decided to walk over to them and take a look. Even though it was fairly warm for a winter day it still felt a little cool just sitting. It would be better to be moving around. I kept my eyes on the ground as I walked. Between the well and the rocks there was an almost continuous scatter of broken glass, a few old solder dot cans, and assorted small pieces of metal.

The rocks appeared to have been arranged in a square. I wondered if the Civilian Conservation Corps crews had used them to hold down the sides of a tent. Putting in the well and associated pipeline and drinkers would have required them to be out here for an extended period of time so they must have had a work camp set up.

There were enough small pieces of junk laying around on the surface near the rocks to keep my interest for a while. Plus, it sure was nice being out a little farther from the sound of that old pump motor.

As I started back towards the well I reached up and unzipped the pocket holding the watch. Checking the time I was happy, and a little surprised, to see that an hour had passed since Dad had started the old engine. I hopped on Bucky and headed to the first drinker to see how high it had filled.

After all of the horseback riding Lenny and I had been doing lately checking waters for ice and general ranch work it felt good to have my butt back on the soft leather saddle of my Schwinn and zooming along a relatively smooth and level ranch road. The only thing I had to remember was to watch out for the occasional dried, hard ruts. If the front tire caught the side of one of them it would cause a crash. I didn't want to have another wreck with my bike like I had had late in the past summer. As I already mentioned, that wreck had damaged Bucky to the extent that several new parts had been necessary, plus I had to get several stitches to close a cut over one of my eyes.

Also, I was aware that if I did have another crash on the bike and Lenny or even Lynda ever found out about it I wouldn't hear the end of it. I sure didn't want Lenny telling me that I should get training wheels for my bike.

Down at the first drinker I was pleased to see that it was a little more than half full. I pushed the cutoff float down and the water flow stopped just as it was supposed to. It resumed flowing when I released the float. Walking around the drinker I looked for any leaks and was happy not to find any. I could report to Dad that this drinker was working okay. I pulled out my little tally book and made a note on it with the number of the drinker at the top of the page. I was thinking about how later that night after supper Dad and I could sit at the kitchen table and go over what I had found and I could refer to my notes just like he did with his tally book.

Back at the South Pasture Well I waited around a little past the two-hour mark and then made a fast trip back down to the first drinker and made sure that it was full before shutting down the engine. The drinker was full and the shutoff float had stopped the flow of water. Perfect, I thought as I made another note in the little pad. Riding back towards the well I looked for any wet spots on the surface above the pipeline that would indicate a leak. The ground was dry.

Arriving back at the well I was warmed up enough from the ride to take my coat off for a little while. However, it didn't take long standing around before I put it back on. Before shutting the pump motor off I waited another 15 or so minutes to make sure that enough water had reached the farthest drinkers on the pipeline.

I sure was glad when I shut that engine off and the god-awful noise it was making stopped. I was getting a headache having to listen to it run. As I rode off on my bike I thought that I could still hear the popping and whooshing in my head.

My inspection of the pipeline route and the other drinkers went fairly fast and for the most part was uneventful. I did manage to get my front tire on the steep side of a rut when I wasn't watching and the bike sort of slipped out from under me. Instead of landing on my face like I had last summer I rolled a few times after clearing the handle bars and came to a stop with no apparent damage to me or to Bucky. After dusting myself off and seeing that there wasn't any evidence in the way of damage to me or my bike and more importantly, no witnesses, I decided to keep the crash to myself.

I made sure the float valves were working and that there were no leaks in the troughs or anywhere along the entire length of the pipeline. I had to bend the rods on a couple of the floats to get them adjusted correctly. They had allowed the water to get high enough that it had overflowed the drinkers before shutting off the flow. I had watched Dad and Jay do the same thing at other water troughs and drinkers and knew how to do it. I would be able to tell Dad that everything was working good when I got back to the headquarters.

I jotted down a few more notes in my tally book and then sat on the rim of the last trough on the pipeline and ate the cookies I had brought plus a few pieces of candy.

Looking back along the pipeline I saw a small herd of antelope and a few deer at one of the drinkers. It hadn't taken the wildlife long to smell the water.

I still had plenty of daylight left for the ride back to the headquarters so I took my time. Dad already knew that the old hit-and-miss motor was running okay and he sure looked relieved when I reported to him that he wouldn't have to go out and do any repair work right away on the drinkers or pipelines. Not having to spend time and money on repairs was always welcome news on a ranch.

Shortly thereafter Dad found a herd of cattle, owned by a person who operated a feedlot near Prescott, to put out on the South Pasture for six months. The cattle were on a ranch on the desert southwest of Prescott at the time and the feed had pretty much been depleted.

The income from pasturing the cattle would sure come in handy. The herd was scheduled to arrive shortly after New Year's. At least that was the time of arrival agreed upon by Dad and the feedlot owner when the deal was closed.

That night, after riding the pipeline, it was hard going to sleep. Whenever I closed my eyes I could hear the popping and whooshing of that old hit-and-miss motor.

Chapter 5
Road Trip

Although I was still trying to think of a good Christmas present to buy for Lynda as well as presents for the others on my list I hadn't had a chance yet to do any shopping. I was thinking that it would help if I was just able to spend some time looking around in a big department store. Then I might just be able to find the perfect presents for everyone.

The Howard kids got frequent opportunities to shop for presents when their mother would take them to Flagstaff where Mr. Howard spent most of his time running a bank and the family maintained another house. However, my one and only home was on the ranch which sure didn't provide me with the same shopping opportunities.

My chance to do some Christmas shopping came up when Dad announced one evening after supper that he was going to have to make a trip into Prescott to pick up a few supplies for the ranch. When Mom suggested that she could go with him and do some Christmas shopping I asked to go too. They both realized then that I also had shopping to do for Christmas so it was agreed that we would all go and make the trip an overnighter so we wouldn't be rushed. Spending the night and eating in restaurants would make it a nice family outing for us. Dad would let Jay and Clay know that he would be gone for a few days. It was understood that Jay was always in charge whenever Dad was gone from the ranch.

Dad admitted that he could use a little time to browse around Goldwater's and perhaps a few other stores on his own to look for something for Mom. When I heard Dad say that I realized that the stress I was feeling about picking out a present for Lynda wasn't something I could expect to outgrow. Men had the same problems picking out gifts for the women in their lives. At least since he had lined up the pasturage agreement for the first of the year Dad probably felt like he had a little more money to spend on Christmas presents.

My mom suggested that we take her 1936 Ford four-door convertible on the trip since it had a trunk for storing presents and a backseat so we wouldn't be crowded together on the single bench seat of the pickup. Dad, who didn't have much faith in that old Ford insisted on taking his Chevy truck.

I listened as Dad told Mom, "Betsy, I figure that I can find us a big box for free at one of the hardware stores in Prescott that I can get to hold any purchases we make. I will tape it up real good before we head back to the ranch so nothing gets dusty in the back of the truck."

The weather had been dry and no storms were coming in so stuff getting wet in the back of the truck wouldn't be a problem. Besides Dad always had an old tarp behind the truck's seat for emergencies that could be roped down around the packages in case some bad weather blew in while we were on the road.

Mom felt her car would be more comfortable for the relatively long drive back and forth to Prescott, but she decided to drop the matter. However, I don't think she was aware of the real reason that Dad didn't want to use her car for trips. He just didn't trust Fords, especially old ones.

The morning we were to leave on the trip I noticed that Dad had a trash can next to the cab of the truck and was filling it up with debris. Old stock magazines, tobacco tins, wrappers, papers, a few beer bottles, a Pepsi bottle, and other discarded items went into the trash can until it was almost overflowing. He didn't clean out the cab very often. He must have considered our family Christmas shopping trip to be a special occasion. Most likely he was trying to avoid Mom making comments.

Once our overnight bags were packed Dad used a fairly new, clean tarp he had gotten out of the supply room and wrapped them with it before placing the bundle in the truck's bed up against the cab. Before long we were headed north up to Route 66.

During the drive to Prescott that day Mom asked me what type of things the Howard kids liked to play with. She thought it would be nice to buy each of them presents along with something for their parents.

I told her that I was planning on buying Lenny, Lynda, and Mick presents, but didn't know what yet. About then Dad asked her something and they were soon discussing something to do with some bills that would be coming due toward the end of the month.

We had stopped at a café along Route 66 in Ash Fork for a late breakfast. Mom thought it would be a good idea so we wouldn't be hungry while we were shopping. Then we would have a combination late lunch/early supper sometime in the late afternoon.

In Prescott we parked near the courthouse square and headed out to do our shopping. Dad needed to pick up several things at the Sam Hill Hardware store and he told Mom and me that we could all meet back at the truck around 3:00 p.m. Then we would find a place to spend the night and look for a restaurant to have a nice meal.

As Mom and I were walking over to the Goldwater's department store I bought up the subject of what to get Lynda by including her brothers in the statement, "Mom, I am not sure what to get Lenny and his sister and little brother for Christmas."

I was hoping Mom would come back with some gem like, "I have an idea for the perfect gift for a twelve-year-old girl" but that wasn't the case. I should have known, since she had asked for my advice earlier on what she should get them.

Instead of providing me with an answer to the problem Mom just said, "Oh, I am sure you will be able to find something that they would each like once you look around in a few stores here. We will compare our purchases later so we don't end up buying the three of them the same gifts." With that Mom and I split up near the front door of the big department store.

The truth was that gifts for Lenny and Mick weren't real high on my priority list. I figured that I would just grab the first thing I saw for each of them and then concentrate on Lynda's gift. And that was pretty much what I did. I selected a set of Lincoln Logs for Mick and two large packages of BBs for Lenny. Thinking about it I also got a pack of paper targets for Lenny. I thought the extra cost would be a small price to pay for being able to tell him something like, "Now maybe you won't be shooting birds and getting in trouble with your mom."

Then it was over to the jewelry and perfume counters to look around. I felt like I was exploring Mars. It was definitely an alien environment for a twelve-year-old boy.

Fortunately a sales lady saw my rather bewildered look and asked if I could use some help. I produced a grateful smile and said, "Well, madam, I sure could. I am trying to find presents for my mom and for a friend's sister … she's twelve."

The sales lady helped me pick out a heart-shaped pin that had "Mother" written across it that I was pretty sure my Mom would like. It looked like something she would wear on one of her blouses or maybe on the collar of a jacket. Then it was on to the hard work. I wanted something nice for Lynda but at the same time it needed not to be anything remotely mushy. I didn't think Lynda would like it if I ended up having to take a swing at Lenny on Christmas morning if he was kidding me about a gift to a girl, even if she was his twin sister.

The sales lady was patient with me as she showed me a number of pins, necklaces, perfume, hats, scarves, and rings. But I didn't see anything that jumped out at me ... that I could afford anyway. So I took a break and walked over to the men's department to look for something for Dad. I found a brown leather belt with four silver conchos that I thought would look good with his silver rodeo buckle. Luckily I had thought about a belt for him earlier back at the ranch and had taken a look at one of the almost worn out ones that he had in order to get the size. I got him the belt in the 36-inch length.

After selecting the belt for Dad I wandered back across the store and by chance happened to find myself in the stationary department. I then flashed on what would be the perfect gift for a girl who liked to write. I remembered the spooky story that Lynda had written and had read to me when we had ridden horses out to Heckler Tank in the summer. She had told me then how much she enjoyed writing and how she hoped to be a professional writer someday. That horseback ride had been the first time just the two of us had done something on our own and I had been surprised at how much I had enjoyed spending the day with her. Things in my world hadn't been exactly the same since.

I picked out a thick notebook with a fancy brown leather cover embossed with pink flowers on it and then I found a pen and mechanical pencil set that was also pink. The pen and pencil set was a fairly expensive brand but it went perfectly with the cover of the notebook. Even at age twelve I was observant enough to have noticed that girls, as well as grown-up ladies, seemed to like things that matched. I got a refill for the ballpoint and a package of extra leads for the mechanical pencil.

Gathering my selections up I felt a certain amount of relief as I started towards one of the cashiers to pay. I knew for certain that I had found something that Lynda would like. I was also pleased with myself for the gifts I had found for Mom and Dad. The ones for Lenny and Mick would do.

The store even provided free gift wrapping for the presents so I had them do that after I had paid. I was careful to fill out and tape the gift tags the sales clerk provided, onto the various packages so they wouldn't get mixed up. Then everything went into a couple of large shopping bags that had "Goldwater's" emblazoned on their sides.

Mom always took care of selecting and buying gifts for me to give to my grandparents so I didn't have to worry about what to get for them. With my shopping finished I wandered over to where the store's Santa Claus was sitting in a big chair amid fake snow and large boxes decorated with bright Christmas wrapping. It occurred to me that the big boxes were probably empty so everything was make believe.

There was a line of a dozen or so younger kids waiting for their chance to tell Santa what they wanted for Christmas. My parents had never told me the truth about Santa, but rather just let me enjoy that part of Christmas for as long as I could. Eventually my friends and I figured it out on our own and Christmases never felt as magical again. But I guess that comes to everyone in time.

I still had a half hour or so left before I had to meet Mom and Dad back at the pickup so I walked over to a newsstand down the street that also sold comic books. After the gift purchases I was running a little low on money but I still had enough to buy the latest issues of the Roy Rogers and Superman comics with even a little left over.

Dad was sitting in the truck listening to the radio when I got back a few minutes before 3:00 p.m. I didn't have a watch but I had kept looking out across the square at the big clock on top of the courthouse from time to time while I had been shopping. We only had to wait a few minutes for Mom to appear loaded down with several packages and bags. Dad looked up at her as she approached and then turning to me said, "Well, I guess it's a good thing we brought the truck." Mom didn't hear the comment.

We then drove out on one of the main streets a few blocks from the downtown area and found a motel. Once we had gotten a room we put our packages and overnight bags in it and then headed out to find a restaurant. The late breakfast had worn off and we were all ready to sit down to a big feed.

After we had finished eating the rest of the afternoon and a little bit of the evening was spent on doing more Christmas shopping. It seemed that we had hit most of the stores in Prescott before Mom and Dad found presents for their parents, each other, and a few other people they were shopping for.

At a home appliance store Dad got a large, sturdy cardboard box that had been used for shipping a kitchen stove. He put it in the bed of the pickup and placed all of the packages and bags we had acquired during the late afternoon and early evening into it.

Turning to Mom he said, "Betsy, it looks like this box will be more than big enough to contain all of the earlier purchases that are back at the motel, too, without anything getting squashed." After a pause he added with a chuckle, "Oh, oh, forget what I said about it being more than big enough … we probably have brought more than enough presents already. Let's just pretend that there's no room for anymore."

Dad told us that he would get a roll of strapping tape before we went back to the motel so he could seal the top of the box to keep everything inside it from getting dusty on the drive back to the ranch. He had a coil of rope in the bed of the truck that he could use to secure the box with.

One of the last stops we made that day was at a saddle shop. Dad told us that he had to pick up something he had ordered for Jay. It was a custom made leather wallet with

Jay's initials embossed on it. He showed it to us after he had gotten back into the truck's cab.

It was early evening by the time we made it back to our motel room. Dad and Mom emptied the bags of presents out of the box and carried them into the room. I had started to help but Mom had told me they would do it since some of the bags contained presents for me that were unwrapped. Mom preferred to wrap presents herself and had declined the store's cashier's offer to wrap them. Once the box was empty Dad found that he had to collapse it some to get it to fit through the door of our motel room. He told us that it was no big deal since with the strapping tape he could put it back good as new tomorrow morning when he had it in the back of the truck.

Once the presents and flattened box were in the room we washed up a little and then went out and stopped at another restaurant for a light supper. Afterwards we went to a theater to see a movie. The Deans were really doing the town.

The next morning we had breakfast at a café next to the motel. The three of us loaded up on pancakes, eggs, and bacon.

As far as I knew the only thing we were going to do that morning was take a leisurely drive back to the P Bar J Ranch. However, Dad had made plans to check out two frontier era army camps along the way.

After breakfast, as we were walking out onto the sidewalk in front of the café and heading toward the pickup Dad let us in on what he wanted to do. He wanted to look for Camp Hualapai and another army camp that he didn't know the name of at the time.

Dad had always had an interest in old military forts and enjoyed exploring abandoned ones. He was a big fan of John Wayne and usually took me with him to see his movies. Dad's favorites were the ones set during the Indian Wars in which Wayne played cavalry officers.

I remember going with Dad in the late 1940s to see "Fort Apache" and "She Wore a Yellow Ribbon." So when he told me about how we were going to go by the ruins of old army camps I was expecting to see stockade walls. However, the real West wasn't like the movies. Years later I learned that Fort Whipple in Prescott was one of the few frontier army posts that had actually had the stockade walls at one time.

Instead of taking the highway north from Prescott Dad showed us another route on a dirt road that came out on Route 66 at Seligman. The road was named Williamson Valley Road.

Jay had worked for a ranch along this road back in the early '40s and knowing of his interest in such things had told my dad about one day finding what he thought was the site of an army camp while he was out riding a fence line checking for breaks. He had even drawn a little map that Dad produced from a shirt pocket once we were heading northwest out of Prescott on Williamson Valley Road that morning.

He handed it to me and said, "Since we have the time this morning the first thing that I want to do is make a little side trip off this road and try to find an old army camp that Jay told me about a while back. This here is a little map he put together for me."

Dad had me pass the map to Mom and then told us both, "Betsy ... Jeff, I want you two to be looking for those hills that Jay drew off to the east there," as he pointed at the spot on the map. He then added, "A few miles or so farther north we should see a ranch road taking off at an angle to our right. According to Jay the site of the army camp is less than a mile off to the east. It's on a slight rise and from the sound of it there's not a lot left but I just want to take a look at it."

As we continued north Mom and I kept our eyes toward the northeast trying to catch a glimpse of the hills. At the time I didn't know their name but I later learned they were called Sullivan Buttes. I also eventually learned the name of the camp we were looking for that morning. It was Camp Rawlins. The post was established in February 1870 and had been abandoned by the army in September of the same year.

Jay's map included a rather detailed depiction of the distinctive peaks of the hills. Mom and I spotted the hills at about the same time and pointed them out to Dad. Sure enough a few miles farther on we saw a ranch road leading off to the east just like Jay had drawn on his map.

It was late morning and already getting cloudy and windy by the time we turned off onto the rutted, two-tracker ranch road. Dad had told us that we were looking for rows of short juniper posts near the base of a gentle slope. Since this was a minor, temporary encampment the soldiers didn't have barracks for shelter. Instead, the posts had been put in the ground as a base to set a wooden platform on. Then a tent was placed on the platform.

We had to pass through two or three gates that Dad had me open and close. After only about ten minutes of looking I spotted the site. I yelled excitedly, "Dad, there it is!"

Dad hit the brakes and he and Mom looked to where I was pointing. What I had seen was an alignment of short juniper posts on a small southwest facing slope. Also, there were six fence posts that looked like they were the same age, a few hundred feet farther to the southwest.

As we piled out of Dad's pickup he grabbed Mom's Kodak camera from the glove box. He took photos of Mom and me next to the rows of posts with Sullivan Buttes in the background.

As we were standing there looking at the short posts sticking out of the ground Dad said, "Just think, those posts were cut and put in the ground by soldiers in the late 1860s or early 1870s." As he tapped one with the toe of his boot he added, "And they are still strong enough to do the job they were intended for."

Luckily the soldiers had used junipers for their tent platform supports. If they had used pine or cottonwood they would have been long gone without a trace.

We spent a few hours or so just wandering around the site. One of the first things that I found was a barrel ring laying in the gully below the fence posts. I found probably a dozen barrel rings that day. I also found lots of square nails as I walked around the site.

Dad took a photo of me kneeling within the westernmost tent platform. There were two sets of what Dad identified as tent platform posts down low on the slope. Upslope from the easternmost platform I found a can that had a square metal patch soldered on the bottom. As I dropped it back onto the surface near where I had found it I could only wonder what the patched can had been used for.

At the top of the ridge there were more posts in the ground in a group, presumably for another tent platform ... making a total of three that we found. Perhaps this tent had been for the officers. Up high on the ridge there probably would have been more of a breeze, plus it was farther away from the corral on the flat where the livestock were kept. So the officers wouldn't have had to deal with the odors.

On the ridge I found the top of a brown bottle, the top of a blue bottle, and a large solder dot can. Square nails were scattered around. Dad took photos showing all three groups of posts/tent platforms.

Farther to the north on the same ridge there were three large posts in the ground; one was about seven feet tall. The posts had square nails in them. There were pieces of glass and white China scattered around near these posts.

Dad made the observation that there seemed to be a higher concentration of winterfat, snakeweed, and wolfberry over the site of the camp than on adjacent areas.

Upslope from the easternmost platform there was a large, old Utah juniper with a stand of wolfberry bushes all the way around beneath its canopy. As Dad and I walked up to the big tree he turned to me and said, "This old tree saw the army troops come and go."

The site of the camp was spread out mostly on the south-and southwest-facing slope of the small gentle hill we had climbed. The hill provided a commanding view to the east and south. Sullivan Buttes were to the southeast and looking out at them I thought how a soldier could have been placed on one of the peaks to relay signals or act as a lookout.

There was a ruin of a small structure that had a stone foundation out on the flat. It was on the opposite side of a small gully from a group of tall posts that Dad thought could possibly have been the camp's corral. Dad speculated that the little building might have been where the soldiers stored supplies including extra ammunition. There were lots of square nails scattered near the stone structure. The structure's foundation was built from limestone that had been collected from the surface of the nearby slopes and ridges. We could see that some of the rocks had been cut and shaped so they would fit together with very little gap. At least one of the soldiers must have been a skilled stone mason.

The building was on a little mound and Dad told Mom and me that the "mound" might be the result of adobe walls melting. The ruin, as I remember it, was approximately ten by twelve feet.

There was a network of small and large gullies cutting through the area, especially where there was a runoff slope. Dad wondered aloud if some of the gullies had originated from footpaths worn onto the surface by the soldiers.

There were several large junipers on the site and on the adjacent areas. It looked like there had once been many more judging by the numerous large stumps that we saw on the slopes and ridges while we were exploring. The cut trees would have provided abundant fence posts, building material, and firewood for the troops during their brief occupation of the camp.

In addition to the things left by the soldiers there were lots of prehistoric artifacts that we noticed on the site. These included pieces of metates, several pieces of flaked stone, and fragments of gray pottery that I found sticking out of the side of a gully.

While Dad and I were distracted by what looked like an old can dump Mom slipped away. She really didn't have much interest in these historic sites. When we noticed that she was no longer with us we looked around to see where she had gone.

Looking back toward where the pickup was parked we noticed Mom sitting on the open tailgate. When she saw us looking she waved with a paperback book in her hand and hollered, "I am just taking a little rest break. You guys look around at the old junk all you want."

So with Mom's blessing for us to do some more exploring Dad and I followed the ridge to the west towards the main north-south road that we had taken from Prescott. Every few steps we noticed something interesting on the ground and one of us would bend over, pick it up, and examine it before passing it on to the other person. Darkling beetles were commonly encountered. Those and cottontails were the only wildlife that we saw, although Dad pointed out numerous groups of deer pellets and even what he identified as mountain lion and bear tracks. The lion and bear tracks were on a heavily wooden ridge with some rock overhangs that would have afforded cover and shelter for the big predators.

There were a few old shell casings on the ground. Dad found a 56-50 Spencer cartridge case on the ridge. It had "F V & V & Co" on the cap. Dad explained to me that it was a rim fire type rather than a center fire cartridge.

Solder dot cans, tobacco cans, and pieces of white China were scattered around. There was another barrel ring near the ranch road along with numerous pieces of green glass on a rocky section of the ridge. It looked like someone had either thrown or dropped a whiskey bottle and it had shattered on the limestone rocks. . .

There were pieces of broken glass in various colors ... pale blue, dark green, brown ... scattered throughout the site. Square nails seemed to be just about everywhere. I noticed that some of the solder dot cans appeared to have been opened with a knife. The soldiers probably didn't have a can opener handy and made do with what they had.

We found a metate in two pieces next to a juniper stump. There was a large piece of a white China cup nearby. It was at that point in our exploration that I had to stop to get some three-awns out of my tennis shoes. The sharp pointed seeds and their awns were working their way through my socks and were hurting me.

While I was taking care of the troublesome seeds Dad had continued scanning the surface as he walked around the stump that I was sitting on. I knew he had found something different from the nails and broken glass when I heard him exclaim, "Damn, if that don't beat all!"

Looking over I saw him pick up what looked like two or three pieces of dull gold-colored metal. After quickly examining them he brought them over and handed them to me.

"Jeff, take a look here at what I just found. These are insignias from the hats of the soldiers that were stationed here." After a pause he pointed at each piece in turn and said, "That letter C was a troop designation and the twelve and three refers to the number of the infantry or cavalry. So the C and the three could mean that Troop C of the Third Cavalry was here."

We spent several minutes looking at his find and discussing each piece. Dad told me that soldiers didn't like them since the metal when new and shiny or freshly polished gave off a glare in the sunlight and made a good target for a hostile Indian to aim at.

Since Mom was waiting at the pickup Dad suggested that we probably should head back that way. But once we had hiked back down the slope Dad noticed something else that caught his attention fifty feet or so from where we had parked. He had noticed a piece of tarnished gold metal like that of the insignias he had picked up earlier. He walked over and saw that it was an infantry bugle that attached to the front of a solder's hat.

As he was walking back to us he had a big grin on his face. Holding the little metal bugle up he said, "Take a look at this. Now all I need to find is a cavalry insignia." The cavalry's symbol was crossed sabers, but he didn't manage to find one of them that day.

By the time we got back to the truck and headed out toward the main dirt road it was starting to sprinkle large flakes of snow. Due to how much time we had spent at the first site and the deteriorating weather Dad said that we would just make a quick stop at the site of Camp Hualapai.

The turnoff for that camp was north of a bridge over Walnut Creek. As we crossed the bridge Dad pointed out a large Indian ruin on a bluff east of the road. It was a hilltop fort or pueblo. If not for the snow, which seemed to be increasing Dad and me probably would have climbed up to it and checked it out.

Just a little farther north the road forked and we took the one headed west a few miles to the ruins of Camp Hualapai. Compared to the other site the ruins of this one were quite extensive. Camp Hualapai had been a major camp that had been occupied by the army for several years during the Indian Wars. It had originally been named Camp Tollgate. The site had been used by settlers after the army left.

However, due to the snow and a cold wind that had come up Dad and I only took a quick walk around the ruins of a few buildings before climbing back into the warm cab where Mom had wisely chosen to stay. She shook her head at us as we got in after shaking the snow off our hats and jackets.

We then continued north into Seligman and had supper at a café on Route 66 just west of town. By the time we had finished eating the snow had stopped.

Chapter 6
The Horse Wreck

The ranch work that Lenny and I had to do every day made the days go by pretty fast even with all the anticipation for Christmas morning to hurry up and arrive. There were a few snowstorms that dropped a couple inches or so, but then it would warm up and the snow would mostly be gone.

Lenny and I would have to go out and chop ice on the cold mornings, but at least there would frequently be mornings where it hadn't gotten really cold due to a heavy cloud cover. Sometimes a warm spell would occur. But even if we didn't have to go break ice Dad saw to it that we usually had plenty to do.

Mom and Mrs. Howard had made plans to cook a big Christmas dinner together and we would all eat at the Howards' house since it was bigger than ours. Both sets of my grandparents were going to be there.

After spending Christmas on the ranch the Howards were going to drive down to the Wagoner area south of Prescott to spend New Year's Day with Mrs. Howard's folks at their ranch on the Hassayampa River.

My Aunt Christy and her husband, who was working on a ranch near Las Cruces in southern New Mexico, were spending Christmas with his folks who lived near Albuquerque. Then they were going to drive to Winslow in time to ring in the New Year with her parents. Dad had written his sister and invited them to come out to the ranch if they had time before they had to head back toward Las Cruces. With the pasture cattle scheduled to arrive just after New Year's he wouldn't have the time to take us to Winslow for a visit.

Dad had given Clay some time off for Christmas so he could go visit his kids in Cheyenne. With his helper gone Jay asked Lenny and me one morning to help him push some cattle between pastures west of the headquarters. Naturally we agreed to ride with him.

It was cold when we headed out from the headquarters but I was thankful that the wind wasn't blowing. The ground that early in the morning was still frozen, but at least there wasn't much snow, just patches here and there. The hooves of the horses made a crunching sound when crossing over the scattered patches of crusted snow.

As we approached the north-south running division fence separating the pastures Lenny and I both raced each other to it. Among the many pieces of cowboy etiquette that I had picked up the previous summer was that the younger cowboys opened the gates for the older ones. The race was pretty much a tie and when we both climbed down and started to open the gate Jay rode up and said, "Boys, I figure it's going to take both of you to open that sucker. The wire loop is pretty tight."

I grabbed the gate post on the side where it was secured to the adjacent fence post by loops of barbed wire at the top and bottom to check to see just how tight it was. Once I saw that barbed wire had been used for the loops rather than smooth wire I wished I had thought to bring along a pair of work gloves.

These wire gates are opened by pulling the gate post towards the fencepost and then lifting the top loop off the post. After that you lifted the bottom of the gate post up out of the lower loop. To fasten the gate the procedure is reversed. The use of barbed wire for the upper loop made it a little more difficult to do without cutting your hands. For some reason one of the former owners of the P Bar J or their cowboys had used barbed wire for loops on a regular basis.

Dad was replacing the upper loops with smooth wire whenever he needed to do any repair work on gates, but he hadn't gotten to all of them yet. He thought from the ranch's standpoint it made sense to have the gates as easy as possible to open and close. That way people passing through for one reason or another weren't so likely to leave a gate open. It was unrealistic to expect someone to have to cut their hands up or rip their shirt or coat on a piece of barbed wire just to close someone else's gate.

Lenny had work gloves with him so I told him that I would put a shoulder into it and once I had gotten some slack in the top loop he could pull it up and over the post. I grabbed a hold of the thick juniper fence post and pushed the gate post toward it with my right shoulder. I was glad that it was cold enough for a heavy coat since it provided a little padding. We succeeded in getting the gate open and Jay told us to just lay the gate back against the fence so it would be out of the way when we drove the cattle back through.

Once we were over in the pasture we were moving the cattle out of we didn't have to spend much time looking for them. Out to the west of a small creek we found the majority of them bunched up near some salt blocks in a small clearing that was sheltered by a thick stand of junipers. Splitting up we got around the main bunch and started pushing them along with others we were able to gather along the way, toward the gate we had left open. Once through the gate they would be in the pasture that Dad wanted them in.

After we had started out that morning Jay told us about something else that he had to do once we got these cattle moved. He had gathered some strays from the Holden Ranch, which bordered the P Bar J to the south, late the day before and had left them penned in a water lot. He told us that he planned on making a quick ride down there in the afternoon and pushing the bunch back to the Holden Ranch. Since it was a small bunch he said he wouldn't be needing our help.

Everything was going pretty good as we crossed the dry rocky bed of the small creek with the cattle out ahead of us.

We were a little farther north of where we had crossed the creek earlier that morning. The bedrock over which the creek flowed in that stretch during runoff events was shaded by junipers, which like other trees tended to be larger along water courses, and as a result of the shade the smooth rock still had a heavy layer of frost covering its surface. The frost wouldn't melt until the sun got up high enough to clear the tops of the junipers.

Jay was watching to make sure none of the cattle decided that they would just as soon stay in the pasture they were in and take off from the bunch. In a bunch or herd of cattle being pushed there were at least a few that would try to break away. They were called bunch quitters. As Jay's horse started across the creek bed its front hooves hit a section of the smooth frost covered bedrock and its legs slipped right out from under it.

Lenny and I had been riding off to either side and ahead of Jay when his horse fell and we heard the crash before we saw it. We only turned to look upon hearing Jay exclaim, "Oh, hell!" as he was falling.

The horse fell on its right side and caught Jay's foot, which was still in the stirrup, between its body and the bedrock. Jay's upper body was slammed against the bedrock surface of the creek bed. After the horse had crashed, Jay's cowboy boot luckily slipped out of the stirrup, so the horse didn't drag him as it started getting back up.

I remember being scared as I rode up quickly to where Jay was laying. He wasn't moving, and all I could think of was how Michael T had been killed the summer before.

Lenny dismounted from his horse and went running after Jay's. The horse was standing off fifty feet or so from where the wreck had occurred. It didn't seem to be hurt.

I climbed down from my horse as I was yelling, "Jay, are you alright?" I was thinking that things could sure go wrong fast. Damn!

Reaching him I was somewhat relieved when I saw that he was conscious. Jay had risen up a little on his right elbow and was staring at his right leg as if trying to will it not to be broken. He mumbled, "Son of a bitch, goddamn it all to hell" as he looked at the injured leg.

Jay then looked over towards his horse. Seeing Lenny walking up to it and taking hold of the reins he called out, "Lenny, walk him around a little to make sure he's okay." The old cowboy seemed visibly relieved when he saw that the horse hadn't broken one of its own legs in the fall.

After I reached his side Jay calmly told me, "Jeff, you and Lenny need to catch up to that bunch of cows we gathered and finish pushing them through the gate. Then I want you to light a damn shuck back to the headquarters and tell your Dad what happened. He will know what needs to be done."

I wasn't surprised that Jay wanted us to tend to the cattle before going for help for him. He was a cowboy and the boss had given him a job to do. We weren't very far from the gate so completing the job would only take a few minutes.

"Okay," I told Jay, knowing it wouldn't do any good to argue, and then added, "but once the cattle are through the gate Lenny will come back to stay with you while I go and get help." I was expecting an argument, but he just managed a smile and nodded.

As I started to climb back up on my horse Jay pointed down the creek and said, "Before you take off could you go over to that stand of willows and break off a few small branches and bring them to me? Right now everything feels pretty numb but once that wears off I have a feeling I am going to be hurting pretty much all over this damned old body of mine."

I had heard cowboys talking about various natural medicines and chewing willow stems was something they did for headaches and other pains. I rode over to the willows and reached out and broke off some small branches and took them back over to Jay.

Once the cattle were in the pasture they were to be moved to I looked around and found a piece of barbed wire that had been tossed on the ground that looked long enough for me to make a loop out of it that would be slightly longer than the top one that was presently on the gate. Using it for at least a temporary replacement would make the gate a lot easier for one person to open and close. We didn't have time to be fooling with an overly tight gate. And we couldn't just leave it open since the cattle we had moved would just drift back through it if given the chance.

After I had secured the gate with the new loop I took my jacket off and handed it over to Lenny who was standing on the other side. Before turning my horse towards the headquarters and giving it a kick in the ribs I told him, "Use this to help keep Jay warm. You might want to gather up some wood and see if you can get a little fire going. I am sure Jay has some matches on him. I will get my Dad and he will bring the pickup out here to get him."

For once I wasn't worried about falling or getting bucked off. I had just one goal and that was to get help for Jay as fast as possible.

As I urged the horse into a gallop I remember thinking that at least Dad wouldn't be able to blame himself for Jay's accident like he had with Michael T's. The summer before Dad had taken Lenny and me, along with his two hired hands, Jay and Michael T to help out on a roundup on the neighboring R_X Ranch. Michael T had been out by himself chasing a few head of pretty wild cattle when his horse stepped into a prairie dog hole and fell, slamming him into the hard ground on his stomach. A pistol he was carrying in a front pocket of his chaps discharged from the impact. The bullet severed an artery in one of his legs. Knocked out from the fall he bled to death without ever regaining consciousness.

Dad and some other cowboys went searching for him when he didn't meet back up with them as planned. They found his horse, a paint, wandering and then backtracked it to the body. Dad would have been torn up about what had happened to his employee regardless but what kept eating at Dad long after the wreck was that he had noticed earlier when Michael T had shot a rabid bobcat that he carried the six-shooter fully loaded which most westerners knew was dangerous.

If the hammer of a revolver was resting on a shell and the gun was dropped or something happened to knock against it there could be an accidental discharge. Michael T was still in his twenties and originally from the Mid-West and must not have been aware of the danger. Dad had meant to talk to him about just keeping five shells in the gun as a safety precaution but hadn't gotten around to doing it since he didn't want it to seem like he was reprimanding or lecturing his young cowboy employee. Then after Michael T died Dad had a lot of "what ifs" to have to deal with.

I was brought back to the situation with Jay as I rode into the headquarters and heard Dad calling to me. Dad was down at the barn as I came galloping into view and seeing me alone he immediately knew that something had gone wrong. He dropped what he had been working on and ran out to meet me.

After I told Dad what had happened and where Jay was he said, "Jeff, don't bother unsaddling your horse, just turn him into the corral, slip his bridle off, and come with me." Dad then went over and got in his pickup and started it up.

I did what Dad had told me to do with the horse and latched the corral gate. I tossed the bridle over a saw horse that was sitting in front of the barn and then jumped into the truck with him. He then drove up to the Howards' house where both Mom and Mrs. Howard were and told them what had happened.

Dad asked Mrs. Howard to drive into Seligman to see about getting an ambulance out to the headquarters and then asked Mom to drive over to the R_X Ranch and see if Doc Thorpe was there. If he was, Mom was to ask him to grab his bag and anything he had to stabilize a broken leg and get out to the headquarters of the P Bar J as fast as possible.

Since Clay had left the day before to drive up to Cheyenne to spend Christmas with his family there wasn't anyone else at the ranch to send to get help. The women were shaken at the news, but did as Dad requested. They both also remembered what had happened to Michael T.

Dad then swung the pickup down to the bunkhouse where some extra single-bed-sized mattresses were stored in a small back room. As he started into the storeroom he said to me, "Jeff, while I grab a couple mattresses climb up into the truck's bed and toss out everything you can. It's just going to be in the way."

The first thing I did was roll an extra spare tire out over the open tailgate and that was quickly followed by a few fence posts, a roll of wire, a sledge hammer, and some tools. I tried to put them into a single pile so it would be easy to put them back into the bed later.

I had the bed emptied out by the time Dad got back carrying two mattresses which he tossed into the rear of the truck. I was jumping back into the cab when I heard him slam the tailgate. A few seconds later he was back behind the wheel and we were racing out of the headquarters in a cloud of dust kicked up by the spinning rear tires. Mom and Mrs. Howard had left in their cars a few minutes before while we had been getting the mattresses. Lynda and Mick had gone with their mom. Dad told me that he sure wished that Clay were there to lend a hand.

I told Dad how I had modified the wire on the gate to make it easier to get through and how I had told Lenny to build a small fire. I figured it would help keep Jay a little warmer, plus the smoke would help guide Dad to where he was. Dad told me that I had handled things just right and that he sure was proud of me.

There weren't any roads leading back to where Jay was but since the ground was frozen and dry Dad was able to get the pickup across the country without getting stuck. However, he did manage to knock off the mirror on the passenger side when he flew too close past a juniper. Dad just glanced over after hearing the impact of the branch and saw that the mirror was gone but didn't even slow down until we reached the gate to the east of where Jay was lying on the cold bedrock. I quickly jumped out and opened the gate.

From the gate we could see the smoke from the fire Lenny had built. I told Dad as he drove through, "Go on to Jay, I will get the gate and run over there."

As I had suggested Lenny had gotten a small fire going on the smooth rock next to where Jay was laying and the smoke from it helped guide Dad right to him. He skidded the pickup to a stop next to the creek crossing and was immediately out the door running to where Jay was laying. I was only a few minutes behind him.

While Dad talked with Jay and assessed his injuries he had me find a couple stout and reasonably straight branches two or three feet long. Then he asked Lenny to get a coil of rope from behind the truck's seat.

With all of the junipers in the area it was pretty easy to find suitable branches. I broke off a couple that I thought would work. I had seen enough westerns to know without asking what Dad intended to do with them. I started to hand them to him as he was bent over Jay examining the broken leg.

Dad looked up at me and said, "Son, just hold them on either side of Jay's right leg." Lenny had fetched the rope as requested and Dad wrapped it around the leg and the two sticks so they would act as a splint to help keep the leg from moving much on what was still going to be a painful ride back to the headquarters for the old cowboy. There was really no way around that.

Once the makeshift splint was securely in place Dad gently lifted Jay up and carried him to the rear of the truck. He placed him down as carefully as he could on the mattresses in the pickup's bed.

The ride back to the headquarters was going to be rough on Jay but the mattresses would at least help cushion the bumps a little. Dad knew that it would be easier on him to lie in the bed of the truck rather than try and sit up in the cab.

After he had gotten Jay settled on top of the two mattresses Dad said, "Jeff, you hop in with Jay and try to help steady him a little so he doesn't get knocked around so badly on the way back to the headquarters. Lenny, I want you to ride your horse back and lead Jay's horse."

Lenny responded, "Yes sir, Mr. Dean. Except for a few cuts on his legs the horse looks okay. But I will go easy with him on the way back in." Dad had been so worried about Jay that he hadn't even asked about the horse.

I could only imagine how bumpy the ride cross-country back to the nearest ranch road in the pickup bed was going to be. Hell, it would be rough enough even after we reached the rocky and rutted road.

Jumping up in the bed of the truck I knelt down next to Jay. Then we were on our way back to the headquarters. I sat down and grabbed onto him to help hold him in place like Dad had told me to.

Jay was tough and he accepted the whole thing as just part of being a cowboy. I could tell he was in a lot of pain but he never once cried out, even when the truck would hit a bad rut or rolled over a rock, which caused his right leg to be bumped or jerked.

I was trying to steady him as much as I was able to. Jay could see that I was worried about him and told me, "Jeff, don't you be fretting about this too much. Remember that wreck I told you about on the Mimbres? Well, hell, this here ain't nothing compared to that one."

"Yeah, Jay, I remember," I answered. Indeed I did remember Jay telling me about that wreck but I also knew that he had been a lot younger when that one had happened.

Back at the headquarters we were all happy to see that Doc Thorpe was already there and waiting for us. He checked Jay's right leg and looked for other signs of injury. Then Dad and the doctor carefully removed Jay from the back of the truck and placed him on a cot that had been set up for him. They then covered him with a couple of heavy blankets.

Doc Thorpe determined that in addition to the right leg which was broken in at least two places, Jay had probably cracked a few ribs and might even have broken his right hip when he came down onto that bedrock. They wouldn't know the full extent of his injuries until they had gotten him to a hospital and he had had x-rays.

Doc Thorpe gave Jay a shot of morphine for the pain and something to make him fall asleep. The doc figured that Jay had already had to endure enough pain and the trip out in the ambulance would be a lot easier if he was out cold.

The ambulance arrived about an hour or so after we had gotten Jay back to the ranch's headquarters. They took him to the hospital in Kingman. Dad had driven his truck and followed the ambulance. He stayed at the hospital until he was sure his cowboy and friend wasn't in any danger and was going to be alright. Dad had gotten back to the ranch in the middle of the night.

The next morning at breakfast, after just a few hours of sleep, he filled us in. It turned out that Jay's leg was indeed broken in a couple places and he did have some broken ribs. But the good news was that his hip was only badly bruised, not broken. Jay would have to spend at least a couple days in the hospital.

Dad told us that he would go into town and get him and bring him back to the ranch a few days before Christmas Eve. He said when he had come to at the hospital Jay had joked that he sure would be mad about the wreck if it cost him getting to have some of the Christmas dinner that my Mom and Mrs. Howard were going to prepare.

That evening Mr. Howard arrived from Flagstaff. Mrs. Howard had called him from Seligman when she had driven in to get the ambulance and told him of Jay's accident. The Howards had immediately decided that Jay would stay with them when he returned to the ranch at least until he had healed a little and Clay was back from Wyoming.

They converted Joe's home office into a bedroom. Jay's bed was moved from the bunkhouse and put in what had been the office. Once Jay returned to the ranch from the hospital everyone knew he would protest the special treatment but Mrs. Howard would insist and that would be that.

Chapter 7
Pushing Cattle

Dad was shorthanded with Jay in the hospital and Clay off visiting his family in Cheyenne. So the morning after Jay's wreck he came over to the barn looking for some wranglers after he had seen to the generator. That was something the hired hands usually took care of the first thing in the morning, especially during winter time. The generator motor had to be serviced and the fuel tank filled frequently.

Lenny and I were busy putting out feed for the horses and breaking a thin layer of ice in the troughs when he came walking up to us from the generator shed. Lynda and Mick hadn't come down yet to start their chores.

When we looked up at his approach Dad said, "Boys, I got a job I need you two to do this morning. Jay had planned on having it done by now but the wreck stopped him."

"What do you need us to do, Dad?" I asked.

Lenny also jumped in with, "Anything you need us to do, Mr. Dean, just tell us and we will sure do it."

"That's what I like to hear, boys." Dad said. He then continued, "The day before yesterday Jay rounded up a small bunch of cattle from the Holden Ranch that had gotten through a break in our south boundary fence. He gathered them and corralled them in one of our water lots for safe-keeping not far from the south boundary. I need them moved and pushed back onto their home ground."

I knew that these were the cattle that Jay had told us that he had intended to move yesterday afternoon. But he hadn't provided all of the details. I told Dad that Jay had mentioned the strays to us before the accident. Then he told us a little more about the Holden Ranch cattle that he had heard from Jay at the hospital. He also explained why they needed to be moved from where Jay had left them.

Dad explained how two days earlier Jay had been out checking waters and fences to the south of the headquarters and had come upon a bunch of Holden Ranch branded cattle late in the day. They were near a fenced water tank, so he drove them into the water lot and closed the gates since none of the P Bar J's cattle were currently using that range.

It was in the pasture directly west of South Pasture. Jay's thinking had been that after finishing the cattle move that we had helped him with the day before he would ride on down and push those cattle back to where they belonged. The wreck had caused that plan not to work out.

After Jay had come out of the operation to reset his leg and his ribs were taped, Dad sat in his room with him until he came to and they talked for a while before Dad headed home. It must have been around 2 or 3 a.m. before Dad had gotten back to the ranch last night. I had heard his truck when he got back. It had been another long day for him.

The first thing Jay did after regaining consciousness was tell Dad that those cattle needed to be moved since they were penned up in the water lot without much feed. They would have had block salt and whatever browse they could get from the brush growing within the fenced area but compared to the open range, pickings for the bunch would start to get pretty damn slim after a few days.

I asked Dad, "Would it be okay if we had Lynda help us?" I knew Lynda had been feeling sort of left out on the cowboy work and she would love a chance to spend a day riding Trixie. Plus, although I wouldn't want to say it aloud, I wanted an excuse to spend more time with her.

Dad said, "Son, I think that is a really good idea. I know Lynda is a good hand on a horse." Lenny also said that he thought having his sister along would be a big help in case we should have trouble keeping the bunch together as we herded them south. While Jay could have handled them on his own we didn't have his experience or confidence.

Now we just had to get the okay from Mrs. Howard. Before heading up to the house Lenny and I set our saddles and blankets out in the sun so they could start warming up.

Then Lenny and I went over to the Howards' to tell Mrs. Howard what my dad needed us to do that morning and to ask Lynda to join us. When I was asking Lynda, with her mother present, I was careful to say it in a way so it sounded like it had been my dad's request for the three of us to herd the bunch of strays. Lynda, of course, was rearing to go on our little trail drive. Lenny backed me up, since he knew his sister wanted to go.

Although Mrs. Howard had things for her to do at the house to help her, she saw how much Lynda wanted to go with us. So when Lynda looked at her mother for permission she just smiled and said, "It sounds like Roy needs your help today, Lynda, so you go on with the boys. I will put some lunches together for the three of you and bring them down to the barn before you are ready to head out."

The three of us then hurried outside and headed down to the barn. Mick followed along behind us. As soon as we got to the barn I put Lynda's saddle and blanket out in the sun next to the ones Lenny and I had put out earlier, so all of the gear would be warmed up by the time we saddled the three horses. I would have done it earlier when Lenny and I were putting our stuff in the sun, but I hadn't known for sure if Mrs. Howard would give her permission. If Lynda hadn't been allowed to ride with us seeing her saddle and blanket out when she came down to do her chores would have just made her feel worse.

Since Lenny and I had gotten a head start earlier we quickly finished our chores. Then, anxious to get saddled up and headed out, we helped Lynda and Mick with theirs.

When he had given us the task of moving the cattle back to the Holden Ranch, my dad had told us to be sure to take along a couple lariats. They would be needed in case we had to lead any of the Holden cattle in order to get them where we wanted them to go. Plus, he said we would need a pair of fence pliers and a length of wire to use for any necessary fence repairs.

Dad told us to head the cattle southeast a little, toward Bobcat Draw once we had them out of the water lot and moving. When we got close to the south boundary, one of us would need to ride ahead to the east-west running fence and take out the wires between a couple posts so the cows could go through. We would then use the pliers for putting the wires back together and making sure we got them tight enough.

Once the cattle were pushed back through the fence onto their home range Dad wanted us to ride the fence line to find where the bunch had come through and then fix the break. He had gotten a small roll of heavy wire and the pliers from the tool room and had me put them in my saddlebags for use in making any needed fence repairs. Also, we might end up needing the extra wire for repairing the portion of fence we were going to cut for moving the cattle through.

We were taking Skipper and Jenny with us. The dogs would be able to help hold the bunch together as we pushed them toward the south boundary fence. There always seemed to be at least one bunch quitter.

Mrs. Howard walked down to the barn with lunches for us just as we were ready to saddle up and ride. We headed out to the south from the headquarters while it was still early morning. The lunches were stuffed in our saddlebags.

It took us a little over an hour to reach the water lot where Jay had left the stray cattle two days earlier. As we rode up to the main gate we could see that there were a total of nine cows inside. The dirt tank wasn't very good and I had heard Dad and Jay talking about its leaky bottom and how it needed to be cleaned and have some bentonite put down before it would be dependable and hold water for very long.

Bentonite spread over the bottom would serve to seal it. The water in the tank was at the time down to about a third of its capacity which meant that a cow wanting a drink had to go through a fair amount of partially frozen mud before reaching the water.

As we stopped at the gate I noticed that one cow appeared to be stuck in the shallow, muddy water. There was a little ice around the edges and the cow had to get out past it in order to reach the water. I remembered that this was the same tank where I had watched Jay drag a stuck cow out of the mud the previous summer.

The first thing we did was check the brands on the cows to make sure they all belonged on the Holden Ranch. It turned out that only seven of them, including the one stuck in the mud, were Holden cattle. The other two belonged to the P Bar J. Those two had probably gotten through a break in a division fence somewhere and had gotten into the water lot through a trigger after Jay had closed the gate on the strays.

I wrote down a description of the two cows in the little pocket notebook that I had gotten into the habit of always carrying since Dad had given it to me. With that information he would later be able to tell where the pair belonged. For now we would just leave them in the water lot.

Dismounting near the water lot's gate we stood looking out at the stuck cow and wondered how we could best go about freeing it. I told Lynda how Jay had gotten a stuck cow out of the same tank and we decided to give it a try. I knew that Lenny was familiar with the technique from the comment he had made about pulling me out of a tank with a rope when we had been out chopping ice. He had probably watched a cowboy do it the same as I had.

We each took turns trying to drop a lasso over the cow's horns. After several tries and misses we were about to give up when Lynda's lasso dropped neatly over the horns. I had been about ready to remove my boots and wade out in the mud and water to put a rope around the horns. I was glad it hadn't come to that. I knew the water would have been pretty cold.

Lenny was riding the biggest horse and he volunteered to try and pull the cow out. I had told him how Jay had done it. I didn't know who Lenny had seen do it but I felt Jay's technique would be the one to copy. Lenny positioned his horse so that when he pulled the rope with a strong jerk the cow would be flipped over on its back and he could then basically slide it right out of the tank. I think the three of us were amazed when it actually worked!

Even though what we had done had most likely saved the cow's life she didn't understand why she had been roped and then dragged on her back through the mud. I knew that the old cow was going to be mad and looking for someone to take it out on. So I had Lynda hold my horse's reins and as soon as the cow came to a sliding stop I had run over and removed the rope and then ran back to my horse and jumped up in the saddle.

The cow got to her feet and started to charge Lenny since he was the closest. However, I had told him what to expect once we had freed the cow and he has ready. He had dropped his end of the rope as soon as I had removed the other end from the rescued cow. The three of us took off fast and rode up to a far corner of the water lot and waited for the cow to cool off a little. It soon joined the others on the far side of the tank. Lenny walked over to where the lariat lay and picked it up. He coiled it as he walked back to his horse. He then fastened it back in place near his saddle horn with a piece of rawhide.

By then we had all worked up an appetite. We tied our horses to a fence rail and sat on the H-brace and watched the bunch while we had a little snack from our lunch sacks. Mrs. Howard had packed a good lunch!

After ten minutes or so we mounted up and started the task we had been assigned by my dad. Lynda took Jenny and cut out the P Bar J cows and moved them off into a corner. I couldn't help but notice that she made it look easy.

Cutting or herding cattle takes skill on both the rider's and the horse's part. The cowboy, or cowgirl, needs to position their horse even with the cow or calf they are trying to turn. If they get ahead of it the cow might stop and then cut across behind the horse so it can continue in the direction that it had been heading. Or if the rider is behind the animal the cow can simply cut across in front of the horse. Being alongside the chosen cow allows the cowboy to use his horse to "push" the critter in the desired direction.

After Lynda had accomplished her task Lenny and I gathered the Holden bunch. With Skipper nipping at their legs and barking we drove them out through the wide open gate and headed them to the southeast. Once we had the bunch out and moving in the desired direction Lynda rode out of the water lot, closed the swing gate, and quickly caught up to us.

I had been happy to see that the water lot had a swing gate. They are sometimes called a Texas gate. I really liked them. Swing gates are a lot easier to open and close than the wire gates. They can usually be opened or closed without the necessity of even dismounting.

I guess just to test whether we were paying attention every once in a while a few of the cows would try to break from the bunch and head back to the water. One of us or the dogs would speed up and get the bunch quitters headed in the right direction again. Luckily the horses and the dogs were experienced in moving cattle and knew their jobs without a lot of input from us.

Since the pliers were in my saddlebags I told Lenny and Lynda that I would ride on ahead and get the fence down before they reached it. I gave my horse a little kick in the ribs with the heels of my boots (none of us were in the habit of wearing spurs) and galloped toward the boundary fence. I recognized Bobcat Draw as I rode past it and knew I was close to the boundary fence.

At the fence I looked for a place where it had been repaired before and used the fencing pliers to remove the four strands of barbed wire from where they were fastened to some big juniper fence posts. I then carefully folded the wires back out of the way so the cattle and our horses wouldn't get tangled in them. Getting its feet in loose wires could spook a horse and cause it to start bucking, which I really wanted to avoid. Horses could also get bad cuts on their legs from encounters with loose barbed wire. I could imagine the lecture that I would get from Dad or Jay if I ever brought a horse in with barbed wire cuts on its legs.

With the wires out of the way and secured I climbed back up on my horse and moved off a little ways and waited between two large alligator junipers. I needed to be out of sight so that the cattle wouldn't see me as they were approaching the fence and get spooked away from the opening I had made.

I only had to wait a few minutes before Lynda and Lenny arrived with the bunch. They scanned the fence line and quickly saw the opening and guided the cattle to it with the help of the herd dogs.

Once the cattle saw the opening in the fence as they got close they headed for it on their own. They quickly charged through it and back onto their home range. As Lynda and Lenny held their horses up at the fence line and watched the cattle disappear amid the junipers and brush beyond I rode up to join them.

I reached behind me and grabbed the pliers from one of the saddlebags, and started to climb down. I figured we would get the fence put back together and then head west along the boundary fence looking for the break. Once we had found it and did the necessary repairs we could head back to the headquarters.

It was getting on towards late morning and Lynda asked what Jacks Canyon looked like since she knew Lenny and I had both seen it. She assumed there would be a stream with water so before we could answer the first question she added another one, "Hey, since it's about time for lunch why don't we ride down into the canyon and eat next to the creek?"

"It sounds good to me, Lynda," I answered and then added, "but we will need to put these wires back up after we ride through, so the cows we pushed won't try getting back onto the P Bar J."

We moved our horses through the opening in the fence onto the Holden Ranch. With the fence pliers already in hand I jumped down from my saddle. I handed Lynda my reins.

The strays had been heading south when we had last seen them and were most likely on their way down to the creek in Jacks Canyon for a drink. I thought there wasn't much chance of them going back through the break in the boundary fence they had come across earlier anytime soon, so we could afford to take a little lunch break before riding the fence line to look for it.

With Lenny's help the four strands of barbed wire were soon reattached to the juniper posts well enough to hold until we got back. Later when we were back on the north side of the fence we would be sure to attach them more securely and tighter. Dad had explained to me the importance of keeping fences tight so deer wouldn't get their legs tangled up in slack wires while jumping them.

Saddled back up we slowly wove our way between the junipers toward the south. Jacks Canyon was only about two miles south of the boundary fence. We were riding along, talking and enjoying the ride and our success at moving the cattle, when we noticed what looked like traces of an old road.

We had ridden about a mile since going through the fence and had drifted a little to the west from the route Lenny, Jay, and I had ridden the past summer. It looked like the road hadn't been used in a long time and it had been colonized by bushy junipers.

Lenny said, "Let's do some exploring and see where this old road leads." Lynda and I were both thinking the same thing and immediately agreed with him. So we started heading in, what I guessed to be a southwesterly direction. At times I was pretty sure we were headed due west. The road followed a ridgeline for a while. Then it dropped down a slope to the south of the ridge and to our surprise ended on a flat at an old cabin that appeared to be fairly intact. The flat looked to me like it had been cleared at one time but junipers had since reclaimed it to a point where it would have been difficult to spot the cabin from any distance.

"Wow!" Lenny exclaimed and then continued, "Take a look over there … it looks like a Model T truck!" I looked over to where he was looking and pointing. Sure enough there was a Model T, with a pickup bed, wedged between a couple junipers that had most likely grown considerably since the old Ford had last moved. It looked like the trees had the truck trapped.

From the looks of things we were the first to stumble upon this place in a lot of years. Dad had mentioned that the Holden Ranch didn't have cowhands that regularly rode their range and that the owners lived in Phoenix and only came up to the ranch when they had to. That's why they hadn't known about the bunch of their cows that had ended up on the south end of the P Bar J.

Also, this little strip of juniper-covered land between Jacks Canyon and the boundary fence would have been fairly unimportant to them. Dad had said that the owners of the Holden Ranch didn't even have any interest in helping to keep up the shared boundary fence and left the maintenance of it to the P Bar J Ranch.

Riding up to the little cabin Lynda said, "Let's see what's inside," as she jumped down from Trixie. Lenny and I followed her lead. There was a rickety looking hitch rail in front of the cabin and we tied our horses' reins to it before stepping up on the cabin's small porch. The front door was hung on dried and cracked leather hinges. The top hinge had broken apart, leaving the door hanging inward. Opening it all the way we stepped into the one room cabin.

There were a couple of wooden framed, single beds against two of the walls. A pot belly stove was next to the back wall, with a pipe going up through the roof above it. The walls had been papered with newspapers, with dates from the late 1920s and early '30s. I noticed an ad on one of the pages for a La Salle car and another for Reo trucks. They caught my eye since I wasn't familiar with either brand.

A calendar on the wall was opened to July 1934. A can of Arbuckle's coffee was on a shelf near the stove. There were a few cans of soup with tops that were puffed up on other shelves. I knew that was caused by whatever was inside spoiling. Old clothes were scattered on the floor.

There were a few pieces of homemade furniture, including a table, a bench, and a couple chairs. The cabin reminded me of the ones the bad guys always seemed to use for a hideout in the B Westerns. It would be easy to picture Roy Barcroft sitting at the table waiting for his henchmen to arrive with a stolen mine deed or the loot from a bank or stagecoach holdup.

Standing near the stove I happened to glance out the little window on the rear wall of the cabin. Through the open window frame there was a view of what lay behind the cabin. What I saw gave me a chill.

Walking up to the window to get a better look I noticed that it looked like the panes of glass along with the wood framing had been pushed out from the inside. Glancing through the opening I saw them laying in pieces on the ground. A broken out window in a deserted cabin wasn't big news so I didn't mention it to my companions. But the graves I found myself staring at were another matter.

"Look, there are a bunch of graves out there," I said to Lynda and Lenny. They looked out and saw them. Then we were all pretty much ready to leave. Our curiosity about the old cabin was satisfied. But we did want to take a look out back before leaving. We walked around the side of the house and stood looking at a row of half a dozen graves mounded with rocks. A couple of them still had crude wooded crosses on them. But the one that caught my eye had several dried flowers on it.

It appeared that someone had also tried to transplant a wild rose bush on it. The plant had dried up and died. Something else I noticed was that it appeared that all of the graves were being cared for. There were dry weeds and grasses on adjacent areas but not on the graves. None of the rocks piled on the graves were scattered as would be expected after a number of years. The rocks around the edges of the individual graves had obviously been aligned with care. Someone had been tending these plots.

After the quick look at the graves we decided that we hd best be going. Our excuse was that we were all ready to get to the creek and have lunch. But truthfully this old homestead had suddenly acquired the feel of a graveyard that I don't think any of us wanted to linger at any longer.

Back on the horses we quickly rode away from the cabin without talking. We headed south. Before long the tops of the leafless cottonwoods could be seen sticking up over the basalt rim of Jacks Canyon. We hunted around and found a spot where the rim was broken down enough that we could ride down to the bottom and water the horses at the creek.

There was a pretty good flow in the creek. We tied the horses to some low-hanging cottonwood limbs and got our lunches out of the saddlebags and sat on some rocks at the edge of the water and ate.

The dogs waded into the creek to drink and then found spots to lie down and rest. After a while, we started talking again about successfully moving the cattle and how we were enjoying handling cowboy work just like the adults. There was also some discussion about our discovery of the homestead and the graves.

After lunch we headed north back to the P Bar J and after a little searching found the spot in the fence we had come through. I got off my horse and quickly took it apart just as I had earlier.

Once we had gone back through the opening Lenny and I put the fence back together and made sure it was tight. Lynda stayed mounted while she held the reins of our horses. The job only took us a few minutes.

We then started riding west along the fence line. We ended up riding three or four miles before we found the break. Using some of the wire on the roll Dad had given me Lenny and I soon had it repaired and were in agreement that nothing was going to be able to get through it again.

We then turned north toward the P Bar J's headquarters. We rode along side by side so we could talk. The dogs were finding occasional cottontails and jackrabbits to chase. If Lynda saw that it looked like they were going to catch one she would yell at them to come back.

As we rode along talking I thought I heard a clicking sound about the time Lynda asked, "Jeff I think I hear a noise that seems to be coming from one of your horse's hooves."

"Yeah, Lynda, I am hearing it, too," I replied. I think I would have ignored it if she hadn't said anything.

The three of us pulled up and I climbed down. Leading my horse by the reins I listened for the sound. The clicking noise was coming from the left rear hoof each time it came in contact with the rocky ground. I asked Lenny, who by then had also dismounted, to hold the reins while I checked the hoof. The horseshoe was just barely attached ... two of the nails had completely fallen out, and the remaining ones were loose.

We didn't have any extra nails with us which probably was just as well since none of us were exactly sure about how to shoe a horse. I made a mental note to ask my dad to show me how, since it was a skill that would be handy for a cowboy to know. Once I could do it I would make it a practice on horseback rides to carry the necessary tools to reattach a horseshoe, and even an extra shoe in case one got lost. But that was in the future ... this particular day it looked like I would be walking.

At least it wasn't very far. We were only a mile or two from the headquarters so I told Lenny and Lynda to go on ahead and I would lead my horse. They both pretty much answered at the same time and said that they would walk with me. I just smiled and thanked them for offering to keep me company on the walk back, but truthfully I would have preferred it if only Lynda had made the offer.

Still holding up the hoof with the loose shoe with my left hand I grabbed one edge of it with my right hand and pulled it off the rest of the way. I slipped the horseshoe into one of my saddlebags after pulling out and tossing the remaining bent and worn nails.

With the three of us walking along leading the horses and talking it didn't really seem to take long before we were at the barn and corral. Dad was in the barn when he saw us and came out to see why we had been walking instead of riding.

Looking at me and grinning Dad said, "Jeff, I know that you and your partners there are still learning the ropes, but the first thing a cowboy learns is never walk when you can ride." I told him about the loose shoe and how I, at least, hadn't had any choice but to walk back to the headquarters. He told me that he had figured that something had happened to put us afoot but he couldn't resist the little joke. He knew there were good reasons for us not to be riding.

As he started to look at my horse he told Lynda and Lenny to see to their horses. That meant unsaddling them, giving them a good brushing, and then putting them out in the corral with some oats

Dad picked up the horse's left rear hoof and took a look. After making sure the hoof wasn't damaged he went around and checked the other three hooves and shoes. While he was doing it he had his pocket knife out and removed a few small pebbles. Afterwards he said that the other shoes and hooves appeared to be okay.

"Jeff, you did everything just like you should. You removed the loose shoe and you walked your horse ... you are getting to be a real cowboy," Dad told me after he had finished his inspection of my horse's hooves.

I remembered hearing how years earlier on one of the first ranches where he was the foreman he had fired a cowboy who had lamed a horse by riding it with a missing shoe over some rocky country.

The cowboy had tried to justify injuring the horse by telling my dad that he had work to do and he didn't care very damn much for walking. That turned out to be pretty much the worst thing to say to my dad while he was still examining the horse's injured hoof.

He turned to the cowboy and said, "A real cowboy would rather lame himself by walking several miles in his boots than risk harming his horse, you damn fool ... you go down to the bunkhouse and grab your gear, I am firing your dumb ass."

Even if I hadn't heard that story I would have still walked the horse after discovering the loose shoe. It seemed to me even at the age of twelve just to be common sense. But as I got older I would come across lots of people that were totally lacking in that department.

Dad said that he had time right then to replace the shoe. He told me to go ahead and get the horse unsaddled and then lead him over in front of the workshop.

"Okay, Dad. Here, let me show you the shoe that came off. I thought you might be able to reuse it," I said.

I then dug the horseshoe out of my saddlebag and handed it to him. He examined it and shaking his head he tossed the shoe over next to the edge of the front wall of the workshop where it would be out of the way.

"It was good thinking, son, that you saved the shoe but it looks like it's worn to the point that it doesn't make sense wasting the time to reattach it. I will just go ahead and fit a new one while I am at it," he said.

He then went into the workshop and grabbed the tools that he would need for the job. As he stepped out of the workshop with a metal tray holding several tools he turned and walked over to where Lynda and Lenny were tending to their horses. He told them when they were finished feeding and watering their horses to join us over in front of the workshop. He said that he was going to put a new shoe on the horse that I had been riding and figured that while he was at it he would show all of us how to do it ... at least the basics.

I would brush my horse and feed him after Dad was finished with the shoeing. He said it wouldn't take very long to attach one new shoe.

Whenever I think of horseshoeing I remember how Dad, like most cowboys, always carried a few extra shoeing nails in the rolled up cuffs of their jeans to have them handy whenever they were needed. And of course like most cowboys he routinely forgot about them when the jeans were tossed in the dirty clothes hamper.

I remember Mom frequently complaining about the nails that ended up in the washing machine and how they would put holes in the clothes. She always tried to remember to unroll and empty out cuffs before sticking jeans into the washer. If they didn't have nails, they usually had dirt, bits of twigs, cigarette butts, etc. that didn't need to go in with a load of clothes she was trying to get clean.

Dad had explained to me previously that along with nails it was good to carry a pair of needle nose pliers in your saddlebags. The pliers were necessary for holding a nail in place while you hammered it in. However, it wasn't necessary to carry a heavy hammer along on rides, since usually a rock would be handy for that job.

With Lynda, Lenny, and I gathered a safe distance from the horse, my dad picked up the horse's rear hoof that needed to be shoed and began the process, while explaining each step to us. He started off by telling us, "Now, I don't expect any of you to be shoeing horses on your own for a few years but it won't hurt for you to have an idea of how it's done."

The first step was to check the hoof for any small stones or other debris and to check for any injury. Dad used a small pick to remove a few pieces of gravel that he had missed when he was using his pocket knife earlier. Once the hoof was cleaned he grabbed what he told us was a hoof knife and used it to remove some excess sole from the bottom of the horse's foot. He followed that by using nippers to trim off excess hoof wall around the edges of the hoof. After that he picked up a rasp and filed down the edges of the hoof so there was a flat surface.

As Dad was using the rasp he looked up at me and said, "Jeff, go over to the bin where we keep new horse shoes and grab half a dozen."

I did as he asked and laid them on the ground next to where he was working. When he had the hoof properly prepped he picked up a couple of the shoes and set them on the hoof one at a time to gauge the fit.

The shoes had a little variation in their size just like horse's hoofs do. Neither of the first two he picked up seemed to fit right but the third one he tried was apparently pretty close.

Holding it up so we could see it Dad told us, "This one will do the job with just a little fine tuning." With that he let the horse's leg drop down to the ground and he took the selected horse shoe over to the work bench. A heavy anvil was attached to a thick block of wood that sat on the floor next to one end of the work bench.

Grabbing a large hammer from a peg on the wall over the bench Dad laid the shoe on the anvil and gave it several good whacks. He inspected it, gave it a few more slightly lighter strikes with the hammer and then started back to the horse with a satisfied look on his face.

"Now it should be just about perfect," he said as he bent down and picked the horse's leg up again. Then he attached the new shoe with a small hammer by driving nails on an outward angle so they came out through the wall of the hoof. He tapped the ends of the nails so that they lay in closely against the hoof instead of sticking outward. A driving hammer was used to hit the heads of the nails to set them. He used the rasp again to file grooves below the nail heads and then using clenchers he set the nails so they would stay on.

Dad finished the lesson with, "Now ... again I don't want any of you trying this for some time. If it's not done right the horse can end up crippled."

I had seen enough cowboys with cuts on their arms and even missing teeth from being kicked by horses they were shoeing that I wasn't in any hurry to try it myself. I don't think Lynda or Lenny were anxious to give it a try either. But the lesson had been interesting and I thought it was useful information for a budding cowboy to have.

Since Dad knew we wouldn't be jumping right into careers as farriers he glossed over or simplified some of the steps such as setting or seating the nails. But how I related the lesson we received that day was pretty much how he gave it to us while he did the work. When he was finished and released the horse's leg it was all ready for me to ride the next day.

That evening at supper I told Mom and Dad about the cabin and all the graves behind it that we had found on the Holden Ranch. Mom told me that she hoped I was careful looking around old places like that since there could be an open well, or a mine shaft, or any number of other dangers that mothers seemed to worry about.

Thinking about the old cabin she said, "It was probably full of pack rats and you kids could have gotten bitten by one. There could have been bats in there too." Since it was winter at least rattlesnakes weren't a worry.

Dad said after a few moments of thought, "Oh, it sounds like you kids must have found an old cabin that Jay told me about. Just after I got to the P Bar J, Jay and I were out riding the south boundary fence line when at one spot he pointed off to the south and said that there was an old homestead, or rather squatter's camp a mile or so in on the Holden Ranch. I seem to recall that he called it the "Old Denham Place."

He went on to tell Mom and me the story of the Denhams, and how the whole family had been murdered in the 1930s, as he had heard it from Jay, and later from others in the Seligman area that were old enough to remember. According to Dad it was still a common topic that was discussed in the cafes and bars in the area. It seemed that there were a number of theories as to who had killed the Denham family. But no one really knew for certain what had happened at the isolated cabin all those years ago.

The Denham family had moved into that area sometime after the crash of '29 and built the little cabin. The rancher at the time on what's now the Holden Ranch just figured on ignoring them and that sooner or later they would drift on to somewhere else. There was a mother and father and three or four kids. A couple of the kids were close to being adults. The family poached deer and antelope for food and did some trapping to sell furs, but left the rancher's cattle alone for the most part.

One day the rancher, who hadn't seen anything of the family for a while, decided to ride over and check to see if they had moved on. If they had he was planning on burning the cabin before any other squatters came along. However, what he found was the bodies of the whole family.

The rancher rode back to his place and got his truck and went into town and reported what he had found. A Sheriff's deputy and the county coroner came out with a few others and it was quickly determined that they had all been murdered. The bodies were scattered around and in an advanced state of decay.

A couple of the bodies were inside the cabin, one or two were outside as if those victims had tried to run away, and another was found inside the Model T truck. That was the reason no one had ever salvaged the truck and it had just been left out there. By the time the crime was discovered the inside of the truck had a smell that wasn't going to be gotten rid of. No one had the stomach to even try to deal with it.

Dad said, "I seem to remember that it happened in the summer so the bodies probably started decaying and smelling pretty dang quickly."

At that point I noticed Mom glaring at him and she said, "Roy, I don't think Jeff needs to get such a vivid description of what it must have been like for those poor people ... and for that matter, neither do I ... especially at the dinner table."

After a brief pause Mom added, "Honestly, Roy Dean, you are going to give him nightmares."

Before Mom forced the conversation onto another subject I mentioned the calendar on the wall of the cabin being on July. That seemed to confirm what Dad said he had heard about the crime happening during the heat of a summer.

Dad just gave me a smile and nodded. It was obvious that he didn't want to upset Mom anymore. However, we were able to talk about it later that evening when Mom was over at the Howards' talking to Abby. The two women had become good friends.

Due to the isolated nature of the area and the deterioration of the bodies the Deputy and the coroner, along with a couple men they had brought along to help move the bodies decided at the time to bury them behind the cabin. No next of kin were ever located. No one even knew for sure where the family had come from or even all of their names. It was assumed at the time that all of the victims were members of the same family.

There hadn't been any evidence found at the Denham's cabin and its surroundings, and there were no leads that could be followed. So the crime was never solved.

As far as Dad had heard no suspects were ever even questioned about the murders. There was some speculation that the Denham family must had gotten involved in a feud with one of the other homesteader families that were squatting in the area at the time.

Upon hearing the story I thought about that family from time to time and wondered what had happened out there north of Jacks Canyon. I found the speculation of a feud with other squatters or homesteaders especially interesting.

It had occurred to me that the Owsleys were also in the area in the '30s and had packed up and left, from what I had heard, rather suddenly. Had they been running from a crime that evidently no one had ever even suspected that they had committed?

The two families' homes were several miles apart so what could have been a source of conflict between them? Would it always remain an unsolved crime?

Later that night while lying in bed trying to fall asleep I was still thinking about what had happened at the Denhams' little cabin almost twenty years earlier. Where were their murderers now? What had triggered the murders? Also, who had been visiting the graves and leaving flowers and clearing weeds off them? Was it one of the murderers with a guilty conscience, or perhaps some family members had survived? I had no idea at the time, but I would get the answers to these questions eventually.

However, until then that empty cabin and the row of graves were in my thoughts a lot. That was especially true at night when I was trying to get to sleep. So there I was starting to be a real cowboy, and thinking what I needed to be was a real detective in order to solve that crime.

Chapter 8
New Ranch Hand

Bright and early the following morning, after all of our chores at the headquarters were finished, Lenny, Lynda, and I were once again saddled up and headed south. The dogs were running out ahead of us as if they knew exactly what we were going to be doing.

We were going to collect the two cows that were left at the water lot and push them to the North Pasture where my dad had told us they belonged.

He had told us before we left the headquarters, "The three of you are old hands at this sort of cowboy work now." I think that made all of us feel pretty good. Even better was the fact that Mrs. Howard was letting Lynda ride with us again.

On the ride south I told the twins what I had learned about the Denham family from my dad. Lenny said that he probably wouldn't have even gone inside that cabin if he had known what had happened there and I noticed that Lynda nodded in agreement with her twin.

I answered, "That's just it, Lenny. No one knows what actually did happen and why." That was the part of the story that I found especially interesting and intriguing, and I guess at the same time somewhat troubling. The murderer, or murderers, had gotten clean away with it and could still be around as far as anyone knew. The good guys hadn't caught them like they always did in the movies.

It was scary to me that the killer or killers could still be around. It had only been a little over 18 years since the crimes that had occurred at the Denhams' cabin in 1934 had been committed. The killers could be people we had seen in one of the nearby towns.

It occurred to me that it was the same thing that had happened to the Moore family in what later became Lost Cabin Canyon on the Broken W Ranch. One of Jay's friends had told us the story of the Moores the summer before when we took a troublesome bull out to the Broken W.

That pioneer family had all been murdered and their killers were never caught. But at least those killings had occurred in the early 1870s. So even though the killers hadn't been caught and punished at the time, by 1952 it was pretty certain that they were as dead as their victims and couldn't hurt anyone else.

I was already working over in my head about whether the Owsleys had anything to do with the Denham family's deaths, but I was keeping the thoughts to myself, at least for the time being. After I had told Lynda and Lenny the story of the murdered family, as my dad had told it to me, we rode along in silence until we reached the water lot.

At the water lot I was glad to see that neither of the cows had gotten stuck in the mud. After pushing the seven cows the day before it was relatively easy handling just the two. Within a few hours we had them relocated in the North Pasture where they belonged. Since we were up in that country anyway we took a loop ride through the pasture, checking fences and water lots. We had brought along lunches and found a nice spot to stop and eat. It was close to late afternoon before we headed back to the headquarters.

Weather-wise the past couple of days on horseback had been fairly comfortable. We were in the middle of a warm spell with sunny days and very little breeze. It was cold in the early mornings, but as soon as the sun got up a ways we were able to take our coats off and tie them behind our saddles. It was warm enough that we hadn't needed to do any ice chopping for a while. Lenny and I were grateful for that.

Dad had gone into Kingman early that morning to pick Jay up at the hospital. He had left just after we had headed out on the horses to move the two cows.

As we were unsaddling our horses we saw a cloud of dust on the access road that led into the ranch from Route 66 and figured it was my dad coming back with his senior ranch hand. Sure enough it was them.

Jay had been expecting to be taken down to the bunkhouse when Dad got back to the ranch with him. He was understandably surprised when they pulled up in front of the Howards' house instead.

Noting Jay's expression and knowing the old cowboy was about to lodge a protest, Dad just sort of grinned, gave him a pat on the back, and said, "Abby's idea. Won't do you a goddamn bit of good to argue, old man," as he helped Jay out of the pickup.

Mrs. Howard immediately explained to Jay that she didn't want him down at the bunkhouse by himself when she met him and my dad at the door of her house. I knew Jay always felt uncomfortable whenever folks made a fuss over him, but he gave up because he knew Mrs. Howard had made up her mind and that was that. Just like my dad had told him.

For as long as she lived Abby never forgot how Jay had saved her and her kids and me the summer before when one of the Owsley gang had come charging into her house with a gun in his hand. Jay had blown the intruder out of the house with a blast from a twelve-gauge shotgun before he could hurt anyone.

Dad had told me the night before about Mrs. Howard's plans for taking care of Jay. Lynda and Lenny had also been told by their parents that Jay would be their houseguest while he was recovering from his injuries.

After we got the horses unsaddled, rubbed them down, and gave them some grain we walked up to the Howards' house to see Jay. Abby had a big meal prepared for his homecoming and Jay had already gotten started on it. If Jay was uncomfortable with all of the attention it didn't seem to be affecting his appetite I noted.

Later that day Dad had driven into Seligman and stopped at a couple cafes and bars looking for an out of work cowboy that he could hire to work on the ranch for at least a couple weeks. The idea was to find someone to help take care of things until Clay got back and Jay was up and around. Of course it would be a while before Jay would be able to spend a day in the saddle, so the new hand, if he worked, out could expect to work at least until spring.

Dad found a cowboy that he had hired once before when he had needed extra help during a roundup a few years earlier on another ranch that he was managing at the time. They sat and talked for a while and Dad was pleased to learn that the cowboy, named Johnny Robbins, had actually worked on the P Bar J Ranch once before for a previous owner.

Johnny told Dad that he was familiar with the layout of the ranch and would be able to find his way around on his own. Dad liked that since this being the holidays he didn't really want to be out showing a new cowboy the ranch.

Dad and Johnny arrived at a deal and shook on it. After his task of finding a new cowboy was successfully completed, my dad asked his new employee if he was hungry since it was getting on toward supper time. Johnny answered, "Sure, Mr. Dean, I guess I could take care of a burger, I reckon."

"Okay, then come on and we will head on down the street to the café and get something. And, Johnny, it's still just Roy," my dad responded with a grin.

As soon as they had given the waitress their orders and gotten settled in with cups of hot coffee Dad started in with some more details on the things he would like Johnny to take care of especially during the upcoming holidays. However, the conversation at a table across the room immediately intruded on them to an extent that it was impossible to ignore.

"Well, a military man like Ike is sure a hell of a lot better than Stevenson, who was just another lying lawyer politician," one older cowman said apparently in response to a derogatory comment that had been aimed at Eisenhower.

That seemed to get the attention of some of the other patrons of the café. A few of them walked over and joined the four men who had been sitting at the table. Politics and lawyers always seemed to get a roaring conversation going.

Dad, watching the gathering grow, sat back and said to Johnny, "Well, hell, this just might get entertaining."

One of the men taking up the tone of the last comment declared, "A lawyer should not even be eligible to run for or be appointed to any level of public office. Of course they are dishonest, lying pieces of garbage ... they are lawyers!"

Those sentiments were followed by nods and words of agreement which encouraged an elderly man that appeared to my dad to have been a retired railroad worker to say, "The most galling thing ever inflicted on American citizens is a legal system designed by and for lawyers and judges. Being forced to stand up when a piece of shit in a robe enters or leaves and having to address the pieces or shit as "your honor" when having gone through law school they wouldn't have any honor or ethics intact. The thing to remember, fellas, is that fucking robe they cloak themselves in sure as hell ain't magic! You wrap a piece of dog shit up in a robe ... it's still a piece of dog shit!"

After a pause to make sure he had everyone's attention, the old man added, "And along those same lines, partners, I will tell you another thing while we are on the subject of those miserable pieces of shit produced by law schools. A judge should not be a lawyer; they should be selected from other professions instead ... hell, even a used car salesman or insurance agent would be better!"

At that point all of the men at the table and several others scattered around the café nodded in agreement. One or two of them even voiced an enthusiastic "Hell, yes!"

One of the other men, who said that he had a ranch north of Flagstaff, jumped in and told the others at the table, "And if any of you are in the mistaken belief that there's equal justice for all in this here country you need to get attacked by a crazy lying piece of shit lawyer down in Yavapai County. Have him swear out false charges against you that one of his pieces of shit cronies in a robe will be more than happy to sign. Wait until his lies have slandered you and cost you thousands of dollars and its shown in the goddamn court that the bastard is just lying his ass off under oath and the piece of shit judge still just can't do enough at your expense to make his crazy crony feel better!"

Dad found out later that the cowboy who had added the last bit to the conversation had previously owned a ranch near Paulden. A few years earlier he'd had the misfortune of having a former law professor buy the ranch that joined his. Needless to say he didn't get along with the piece of shit which apparently in itself is a crime in that county. The lying little bastard used his above-the-law status to file false charges against the cowboy and pretty much take away his rights as an American citizen. Yeah, you could say he was pretty well pissed off at the sorry excuse for a legal system. Instead of innocent until proven guilty he was being told "the attorney says you did this."

Of course their system works well for the lawyers and judges. The guy who was victimized by the bastard's lies ended up selling his ranch and moving out of the county since he no longer felt that he had any rights there. And he knew that the lying piece of shit law professor could file additional false charges anytime he felt like it. Unfortunately he also knew that the same situation would be true in any other court system.

The conversation at the other table continued while my dad and Johnny were waiting for their meal to be served. It was still going strong with even a few new participants when Dad paid the check and they walked out the door of the café. Most of the men it seemed had a sour experience with either lawyers or judges ... or both, and needed to vent their anger and frustration at the injustice of the unethical system that had been forced upon citizens.

The conversation they had overheard stuck with both my Dad and Johnny Robbins. I overheard them both telling about it to others including Jay a number of times. Jay especially found it amusing and told it to others whenever he could work some of the quotes into a conversation at a bar.

I knew my dad shared those same views about lawyers and judges and I guess he passed them on to me. I sure wouldn't want one of the vicious, lying bastards for a neighbor.

With supper out of the way Dad took Johnny over to a small rooming house where he had been staying so he could grab his war bag and bedroll. Like most cowboys who moved from job to job he traveled fairly light. He didn't even have a pickup at the time.

Johnny told Dad that his old truck had recently thrown a rod and since the repair bill would have been more than he felt it was worth he had sold it to a salvage yard. Dad told him that he had been letting Jay have one of the old ranch trucks to use for going into Seligman to see his lady friends on occasion. Now with him laid up Johnny could use the same truck if he needed it to run to town for any personal business. He knew that cowboys needed to let loose once in a while.

Back at the P Bar J's headquarters Dad got the new cowboy settled into the bunkhouse and outlined to him what he wanted done the next few days. Then he took him around and introduced him to everybody. It came as no surprise that Johnny already knew Jay.

Among other duties the hired hand would be expected to check waters, break ice in the water troughs, and check fences and gates. He was going to be doing some of the stuff Lenny and I normally did so that we wouldn't have to be doing it on Christmas Eve and Christmas day.

Dad told Johnny that if he did a good job he would keep him on at least through the winter while Jay was mending. Cowboys were usually pretty happy to find a warm bunkhouse for the winter since that's when a lot of the cowboy work tended to get a little scarce.

Chapter 9
Parker and the Owsleys

The day after Jay got back to the ranch from his hospital stay Deputy Parker dropped by the headquarters fairly early in the morning to see how he was doing. The deputy had heard about the horse wreck from someone at a bar in Hackberry and had come out to the ranch to check on the old cowboy who had killed one of the killers of his cousin.

My dad met the deputy when he arrived and walked with him over to the Howards. They visited with Jay for an hour or so and afterwards Dad followed the deputy out of the Howards' house back to his car that he had left down by the barn where Dad had been working when he arrived.

Johnny was just getting back from checking fences and was unsaddling his horse. He would be going out again in the afternoon to do some work on one of the windmills but would take a fresh horse.

Dad told Parker, "There's a new hand that I hired yesterday to fill in for Jay. I will introduce you."

Dad and the deputy walked over to where Johnny was now brushing his horse. "Johnny, I would like for you to meet Deputy Parker," Dad said. The three men then spent a few minutes talking before Parker said that he should be getting back to Kingman.

Just as he started to get back in his vehicle to leave Parker thought of something and turning to my dad said, "Oh, Roy, I liked to have forgot but on the way in to your place this morning I passed Denton, that government trapper. He was heading out to the highway. We stopped and talked a minute. Do you know him? I thought he might have stopped by to see you."

"Nope, haven't seen him and I can't rightly say I know him, Parker. I have seen him a few times on the road and once or twice in Seligman. That's about the extent of it," Dad answered.

The deputy told my dad that the trapper's name was Preston Denton and that he had just been working in our neck of the country for a few months. Parker believed that he had transferred in from somewhere in Nevada.

Dad told the deputy as he was leaving, "Parker, if you should happen to see that government trapper again you be sure and mention that he best keep his ass off the P Bar J." He had seen what happened on other ranches after trappers and hunters would come in and trap, poison, and shoot every predator they could, regardless of any of them being proven stock killers. All the young mountain lions, coyotes, etc. would then quickly fill in the void from adjoining areas. And then you would sure as hell see some goddamn stock killing.

"You got it Roy. I will pass along the warning," the deputy responded as he jumped into his vehicle and headed out. That was the funny thing about my dad and the deputy. While Dad always just called him by his last name, Parker called him by his first name. As a result I don't even know what the deputy's first name was. I never heard it spoken.

We didn't hear about it until a few weeks later but Parker had some excitement, as well as a close call, on the way back to Seligman following his visit to the ranch.

I am going to relate it the way I heard it from others, including my Dad. Some of it I didn't hear until years later and of course with some of it I sort of had to fill in the blanks. Later it became evident that Parker had crossed a line that day that would eventually cost him his life. At least that's what I have come to believe.

Although Parker didn't think to mention it while he was at the ranch visiting Jay and talking with my dad, earlier that day at his station he had read a police bulletin that a stolen black Hudson Hornet had been seen in the Seligman area. The car had an Oklahoma license plate.

All deputies and the state highway patrolmen were being advised to keep a watch out for the car. There was reason to believe some prison escapees had stolen it. Parker's first thought while he was reading it was that the Owsleys were from Oklahoma and the stolen car they had been driving the summer before was a dark green Hornet ... maybe the thieving bastards really liked Hudsons.

Then he had headed out of Kingman in his patrol car with the goal of dropping by the P Bar J Ranch to check on Jay. Whenever he saw a black car approaching in the opposite lane on Route 66 on the drive east he tensed up until he could determine it was something other than a Hudson.

Parker was thinking that it seemed odd that crooks would steal one of the most distinctive cars on the road ... they looked like giant, four-door, upside down bathtubs. But then, too, they were pretty much the fastest damn things on the road, plus their size made them ideal to bust through roadblocks.

Later on his way back out towards Route 66, after visiting Jay and my dad, as he was nearing the turnoff for the old Owsley place the deputy had noticed a black car turn onto that side road and then speed off towards the east throwing up rooster tails of dirt from the spinning rear tires. He hadn't gotten a good look at the car due to the distance and the dust that it was throwing up around it. But it seemed suspicious so he followed the car and caught up to it before it had reached the road that went back to the site of the old homestead.

"Shit, that's a Hudson!" Parker said to himself as he hit his lights and siren to try and stop the car, which he could now see had an Oklahoma license plate. The Hudson's rear wheels again threw up a shower of dirt and gravel as it accelerated and sped by the turnoff and continued east on the ranch road toward the R_X Ranch. Parker could see that there were three men in the car, two in the front seat and one in the back.

The deputy saw the man in the backseat disappear for a few seconds and guessed that he was getting something from under the seat. "Probably a fucking gun" Parker muttered to himself. About then the man's head popped back up and the right rear door flew open.

The man, holding what appeared to be a shotgun, jumped out, hit the ground and after rolling a few times came up on his knees. Parker saw the gun pointing towards him and hit the brakes just as the gun seemed to explode. The man holding it was blown backwards. The deputy seeing that this one was no longer a threat hit the gas and resumed the pursuit of the stolen Hudson. He would figure out what had happened to the jumper later. He would bet a box of donuts that the piece of shit wasn't going anywhere.

The chase came to a sudden end at the east boundary fence. Although Parker figured they would just plow through the closed gate the Hudson skidded to a stop sideways next to it. The deputy brought his own vehicle to a sliding stop amid a cloud of dust and flying gravel and jumped out with his .45 automatic in his hand.

"Okay, you sons of bitches, you have had all the fun you're going to have," Parker shouted, and continued, "If I don't see you both getting out of the fucking car on the driver's side right now I am emptying the clip into both of you!"

At that point the driver started to do as he had been told and opened the driver's door and stepped out. But as he did so the front door on the passenger side of the Hudson flew open and the other guy jumped out and leveled a rifle across the car's roof at the deputy. Ignoring the driver, who had moved toward the left front fender of the car and stood with his hands stretched up in the air as far as they would go, for the moment he pointed his pistol at the passenger and squeezed the trigger as he said, "Holy shit! God damn it!"

Four or five bullets headed for the would-be shooter and reached him before he could fire the rifle. Only two of the bullets hit the target ... one in the gut and the other through the throat. The bullet that hit him in the gut had passed through the car's interior.

When Parker was able to direct his attention back to the driver he saw that the man hadn't moved. He realized that the still smoking .45 being pointed at him by the extremely angry deputy still packed enough shells in the clip to riddle him too.

At that moment Parker was happy that he had decided to carry his own .45 automatic rather than the revolver that the department issued. No way in hell would he have been able to get off so many shots with a six-shooter so quickly.

Holding the gun in his right hand, Parker cuffed the hands of the driver behind him before stepping around the car to check on the other man. The passenger was lying on his back in a pool of blood next to the boundary fence and had probably been dead before he had hit the ground.

Holstering his weapon Parker went back around to the driver's side where his prisoner was standing and patted him down. The deputy removed a folding knife from one of his pockets and a .25 caliber pistol that was stuck in his waist band at the small of his back.

Holding the little pistol in his left hand, he waved it in from of the man's face and said with a sneer, "If you had shot me with this little fucker you would have really pissed me off." He then put the prisoner in the backseat of the patrol car.

Once he had him settled in he asked his name and the names of the two that wouldn't be answering any questions. It turned out that the driver was a younger brother of the Owsleys who had robbed the bank and killed his cousin the previous summer and the one lying dead next to the Hudson was a cousin.

Upon learning the identities of his prisoner and the other one, Parker thought that it was probably a good thing that he hadn't known it when he was ordering them out of the car. If he had known that they were Owsleys he might have just gone ahead and killed both of the bastards and claimed that they had resisted arrest. At least one had given him the justification.

"Okay," he said to the handcuffed man, "who's the asshole that jumped out of the car back a ways?" The driver told the deputy that it was an uncle who had told them before he jumped out that he wasn't going back to prison.

"Well," Parker said, "from the way that shotgun exploded I think he was right. But I reckon we need to go back and collect what's left of him."

Parker walked over to the stolen Hudson and removed the keys and locked it. He would have a tow truck sent out later to haul it to the impound yard in Kingman.

He popped open the trunk of his car and got out a tarp and went over to the body and rolled it up. Then he had a dilemma. Should he haul the bodies back in the trunk of his car or leave them out here to be picked up by a vehicle from the morgue in Kingman? He figured that the latter would be the best way to handle it. He could call on his mobile radio to get the county coroner to meet him to collect the bodies and get his statement on the shootings.

The deputy then turned his vehicle around and headed back toward the west to where the third Owsley lay amid the prairie dog holes and prickly pears thirty feet or so from the edge of the ranch road. Glancing back at the prisoner as he started to open his door Parker said, "Now boy, you behave yourself while I check on your relative over there."

The man was lying on his back and as Parker approached him the deputy knew he was no longer a threat and was most likely dead. The shotgun had exploded inches from the man's face and the blast had taken off most of it. The deputy noticed the ruined gun and picked it up to examine it. The twin barrels were shattered. Parker imagined the barrels being shoved into the dirt when the man rolled after jumping from the speeding car. The barrels must have been packed with several inches of dirt. When the crook had pulled both triggers the gun exploded in his face. As Parker thought this he also couldn't help but think about what would have happened to him if the barrels of the shotgun hadn't been plugged with dirt. That sent cold chills through him.

After the Hudson was towed to Seligman and impounded it was searched. Two loaded .38 caliber pistols and another shotgun were found inside it. The deputy had been lucky that both of the men hadn't decided to put up a fight when he finally stopped them at the gate. If they had both came out of the car shooting he probably wouldn't have lived to tell about it.

Thankfully we didn't know anything about the incident Parker had with the Owsleys just north of the P Bar J at the time, so thoughts of more of their family or gang didn't intrude on our enjoyment of Christmas which was fast approaching.

When Parker did come back out later, after the holidays, to tell Dad about the shooting and arrest there was some speculation that those three had been up to something other than looking for the money from the bank holdup. The deputy told Dad that he thought that they might have been planning some kind of revenge. Parker was convinced after questioning the sole survivor at the Sheriff's office in Kingman that he was hiding something. But at the time no one could figure out what it was.

It turned out that the Owsley that Parker had taken prisoner was on parole from a prison in Oklahoma. With the car theft and other charges he would be going back to prison for a long time. Parker told my dad that he expected it would be several years before that one saw the outside of the prison's walls again. The uncle who had died and the front seat passenger had escaped from the prison.

As far as anyone knew the surviving fugitive never talked about what they had been doing when they were caught driving on the ranch roads with loaded guns stashed beneath their seats. We were left with the mystery when the sole survivor was sent back to Oklahoma to finish his original sentence with some extra time thrown in for the new crimes. It would be several years before we knew at least some of the answers about what they had been up to the day Parker had sort of stumbled upon them. Years later it became apparent that the Owsley that Parker arrested had made a deal with the deputy. But at the time no one had a clue about what had gone on out there on the road near the ruins of the Owsleys homestead.

Hearing Dad and Deputy Parker talking about the Owsleys and the guns that were in their car when they were arrested made me think of something I thought I had heard when Jay had the accident with his horse. When I heard him shout and turned to look, about the same time I thought I had heard a gunshot. It sounded far away and I figured it was probably a hunter or target shooter off to the north the other side of the ranch boundary.

Rushing to check on Jay and then going for help pushed all thoughts of the gunshot out of my mind at the time. I didn't think it was important. After all, hearing gunshots, especially off in the distance was part of ranch life, like the day I had arrived with Dad on the ranch the previous June and he had encountered the drunken hunters at a stock tank. So I sort of forgot about it, at the time. It wouldn't be something I thought much about for several years.

Chapter 9
The Turkey Delivery

When Mom had made the trip to Winslow to drop off Christmas trees and pick up supplies for Christmas dinner she hadn't gotten the turkeys. Grandpa Johnny's boss with the railroad always gave large frozen turkeys to the depot managers for Christmas. Since they would be spending Christmas with us Grandpa had told Mom to hold off buying any and he would provide them. He also assured her that she would have the turkeys in plenty of time to get them ready. Mom knew that her Dad would come through on the promise and get the turkeys out to her on time.

Once Grandpa Johnny received the turkeys he put them on the train to be dropped off at the depot in Seligman. He had been running the depot in Winslow for several years and had been with the Santa Fe Railroad for all of his working life. He knew just about everyone who worked for the railroad east to Albuquerque and west across most of Arizona. He had made arrangements with his friend George Wilkins who worked for the railroad and lived in Seligman to get the turkeys out to the ranch a few days before Christmas so Mom would have a chance to get them all thawed out and ready to be baked.

Lenny and I were down at the barn and corral tending to the horses when a loud engine noise made us look out toward the road that led into the headquarters. A gold colored pickup was roaring down the road stirring up a cloud of dust behind it and heading our way. Dad was out riding with Johnny Robbins, which I thought was a good thing for whoever was driving that pickup so fast. He didn't like for anyone to drive like that on the ranch since you could never tell when a cow or horse might decide to walk out onto the narrow roads suddenly from behind a juniper or big bush.

As the two of us watched the pickup, which I now recognized as a late '40s Ford, came to a stop where the road split with one fork coming down to the barn and corral and the other one going up towards the houses. After the dust settled the driver noticed Lenny and me and drove down to where we were standing in front of the barn. As he pulled up to us I thought that the trucks' color made it look sort of like a palomino ... like Trigger.

"Hello, boys," he said in a friendly voice out the open driver's window, "I am George Wilkins. I got a couple turkeys here that old Johnny Nolan asked me to fetch out here for his daughter and her family."

I answered, "That's my grandpa, I am Jeff Dean and this here is Lenny Howard. We can take you up to the house where my Mom is so you can give her the turkeys." As I said it I pointed off toward our house.

"Boys, I sure would appreciate that. I wasn't quite sure which of the two houses she would be at," Mr. Wilkins replied, and then added, "hop in and we will run on up there."

Getting into the cab the first thing I noticed was how much cleaner it was than the cab of Dad's ranch truck. This pickup probably spent most of its life on city streets in Seligman and roaring up and down Route 66 rather than on dusty ranch roads. I pointed again to our house that sat on a small rise off to the left and Mr. Wilkins let out the clutch and spun out a little as we took off toward the house. The truck had a four-speed shifter on the floor, with a chrome ball on top.

Mom had heard and seen the truck's arrival and she was standing out in front of the house as we pulled up. I told Mr. Wilkins, "That's my Mom, Betsy Dean."

When we stopped Mr. Wilkins jumped out and introduced himself and told Mom the purpose of his visit.

Mom was sort of expecting her Dad to have one of his railroad friends run the turkeys out to the ranch so she wasn't surprised. The turkeys were in a large metal cooler that Mr. Wilkins had lashed down securely in the bed of his truck.

Walking around the back of the Ford I noticed something else besides the relatively clean cab that marked it as a "city truck." The pickup had duel exhausts that came out under the rear bumper and extended a few inches past it. The first time it was driven through a wash or gully the tips of those pipes would get flattened when the back bumper hit the ground. Dad's pickups always had the exhaust exit from the sides, behind the rear wheels so they wouldn't get damaged when crossing through dips.

After I had grown up and acquired some smarts on the long-term durability of the various makes of cars and trucks I became a dyed in the wool Chevy man like my Dad ... at least until I discovered Toyotas. However, as a kid as soon as I got up to the age where I noticed them I sure was partial to the fat-fendered, as they were called, Ford pickups that came out in the late 1940s and were built with only minor styling changes up until '56. I thought that they sure looked a lot better than the Chevy and Dodge trucks of that period. And I still think that the prettiest cars ever built were the '55-56 Crown Victorias. Then Ford had to go ahead and ruin the styling of their cars and trucks with the '57 models.

As far as I knew Dad had never been very fond of Fords. Mom on the other hand always loved the 1936 Ford four-door convertible that her parents had given to her after her high school graduation. She had the car when she and Dad got married so the maintenance on it fell to him. He would gripe, whenever he was sure Mom was out of earshot, about always having to fix one thing or another on "that damn old Ford." He tried a few times to convince her to let him trade it in for a newer, more dependable car for her but she wouldn't even consider parting with the old Ford.

On the occasions when we went anywhere as a family, like the Christmas shopping trip to Prescott, Dad would always insist on taking his Chevy truck. Again, when Mom was not close enough to overhear Dad would lean toward me and whisper something like "I reckon we better take the Chevy if'n we expect to be making it back to the ranch."

Whenever Dad and I were going somewhere on the highways we would talk about the various vehicles we would meet on the road. I think he thought that it was part of a boy's education to be able to recognize the various makes. Sometimes when we would come up on another vehicle or one would pass us heading in the opposite direction Dad would ask, "Jeff, what kind of truck was that?" I got so I could usually give him the right answer.

After the turkeys were unloaded from his cooler and he had carried them into the house for Mom, she asked him in for coffee and big slice of a peach pie that she had baked that morning. He gladly accepted. Lenny and I got in on the fresh pie. Mr. Wilkins was a talker and we enjoyed listening to him talk about working for the railroad. He even had a few stories about my grandfather.

After everyone had managed to get seconds on the pie Mr. Wilkins looked at his watch that he had pulled out of a vest pocket and said that he had better be getting back to town. Soon he had fired up his Ford and was headed back to Seligman.

I can still picture myself standing there watching as he sped down our ranch road and disappeared in the cloud of dust that was being kicked up by the tires of the truck. Of course I didn't know it at the time but that gold 1948 Ford pickup was in my future. It would be parked and waiting for me just a few short years down the road.

On the afternoon of Christmas Eve both sets of grandparents arrived. I heard Grandpa Johnny ask Mom,

"Did George get those turkeys delivered to you, Betsy?" Mom then gave her dad the details of his friend bringing the turkeys out to the ranch.

I was happy to find that both of my grandmas had been busy baking Christmas cookies and making fudge that they had brought along. The goodies were placed on a platter and set on the coffee table for everyone to snack on. However, Mom told me to go easy on them until after I had eaten my supper.

We were a bit crowded but everyone thought it was a small price for having everyone together for Christmas. Among other things adjustments had to be made in the seating and sleeping arrangements in our relatively small house. Dad had me help him put the two extra leaves in the kitchen table so there would be room for everyone. We also had to bring in the extra chairs that we normally kept out on the porch. Mom gave me a wet rag and had me wipe them down. They got mighty dusty out on the screened in porch.

One set of grandparents were to sleep in my bedroom while I used a roll away cot Mom had set up in the kitchen. The other set of grandparents got Mom and Dad's bed while Mom slept on the couch in the living room and Dad spread his cowboy bedroll out on the floor. When his mother saw that he was going to sleep on the floor with just a few blankets to cushion him she expressed her concern.

Dad just smiled at her and said, "Ma, that there old floor won't be any harder than the rocky ground that I usually have to lay it out on when I am working out on the ranch."

Whenever Dad, and most other cowboys, were out working the remote parts of a ranch where a good half day's work was involved in just getting out there, it was normal to just toss a bedroll on the back of the horse or in the bed of the pickup and sleep out. That way they would be able to put in full days of work rather than wasting daylight in travelling back and forth.

She wasn't totally convinced that he would be comfortable, but just replied, "Roy, it's just that your dad and I feel a little guilty taking your bed."

"Don't worry a bit about that, Ma. Betsy, Jeff, and I are just tickled to have our parents and grandparents here to share Christmas with us!" Dad answered. Mom and I nodded our agreement.

Grandpa Johnny had overheard the exchange and he jumped in with, "Well, Emma and I won't be worried none about taking Jeff's bed and putting him on that little cot out in the kitchen," he paused, turned and gave me a wink and continued, "but I am a little worried that he might get into those pecan pies before morning gets here."

I laughed and said, "Don't worry Grandpa, if I get hungry in the middle of the night I will try and save at least a piece of one of the pies for you." I noticed Mom give me a look that said that I had better just be kidding about getting into those pies that were supposed to be dessert for Christmas dinner.

In the evening after supper we all gathered in our living room near the Christmas tree and talked of family, past Christmases, and told stories. I especially enjoyed hearing my grandparents talk of Christmases when they were growing up. It sounded like things had been pretty bleak for them.

Grandma Emma told us how her and her brothers and sisters had been happy to find oranges in their Christmas stockings. They all talked about how their parents had never had a lot of extra money to spend on store-bought presents. Most gifts both given and received had usually been homemade back when they were young. It was alright since none of their friends' parents had much money either, so everyone was in the same boat.

Grandma Clara had brought along an old book of Christmas stories. She passed it around and had everyone take a turn reading a story from it aloud. When it got to

Dad instead of reading a story from the book he told us about a Christmas several years earlier that he had spent snowed in at an isolated line shack on one of the first ranches he worked for. Just after mid-night Grandpa Harold recited "The Night Before Christmas" from memory.

Chapter 11
Christmas Morning!

Christmas morning I was wide awake long before it started getting light out. I didn't want to wake the grownups so I used all of my restraint and just stayed in the cot until Mom came into the kitchen to put the coffee on. She softly asked, "Jeff, are you awake?" and when she saw that I was, she added "Merry Christmas!"

I responded with a cheerful, "Merry Christmas to you too, Mom." I then got up and put on a brown plaid flannel bathrobe over my pajamas and went into the living room to say Merry Christmas to Dad. He had already rolled up his bed roll and stuck it behind the couch so it would be out of the way of all of our company. The living room was crowded enough with the Christmas tree and the presents piled under and around it taking up one corner of the room. I walked over to the tree and checked to see if anything new had been added.

From past experience I knew my parents could be sneaky sometimes during Christmas. When I was younger they would wait until after I had gone to sleep on Christmas Eve and then put out a few large, unwrapped presents for me. Then when I would walk into our living room and discover them by the tree on Christmas morning either Mom or Dad would say something like, "Jeff, look at what Santa brought for you." That had ended after I had figured out the whole Santa thing. So of course this Christmas morning I didn't see anything new. That was definitely a drawback of getting older I thought … Santa no longer brought me any extra presents during the night.

Dad was standing nearby watching me as I checked out the presents. I wondered if he realized what I was looking for but he didn't ask and I didn't say anything. After a few minutes Dad and I joined Mom in the kitchen. Mom put a couple coffee cakes on the table for everyone to snack on. She figured we might be getting hungry for breakfast before all of the presents were unwrapped. Even at the ripe old age of twelve I sure didn't want to postpone opening presents while a big breakfast was being prepared and eaten.

After everyone was up and the adults had each gotten a slice or two of coffee cake and a cup of coffee, except for one of my grandmas who preferred tea, we all gathered in the living room by the Christmas tree to open presents. In order to make it last a little longer Mom decreed that we would take turns opening presents. That way everyone could see what the others had received and be able to give compliments or thanks at the appropriate times.

Being the only kid I did get to go first. That year was the start of a trend as far as my presents went. Toys were replaced in a large part by clothes. Among other things I got a new denim work jacket, a few pairs of blue jeans, a black cowboy hat sort of like the one Dad wore, and of course socks and underwear.

Even Lynda's present for me was something to wear ... black leather gloves. She must have noticed that I wasn't wearing gloves when we were pushing the cattle that had strayed from the Holden Ranch. Mom's parents gave me a real nice wood burning set and a Case pocket knife.

I was happy to get the new hat. The old black one that I had been wearing this winter was a few years old and it had gotten sort of tight on my head. I think I must have mentioned it to Mom or Dad and they had thought "now there's an idea for a practical Christmas present."

Among other things, Dad gave me a book entitled *Triggernometry, A Gallery of Gunfighters*. When I opened the box he had wrapped it in he said, "I got that a few years ago for you, Jeff, and was waiting until I thought you were old enough to enjoy it. It has stories about all of the real gunfighters of the old West." He then reached over and took the book and opened it towards the back and added, "Look at this, it shows how to do tricks with pistols like Curly Bill's road agent spin."

I recognized the name Curly Bill from the book I had read in the Winslow school library on Wyatt Earp. Dad said that he thought the tricks shown or described in the book were something I could practice with my toy cap guns for fun. He added that tricks of any kind were not to be done with a real gun since they could go off by accident.

Grandma Clara gave me a couple books by James Oliver Curwood that were adventure-filled stories set in the wilderness in Canada and the northern states. One of the books I remember I got that year was *The Grizzly King*. I got so I really liked that author and eventually read most of his books. He had written a lot of books and had built a small castle on the banks of the Shiawassee River in Michigan.

Later after I had gone through all of Curwood's books that I could find I asked a librarian about any new ones. I was disappointed to find out that the author had been dead for 25 years.

Eventually all that was left for me to open that Christmas morning was the heavy box from Grandpa Harold. Since I had no idea what it was I had been saving it for last. I had received a few other gifts that were marked from both Grandpa Harold and Grandma Clara, but this present only had his name on it. The Curwood books had been wrapped in a box that only had Grandma Clara's name on it as the giver. Thinking about it later I figured that she was probably trying to counter her husband's present to me somewhat.

I tore off the wrapping paper and then removed the tape holding the top flaps of the cardboard box down. I then reached into the box and pulled out what I knew could only be a gun wrapped up in old newspapers. I remember thinking that this sure is the heaviest cap gun ... I finally got the paper unwrapped and was staring at what sure looked like a real pistol. It was black with a brass trigger guard and brown walnut grips.

I then noticed that there were a few more things wrapped up in the box. The biggest, turned out to be a black leather holster with a flap that had "US" embossed on it. A smaller wrapped package was a tin containing brass caps and another contained a capper, although I had no idea what it was when I first saw it. I was told later that the capper was for securing the caps to the nipples of the gun's cylinder. Looking at the gun in wonder I noticed that on the top of the cylinder there weren't holes for shells to be inserted.

That's when Grandpa Harold told me, "Jeff, that's a cap and ball pistol like the soldiers in the Civil War used. It's an original 1858 Remington."

My mother and grandmothers were all shaking their heads. Grandma Clara looked at the other two women and said, "I got him books."

Seeing their reactions, Dad said, "Now there isn't anything to be worried about, ladies. It's a pretty complicated process to fire one of these old guns and without the gun power and .44 caliber balls it's really nothing more than a big cap gun. You can't load regular cartridges in it."

But turning to me Dad added, "Son, it's true that it is sort of like a cap gun but it's a pretty powerful one. Pieces of the brass caps can get blown out through the end of the barrel so for a while you will only be allowed to fire it when I am with you. We don't want anyone getting pieces of the metal caps in their eyes."

The western movies that I watched were set later than the Civil War and the cowboys all used six-shooters that took cartridges that were kept on loops on the gun belts until needed. I hadn't seen or even read anything about cap and ball guns.

After I received that old Remington I wasn't very interested in my toy cap guns any longer. I studied the diagram in the gunfighter book and used the big cap and ball pistol to practice the road agent spin and a few other tricks. I enjoyed taking it apart and cleaning and oiling the parts. It came apart fairly easily. Once the loading lever was lowered and the cylinder pin was pulled out the cylinder would drop right out of the frame.

After I had grown some more and my hands had gotten bigger and stronger from ranch work I could easily twirl the big Remington. I cut the flap off the holster and punched a small hole through the bottom of it for a tie-down thong so I could practice a fast draw. Of course no one then could guess that years later during another run in with the Owsleys that old "cap gun" would come in pretty handy. As it turned out the Owsleys and their kin hadn't seen a cap and ball pistol before either.

However, that Christmas morning I was thinking about how jealous Lenny was going to be when I showed him the Remington. Then I thought of Lynda and wondered if she had opened my present yet. The grownups had planned for all of us to get together at the Howards in the mid-morning after the families had finished unwrapping their presents. Everyone would visit while Mom and Mrs. Howard, with the help of my two grandmas, cooked Christmas dinner.

But that was still a few hours away and Mom and her mother cooked us a big breakfast of pancakes, eggs, and bacon. While they were cooking my mom had me take the clothes I had received back to my room and hang up the pants, jacket, and shirts and put the socks and underwear in my dresser drawers.

Mom enjoyed working on jigsaw puzzles and her parents had given her a couple along with other Christmas presents she received that year. After breakfast the dishes were cleared off the kitchen table and one of her new puzzles was dumped out onto it. We all gathered around the table and helped Mom work on the puzzle. It was fun with everyone having a hand in putting it together. It helped make the early morning go by quickly. Soon the picture of a large southern plantation house, with white columns in front of it and large magnolia trees in flower next to it, took shape.

Then it was time for all of us to walk over to the Howard's house. As usual we entered through the door that led directly into the kitchen. It was the same doorway that Jay had blown one of the members of the Owsley gang through with a twelve-gauge shotgun blast the previous summer.

I looked around for Lenny as soon as we entered, anxious to tell him about the pistol I had received. My mother wouldn't let me bring it along with us. He appeared to have been working on something that had been dumped out onto their kitchen's linoleum floor. I caught his eye when he looked up as we all walked in. He stood up as I walked over to where he was. I immediately told Lenny about the cap and ball pistol. I told him that I would take him over to my house and show it to him after Christmas dinner.

Lenny had gotten a pretty nice present. His parents had given him a Lionel train set that included buildings, bridges, trestles, and a plastic mountain with a tunnel through it to set over the track. He could pretend the train was going through the tunnel in Johnson Canyon. Lenny's dad told him that he would eventually get him a table to set everything up on.

Lenny and I sat on the kitchen floor and looked at the various parts of the train set. The steam engine was really well detailed and there was a small bottle of oil to drip into the smoke stack to make it smoke.

I liked trains and I was sort of wishing that I had gotten one for Christmas. I always enjoyed visiting my Grandpa Nolan at the railroad depot he worked at in Winslow and watching all the trains coming and going. However, I wouldn't have traded my cap and ball pistol for the world's best train set.

Lenny told me that if he ever got his Red Ryder BB rifle back we could go shoot up some of the BBs I had given him. I didn't say anything but I had a feeling that gun was gone for the foreseeable future.

Mick was sitting at the kitchen table playing with a Mr. Potato Head set. I saw that Mrs. Howard had washed a couple large potatoes for him to attach the various eyes, ears, mouths, and noses to. It would be several years before a plastic potato body was included in those sets. On a nearby chair I noticed that Mick had placed a box containing a double holster set of Roy Rogers cap guns. There was a new Roy Rogers rifle leaning against the chair. Mick had also gotten Silly Putty, a View Master, and several other toys. I noticed the box of Lincoln Logs that I had gotten for him was on the floor. The box had been opened and it looked like he had started building a log cabin with them before going on to another gift.

Lynda was sitting sideways in a big easy chair, with her feet dangling over one of its arms, reading when I walked into the living room. She was wearing fuzzy pink house slippers. It looked like she had received a new Trixie Belden book for Christmas.

Jay was on the couch on the other side of the living room with a coffee cup in one hand and a Christmas cookie in the other. He was wearing what looked like new pajamas and bathrobe that I figured had been Christmas presents from the Howards.

I told Jay "Merry Christmas" and he smiled and told me the same. Jay's broken leg, in a big heavy looking cast, was resting on a footstool in front of him. It looked like he was feeling good; however I was pretty sure that he would rather have been out doing his cowboy work. But he was making the best of the situation that he had found himself in after the wreck.

Jay was a big believer in playing the hand he was dealt. He took things as they came. I like to think that he helped teach me to do the same. The thing none of us realized at the time was that the injuries Jay had received would cause arthritis in his leg and hip to the extent that he would be forced into retiring as a cowboy long before he was ready to quit the saddle. But at the time that was still a few years away.

Hearing me speak to Jay, Lynda looked up from her book and we smiled at each other about the same time. After exchanging "Merry Christmases" Lynda told me that she really liked the writing presents that I had given her. Lynda even added that they might inspire her to write more. I told her that I liked the leather gloves that she had gotten for me and added that they fit just right. They would sure make riding through brush looking for strays easier on my hands. After a few hours of using my bare hands to protect by face from branches they would be pretty scratched up and sore.

I told her about the books that one my grandmothers had given me and she thought they sounded interesting. Later I loaned them to her and we both became fans of James Oliver Curwood. Whenever one of us got one of his books we would always share it with the other one. It got so the hill where we had spent several hours the previous summer reading Roy Rogers, Superman, and other comic books and that we had called Comic Book Hill should have been renamed Curwood Hill by the end of the following summer.

While I was visiting with Lynda my dad had come into the living room and had sat on the couch with Jay. As he sat down he handed Jay a small wrapped Christmas present.

I knew it was the leather wallet that Dad had gotten specially made for him.

I heard Dad say as Jay took the offered gift, "Well, I know that you are already getting this free vacation just lying around the house eating Mrs. Howard's pies and Christmas cookies, but Betsy, Jeff, and I figured we ought to give you something that you can unwrap."

Jay gave Dad a "humph" and followed it with a big grin as he took the present. After unwrapping it and giving it an appreciative look he told my Dad that he sure did need a new wallet or bill fold as he called it, seeing as how a cowboy made so much money.

"Yes siree, Roy, all that money that I have kept stuffed into my old one sure did wear through the leather in no time at all. Hell, I probably haven't had my old bill fold more than twenty or twenty-five years," Jay said.

Gesturing to his pajamas and robe Jay told Dad, "I got these new inside duds from the Howards last night. Abby had them all wrapped up for me with a big ribbon on the box. A man could get plumb spoiled around here if he wasn't careful."

At that Dad shook his head and said, "It looks like it's a tad too late to be worrying about you getting spoiled. I think Abby has already seen to that. It's going to be hell getting a day's work out of you after she's through nursing you."

I managed to talk with Lynda several minutes before Lenny came into the room. Lenny and his dad had gone out to a storage shed behind their house and had gotten a large piece of plywood.

Lenny looked over at me talking with his sister and said, "Hey, Jeff, since you ain't doing nothing help me carry this wood back to my bedroom. You can help me set up my train." Later when Mr. Howard found a table for Lenny to use he would be able to just set the plywood sheet on top of it and not have to take the train track and everything apart.

It wasn't long after we had gotten the piece of wood back to the boy's bedroom that Lynda and then Mick came back to join us and see if they could help with setting up the train. Everyone was anxious to see the train chugging around the track and getting a turn at the controls. I looked at the instructions and saw how much oil to put in the smokestack. I opened the bottle and used the supplied dropper to deposit the recommended number of drops required to produce smoke.

Before too long we had the track set up, buildings, trestles and tunnel in place, and the train was chugging around the layout. We quickly figured out how fast the train could take the curves without derailing. Of course making it derail was the part that was the most fun.

Soon the smells of Christmas dinner cooking were filling the Howards' house. I have always especially enjoyed the smell of turkey roasting. The smells of cookies or even a cherry pie baking are right nice but in my opinion they don't come close to the smell of a roasting turkey.

My mother baked turkeys for Thanksgiving and for Christmas. She would always season them with garlic and I could tell that morning that she had added it even though she wasn't the only cook in the kitchen.

During my growing up years the holidays were always pretty special to me. It's pleasant to look back and think of my mother cooking a big meal complete with favorite desserts, Dad taking a rare day off and relaxing with us, and me just being a kid. Oh, and that smell of garlic-seasoned turkey roasting in the oven.

***

Even now the smell of garlic takes me back to those childhood holidays. It sure enough did the trick that day I had spent driving around looking for a bull that turned out to be long gone … and not on his own power. He had definitely had some help from rustlers.

Well, after stubbornly spending a good portion of the day looking for it I decided to call it quits on trying to find that bull. I would be giving the sheriff a call when I got back to the house and report it as rustled. After enjoying the smell of the garlic seasoned turkey leg warming under the truck's heater vent most of the day I finally got around to eating it as I was driving back toward the house. It tasted as good as it smelled ... and that's saying something.

Driving along and enjoying the turkey leg I was thinking about what I would do once I got back to the house. First I would make a phone call and get the damn sheriff's deputy looking for my stolen bull. Then, I was thinking, since the wind had died down, I figured that I would go out to the garage and get Bucky down from the hooks on the wall, air up the tires and take a little ride. Maybe while I was out riding that old Schwinn I would think of something to get for the wife this Christmas. Every year it seemed I cut it a little closer, but eventually I always managed to find something she liked. So she always says anyway.

Of course the present winter didn't end with Christmas and I found myself drifting back to that first winter that I had spent on the P Bar J whenever I was alone with my thoughts.

That evening I was listening to the news and weather on the radio and they were forecasting that a large weather system packing a wallop was headed for northern Arizona.

And although we hadn't gotten the "snow for Christmas" in 1952 that Gene Autry sang about it was on its way back then. It was just running a few days late.

Chapter 12
The Big Snow

One hell of a big snow fell on the P Bar J as well as the rest of northern Arizona a few days before New Year's of 1953. Clay had just returned from his trip to Wyoming. If he had waited another day he would have been stranded somewhere along the route. Clay was pretty shook up to hear about what had happened to Jay during his absence from the ranch.

Just after Clay's return to the ranch Dad had filled him in on Jay's horse falling on him and how he was recuperating from his injuries under the care of Mrs. Howard. In the short time he had worked with him, Clay had come to respect the older cowboy and had already learned a great deal from him. But that didn't deter Clay from kidding Jay about how he was milking his injuries while being coddled by the pretty Mrs. Howard.

No doubt Dad had mentioned to Clay how Jay was being spoiled my Abby. He explained that at the time of Clay's return to the ranch, the Howards were gone on a little holiday trip and how my mom was watching out for Jay in Abby's absence.

At first the Howards had been going to postpone their trip to see Abby's parents, since she was taking care of Jay during his recovery. However, when Jay had caught wind of it he insisted that he didn't want to be the cause of them changing their plans. Finally, he convinced Abby at least partially that he could take care of himself. Mom had joined in and assured Abby that she would see to Jay's meals and look in on him to make sure he was doing all right.

Mom and Dad had even offered to have Jay stay at our house while the Howards were gone. They told him that he could have my room and I would sleep on a cot like I had when the grandparents were visiting for Christmas. Jay politely put his foot down and assured everyone that he was perfectly capable of surviving on his own for a few days. If it had been his choice he would have just moved back to the bunkhouse at that point and been perfectly happy.

Before they had left, Abby had cooked up several meals for Jay and left them in the fridge so all he had to do was heat them up. She had also baked more than a few desserts for him to have while she was gone. Mom would usually go over around noon each day and either help Jay heat up a meal or bring him something that she had cooked. She also picked up any laundry that he needed washed.

Lenny had been allowed to stay at the ranch to help me with the chores, while his parents were doing their holiday travelling. He would be spending the nights and having his meals at our house.

That first day back from Wyoming, after talking to my dad, Clay walked over to the Howards' house to pay his respects to Jay ... and of course do a little ribbing. Lenny and I had gone over to his house earlier to visit with Jay and to play with Lenny's train set. We were back in Lenny's bedroom when we heard Clay talking with Jay out in the living room. Jay was sitting at what had become his usual spot at one end of the couch. We walked in and joined them since I wanted to ask Clay how the Christmas visit with his family had gone.

Clay, looking at Jay sitting there all comfortable with a homemade apple fritter in one hand, said, "Well, Roy told me I should look in on you. I can see that you have it pretty rough in here, old man."

Jay, looking up with the half-eaten fritter in his hand, said, "Well someone has to hold down this couch and take care of all the treats that Mrs. Howard left for me."

He went on to tell Clay that since Johnny was living in the bunkhouse and now that he had returned from

Wyoming he was more than ready to move back down there himself. The original argument that Mrs. Howard had for Jay staying with them after he returned from the hospital was that he would be alone, day and night, in the bunkhouse and there wouldn't be anyone to help him if he needed it.

Since there were now two other cowboys at the bunkhouse Jay had tried that argument on Mrs. Howard. However, since Jay couldn't get out and work Abby, and my mother as well, didn't want him having to be down at the bunkhouse all by himself while the other two men were out working. Plus the two women knew that since it would be difficult for Jay to do much cooking while on crutches, he probably wouldn't be eating right if left alone.

Abby felt that all in all Jay would be more comfortable at the main house during his convalescence even if she had to be gone for a few days. The storm that was coming would make the Howards' absence stretch out into several more days than they had intended.

After Clay had finished visiting with Jay and of course ribbing him a little, Dad introduced him to the new hand, Johnny Robbins, and they hit it off right from the start. Clay was happy to find that Johnny was familiar with the ranch and was shouldering a full load of the cowboying.

Dad told Clay that he would be his top cowboy while Jay was recuperating and that he could feel free to assign tasks to Johnny that needed doing. He had already told Johnny and he didn't have any problems taking orders from one of my dad's senior employees.

That afternoon everyone was watching the sky as a layer of dark, ominous looking clouds started moving in and the winds, that had been slight all day started picking up. Of course Dad, Mom, and the cowboys had been listening to weather reports on the radio and knew that what sounded like a pretty major snow storm was moving in.

Late in the afternoon, Lenny had walked over to his house just before supper to get some clothes he had forgotten to pack. While he was gone Mom, Dad and I were sitting the kitchen table. Something was troubling Mom. She said, "Roy, I didn't want to say anything to worry Lenny but I would sure feel better about this storm coming in if I knew for sure if the Howards weren't out travelling in it. Before they left to visit her folks, Abby told me that they were going over to Flagstaff from here so Joe could attend to some business at their bank before heading down to her parent's ranch to celebrate New Year's with them."

She went on that she was especially worried that they would get caught in the storm between Flagstaff and Prescott. Even once they got south of Prescott and out of the Bradshaw Mountains they could still run into snow if the approaching storm turned out to be as bad as some reports were indicating.

Mom and Dad had another worry besides the Howards. Dad's sister Christy and her husband were also doing some travelling during this same period of severe weather. After spending Christmas in Albuquerque they were heading for Winslow for New Year's.

I didn't really know much of anything about the dangers of winter driving at the time. All I knew was that I missed having Lynda at the ranch.

Lenny came back a few minutes later and joined us at the table after putting his stuff in my room. He told us that Jay was doing fine. Lenny said, "Jay was finishing his supper when I went over to my house. He had warmed up one of the casseroles that my Mom had left for him."

A little later that evening Dad walked outside to take a look at the weather. Lenny and I followed him out the side door from the kitchen.

The ground was already covered with snow and it was coming down thick enough that we could hardly see the

Howards' house. The lights were out and it looked like Jay must have already gone to bed. I noticed that small drifts had already started to form. The wind was blowing the snow up against any obstacles that were in its way.

I heard Dad mutter, "Oh, shit" and then turning to see Lenny and me following him he quickly added, looking a little embarrassed, "Sorry about the language, boys. But this here looks like a blizzard that is more than likely going to cause us a whole mess of problems before it's all over and done."

Although snows brought moisture that was always welcomed by ranchers, large accumulations of the white stuff also brought a lot of headaches to have to deal with until it melted. That's what my Dad was worried about that night as he watched the large flakes falling from the sky.

Later after we had gone to bed I read some of a James Oliver Curwood novel before going to sleep. I used a Roy Rogers flashlight, with fresh batteries that I had gotten for Christmas, for a light to read by. In the book there was deep snow on the ground that the lead character was trudging through.

After switching the flashlight off and trying to get to sleep I wondered about how much snow I was going to have to trudge through in the morning on the way down to the barn to do chores. It sure wasn't something I was looking forward to having to do. I finally drifted off to sleep to the sound of heavy, windblown snow hitting the side of the house and the windows.

Lenny hadn't done any reading and had fallen asleep before I had turned the flashlight off. He had been quiet after listening to my dad talking about the storm and I thought that he might be worried about his family.

The next morning I awoke to the same noise of the wind and snow hitting the house, grabbed the flashlight, and looked at the wind-up clock on the bedside table. It was a little after 6:00 a.m. and still dark out. I could hear Mom and Dad talking out in the kitchen along with the clanking of dishes and skillets as she prepared breakfast. I woke Lenny up. We were both hungry. Once the smell of frying bacon reached my bedroom we decided to join my parents in the kitchen.

As Lenny and I walked into the kitchen Mom and Dad both looked our way and they both smiled at us. After we all exchanged, "Good Mornings," Dad said, "Looks like the snow dumped on us all night, boys. The two of you are going to have to take shovels with you when you head down to the barn to do your chores since I expect the doors will be blocked by snow drifts ... you guys will probably have to use the shovels to get the chicken coop opened, too."

I turned and looked out the kitchen window. It was getting light enough outside for me to see what he was talking about. Damn, I thought to myself. I was dreading the answer but I asked him, "Umm ... Dad, will Lenny and I have to ride out to the north pasture to break ice this morning?" I knew that with the cold temperatures overnight the surfaces of the tanks and troughs would be frozen over as well as covered by several inches of snow. Hell, I wasn't sure if the cattle and horses would even be able to make it through all of the drifting snow to reach water once we cleared it off for them. The storm had been bad enough that even with the heavy cloud cover the temperatures had really dropped.

Dad smiled, because he had probably guessed what I was thinking as soon as I had looked out the window and before I had asked the question. He answered, "No, son ... at least not on horseback. I have been thinking about everything that needs to be done this morning. In addition to having to break ice, with the snow so deep we are going to have to haul feed out to the cattle since they won't be able to reach any forage."

Dad had gotten up early and had already been down by the barn and corrals checking the depth of the snow on the level areas as well as where it had drifted against obstacles like fences and the sides of buildings. Then he had gone over to the Howards' house to check on Jay and then walked down to the bunkhouse and talked to Clay and Johnny. Clay had just gotten back from the generator shed. He had the dogs, Skipper and Jenny, with him and had let them come into the bunkhouse.

Clay told my Dad that he had taken a look at the lines running to the houses and nothing appeared to be damaged by the snow. Dad was happy to hear that … there was plenty to do without having to repair power lines. He had then told the two cowboys what he planned to do to get feed out to the cattle.

He told the two hired hands that he would need them to help him get the tractor set up with the snowplow and trailer. Then after everyone helped load the trailer with hay he wanted them to get to work shoveling snow off the roofs of the buildings. He was worried that the snow was deep enough to cause the roofs to collapse, especially if much more was added to what had already been deposited … and it was still coming down although according to Dad it seemed to be slowing down at least a little. The wind was also slacking off some.

After he had explained things and started back to our house he told his two hired hands, "Boys, you take your time and have a good breakfast and down plenty of steaming hot coffee. Then mosey on down to the barn. I will meet you there after I eat and let Jeff and Lenny know that they will be going on a little ride with me today."

So there we were at the kitchen table. "I think what we will need to do is fire up the tractor and hook the trailer behind it," Dad started, explaining to Lenny and me what he had already told the hired hands, and continued, "Then we will load up the trailer with bales of hay and head out to feed the cattle and horses and we can break ice in the waters while we are at it. You boys will be throwing out the hay." Dad explained that we would also have to shovel snow off the ice before we could break it.

The tractor was an old green Massey-Harris Challenger that was usually kept parked in the barn. Dad was certain that it would get us where we needed to go to see to the needs of the livestock. I sure couldn't imagine anything that old tractor wouldn't be able to get through.

Dad told Lenny and me that as soon as we were finished with breakfast to hurry and get everything done down at the barn that needed doing, including the chores Lynda and Mick normally took care of. He figured the job he had assigned his two hired hands of shoveling snow off the roofs would take them most of the morning at least … assuming that the worst of the storm was over. It looked to be a long, cold day ahead for everyone on the ranch.

Since there was no telling how long we would be out we would need to pack a good supply of food to take with us. As soon as she had finished washing the breakfast dishes Mom started in frying several pieces of chicken. Dad got out a metal cooler for her to put everything in.

In an attempt at humor he told her as he sat the cooler down on the kitchen floor, "Betsy, you probably don't need to put any ice in it."

Playing along Mom said, "Okay, Roy Dean, but don't you be blaming me if a warm spell comes in and spoils this food before you boys can get it eaten."

"As much as I love your fried chicken, Betsy gal, it would me a small price to pay for a warm spell," Dad answered back to her.

They were both worried about the impacts of the storm on the ranch and livestock as well as on the Howards and Dad's sister and her husband. Being so concerned about these friends and family members, the humor helped relieve the stress, at least a little. With the storm it would be awhile before anyone would be able to get to town to use a phone in order to check on friends and family. Mom and Dad were both careful not to say anything in front of Lenny concerning their worries about his family.

In addition to the fried chicken Mom put a bag of beef jerky, a sack of chocolate chip cookies, and half an apple pie in the cooler. She was determined to pack us enough food to take with us so there wouldn't be any chance of us going hungry. Mom knew that we would be burning a lot of calories with the work we had to do as well as just keeping warm.

After we had placed our breakfast dishes in the sink, Lenny and I went back to my bedroom to get dressed. I dug out a pair of long johns first thing and then got out two pairs of heavy socks and two flannel shirts. I knew that the best way to keep warm while outside in really cool weather was to dress in layers ... and I wanted to stay as warm as possible. Lenny dressed pretty much the same way.

Then it was out to the front porch where we kept the boots and overshoes that Mom had a rule against being worn into the house. I put on a pair of lace-up work boots and then my overshoes that closed with buckles in the front. Pulling a wool hat down over my ears and slipping on the gloves that Lynda had given me I braced myself for the cold that was awaiting us outside. Lenny had his boots and overshoes on our porch and had put them on while I was getting into mine. We then took off through the snow. Of course we had forgotten the shovels that were leaning against the outside of the porch, but remembered them before we had gone very far and went back and grabbed them.

At the barn we quickly cleared the snow away from the doors to it, and then did the same for the chicken coop and the tool shed. We then hurried through our chores. I ran a basket of fresh eggs up to our house. Mom took out just as many as she thought we could use and had me take the rest over to see if Jay could use them. He was sitting on the couch with his broken leg resting on a foot stool. It looked like he had been reading a western novel. Jay thanked me for the eggs and said that he might have a big omelet with ham and cheese in it for his lunch. He added that he was sort of getting tired of casseroles. I told him what the plans for the day were even though I figured Dad had already told him.

Jay told me that he wasn't feeling awfully bad about missing out on shoveling snow off the roofs, but still wished that he wasn't laid up like he was so he could do his share. He said that he didn't feel right not working ... just sitting in the Howards' house holding an old couch down. It was the same thing he had said to Clay ... but in a different tone.

Meanwhile, down at the barn Dad, with the help of Clay and Johnny, was removing the road grader blade from the front of the Massey-Harris Challenger and installing the snowplow blade in its place. The snowplow blade would cut through the snow with a sharp V in front of the tractor. I didn't realize it at the time but some former owner, with considerable skill with a welder and knowledge of mechanics, had made a number of modifications to the front of the Challenger so various blades could be attached to it. The tractor had been originally designed to pull farm implements. How it had ended up on the P Bar J was anybody's guess.

Once the snowplow was attached Dad had Clay fire up the old tractor. That's where they were at when I got back to the barn from delivering the eggs and spending a few minutes visiting with Jay. After the tractor was started Dad had Lenny and me open up the big double doors at the front of the barn to let fresh air in and the exhaust gases out. We propped the doors open with a couple good sized rocks that were kept in front of the barn for just that purpose. Of course we had to find the rocks under the snow first.

Clay then worked the snowplow up and down a little while Dad and Johnny checked all of the controls and hydraulic lines for leaks. Clay then backed up the tractor to the flatbed trailer that was also kept in the center section of the barn.

Dad secured the trailer's tongue to the hitch on the rear of the tractor. With the trailer hooked up the whole rig was pulled over closer to the hay loft. Lenny and I were already up in the loft and as soon as the trailer was positioned we started tossing bales of hay down onto it. Johnny climbed up to help us while Dad and Clay took care of stacking the bales on the trailer.

Before leaving the relative warmth and snugness of the barn we added some salt blocks, and a few bags of grain for the horses that were also out in the pastures. We also got a couple picks, axes, and a sledgehammer for breaking ice on the waters, plus two wide, flat-bladed shovels. Like Dad had said, we would need shovels for clearing the snow off the surface of the ice before we broke it up.

We then stowed the ice box that Mom had jammed full of food in a corner of the trailer along with a couple of blankets and a tarp that Mom insisted we take … "just in case" as she put it. I checked and she had indeed skipped putting ice in the cooler.

Then we were ready to pull out. Clay and Johnny would see to the horses in the corral next to the barn and work on clearing snow off roofs among other chores that needed doing at the headquarters. Dad figured Lenny and I were plenty big enough to toss out the hay bales wherever he told us to.

The last thing we did before leaving the headquarters was to gas up the tractor. There was a large gas tank that stood on thick metal legs that was used for refueling vehicles on the ranch. Dad made sure that the tractor's tank was full to the brim.

Dad had been right about the Challenger plowing through the snow with no obstacles, including drifts, presenting much of a problem for the old tractor. The plow was leaving tall banks of snow on either side of our path. Lenny and I pulled down one bale to sit on and wrapped one of the blankets around us to cut the wind a little. At least the snow had basically stopped ... at least for the time being. However, the sky looked as if it could open up and dump more snow on us at any time.

From the headquarters we headed north on the main access road that led to Route 66. Dad took it as far as the north boundary gate. Lenny and I took turns opening and closing pasture gates. At the boundary gate Dad turned around once he had checked it and backtracked a few miles to the ranch road that led east to the pasture that the majority of the cattle were in. He had mostly just wanted to make sure that the boundary gate was closed.

But there was another practical reason for driving up to the north end of the ranch. The paths we were creating would also be used by any cattle or horses that we missed as travel corridors through the snow. Once they encountered one of the paths left by the tractor and plow it would make it a lot easier for them to walk to the waters. The snowplow was also uncovering forage that the animals could get to along the routes we travelled that morning.

We stopped whenever we saw a bunch of cattle or some horses and tossed out hay until Dad yelled "That's enough, boys ... let's move on to the next bunch." The hay bales were broken apart into chunks before we tossed it out for the livestock. The chunks were called flakes.

Near one of the dirt stock tanks most of the cattle were bunched up next to a stand of large junipers that was thick enough to block the wind. As soon as we pulled up the cattle were heading for the trailer; they could smell the hay. Lenny and I immediately started in ripping bales apart and tossing the flakes as far from the trailer as we could get them. Dad set the tractor's brake and leaving the engine running joined us in tossing out the feed.

At the tanks and troughs we would toss out the flakes of hay and then move the tractor and trailer off a short distance and park. We would then grab the hand tools and clear the snow off and then break the ice up on the waters enough that the cattle could drink. When we encountered horses we would toss them flakes of hay and also clean snow off a piece of ground and put down some oats for them.

When we stopped at Dead Car Tank and had tossed out the hay I was reaching for the shovel and pick when Lenny said, "Now you be careful to not fall in, Jeff. Of course like I said before, I reckon if you do I could just loop a lasso over you, flip you over on your back and pull you out just like a stuck cow."

Before jumping down from the trailer I looked to see if Dad was watching us. He was, so my response to Lenny had to wait.

Instead I simply said at the time, "Lenny, why don't you make yourself useful and grab the sledgehammer?"

It was a long, cold day. We did a lot of throwing, shoveling and ice chopping in between riding in the open trailer. At least Lenny and I could wrap the blankets around us and sit down on the bed of the trailer with the remaining hay bales blocking the wind a little. Dad spent the day up on the totally exposed tractor seat although he did get some of the heat that was coming off the engine.

When we stopped for lunch it was Dad's suggestion that we build a little fire to warm ourselves while we were eating. Lenny and I thought that sure sounded like a good idea. We found a spot protected from the wind by a stand of junipers. After clearing snow off a small piece of ground with one of the shovels we broke off some of the plentiful dead branches from the trees, and built a nice fire, which sure felt good; probably better than any campfire ever had before or since.

After lunch we resumed our work. Out in some open country between a couple of the stock tanks Dad noticed a few mounds on the ground where he knew there shouldn't be any. "Boys," he yelled back to us over a shoulder, "See those lumps in the snow over there? I don't remember any big rocks or bushes to account for them. I guess we better stop and take a look."

Dad pulled to a stop and set the brake and then climbed down. Lenny and I grabbed a couple of the shovels from the trailer before jumping down and trudging through the deep, drifted snow to follow him. "Damn, I got me a bad feeling about what's under that snow," Dad said when we caught up to him,

We had all come to the same conclusion about what we were going to find before we started shoveling snow from the first mound we came to. Sure enough it was a cow that had frozen to death. Checking the other mounds quickly, Dad just had us dig out enough so that he would make a note in his tally book to record the loss. He told us that it looked like the ones that didn't make it were older, weaker cows. The final count was seven dead in that area of the pasture. Thankfully, those were the only dead livestock that we found that day.

By the time we got back to the barn the cooler was pretty much empty. And we sure enough hadn't needed any ice in it that day.

I think Dad must have been at least a little grateful for having so much to do that day. He hadn't been able to sit and worry about his sister and her husband, as well as the Howards, being out travelling during the snow storm. And to make it more frustrating he didn't have any way of finding out anything about where they were and if they were okay. As for the dead cattle we had found, Dad knew that the losses could have been much worse.

With the deep snow still covering the road between our north gate and Route 66 it would be impossible to get to Seligman to make calls to see if anyone had heard anything, unless he drove the tractor all the way ... with the plow down. It would be quite a while before Dad's two-wheel drive pickup could make it out to the highway. Plus, there was no telling if even the highway had gotten cleared yet. It looked like as if we were pretty much going to be isolated for a while from the world outside the P Bar J Ranch.

After a day or two of worrying about family and friends, someone, either Mom or Dad, suggested driving the tractor over to the headquarters of the R_X Ranch and making some phone calls from there. The Thorpes had gotten a telephone line ran to their ranch's headquarters since it was important that the doc's office and patients be able to reach him. The R_X Ranch's headquarters wasn't far from Route 66 and wasn't nearly as isolated as the headquarters of the P Bar J. It would have been a lot more expensive to run a phone line out to our ranch.

Early the following morning Dad and Mom bundled up and left on the Massey-Harris Challenger. Dad left instructions for the hired hands and for Lenny and me. Since it was going to be a slow drive through the snow on the old tractor he had wanted to go by himself, but Mom had insisted on going along since she was worried about Abby who had become a good friend. Also, I think she just wanted to get out of the house after being cooped up since the storm had hit. Everyone was getting a little stir crazy.

Knowing that he would need to take more feed out to the livestock Dad had left the trailer attached to the tractor. The day before he had had another load of hay loaded onto it. One of the hired hands had seen to filling up the tractor's gas tank so it would be ready to go.

Dad figured that as long as they would be going up towards the North Pasture they might as well drop off more hay on the way for the livestock. He even took along hand tools for breaking ice on the waters. He planned on leaving the trailer at the boundary fence between the P Bar J and the R_X and then pick it up on the way back. They would be able to make better time without pulling the trailer.

Mom would ride on the trailer while it was hooked to the tractor. Other times she would have to stand on a step next to Dad's seat and lean against one of the fender coverings. Hand holds had been welded onto the fenders so someone riding with the driver had something to hang onto. They had probably been added by the same person who had done the other modifications to the front of the tractor. Lenny and I had used the handholds the previous summer whenever my dad let us ride with him when he was grading the ranch roads.

When Lenny and I had ridden bikes over to the R_X Ranch the previous summer we had gone north on the main ranch road out of the P Bar J and then cut east past the old Owsley Place. Dad was going to take a more direct route, cutting northeast through the north pasture and going out the northeast corner of the ranch. It would require taking a fence apart and putting it back together, but even with having to do that, it would shorten the trip a little going and coming. Since the surface was covered by snow and frozen to boot there wouldn't be any ruts left by the overland excursion. Dad always frowned on anyone driving off road and tearing up the range.

Clay and Johnny were tending to their duties while Lenny and I took care of all of the chores normally handled by us as well as those of Lynda and Mick. But at least it kept us busy, since we were worried about everyone. I especially missed Lynda. Even with Lenny there the headquarters sure did seem empty and lonesome without her.

Mom had left a big pot of pork and beans for us to heat up for our lunch and she had told me that if she and Dad hadn't made it back by supper time to go ahead and heat up some of the fried chicken that was in the fridge.

In the late afternoon with the shadows lengthening I kept looking out toward the north hoping to see or hear the Challenger. As it started getting dark I got to wondering if that old tractor even had headlights on it.

"Come on, Mom and Dad, you better get to hurrying on home," I hoped under my breath.

The two cowboys had been out a little ways from the headquarters doing some work and had come in a little before 6:00 p.m. They were surprised and more than a little concerned not to see the tractor down at the barn. We all walked over to the Howards' house to visit Jay while we waited. Jay hadn't gotten around to heating anything up for supper so Clay offered to check the fridge and see what was available and then he'd heat it up and we would all have supper together.

Clay heated a tuna noodle casserole up and we sat in the Howard's kitchen and ate it. Clay, Johnny, and Jay each told a few stories while he had our meal. Then it was back to waiting.

The five of us were getting really worried when we finally heard the Massey-Harris Challenger and looked off to the north and saw what had to be its headlights; the question of the headlights thus answered. The two able-bodied hired hands and Lenny and I grabbed our coats, pulled on our boots and overshoes and hurried down to the barn. As we headed out the door Clay turned back toward Jay and told him that he would be back later to fill him in on any news.

Several minutes later the tractor pulled up next to the barn with Mom and Dad looking pretty much frozen. As soon as the tractor had stopped Clay hopped up and told my folks, "Roy, Betsy … why don't you two head on up to your house and get warmed up? Johnny and I will see to unhooking the trailer and getting it and the tractor settled back into the bay of the barn."

Dad answered for both with, "Thanks, boys. We sure would appreciate it. I know I have been thinking of a pot of hot coffee for the past several hours and a warm stove to drink it by."

Mom just smiled and nodded her agreement as she climbed down from the trailer where she had been sitting wrapped in a blanket and tarp. She headed for the house to get a pot of coffee going, while Dad hung back for a few minutes.

First he looked at Lenny and said, "Your family is safe and sound at your house in Flagstaff. They will be along as soon as the roads are clear enough to travel safely." Lenny was happy to hear that. I was, too, knowing that Lynda was safe. It turned out that when they had learned of the storm coming they had decided to stay put in Flagstaff instead of trying to get down to Abby's folks' ranch on the Hassayampa near Wagoner for New Year's.

Dad then told us that they had been late getting back because after coming back onto the P Bar J and hooking up the trailer, he had decided to make another quick check of the gate at the main entry on the north boundary fence. As it turned out it was a good thing he did. He found that someone, evidently in a four-wheel drive, had been tearing down the snow-covered access road heading south from Route 66 when they unexpectedly encountered our gate across the road.

The truck, jeep, or whatever the hell it was had slid through the gate, knocking it off its hinges and breaking off one of the fence posts that supported it. Luckily there had been a couple metal t-posts on the trailer and a sledgehammer that he had brought along for busting ice. With Mom's help they had replaced the broken wooden post with a t-post and had wired the gate back up after hammering it flat. The collision with the vehicle had left it bowed in the middle. Dad had maneuvered the trailer over next to where he needed to pound on the top of the t-post so he could stand on it while hammering. That allowed him to be able to apply enough force to drive the metal post into the frozen ground since they didn't have a post pounder with them. Mom stood on the ground and steadied the t-post with her gloved hands while trusting her husband's aim.

Dad told Clay and Johnny that as soon as the road was good enough to take a ranch pickup on it he wanted them to get one of the extra Texas gates from back behind the tool shed and take it up and replace the damaged one. He also told them to be sure to take along a chainsaw and post hole digger so they would be able to cut and plant another thick juniper post to replace the one that had gotten broken. He didn't consider that the t-post was really strong enough to use at a gate on a permanent basis.

Later I overheard my dad telling his cowboys that he sure hoped that gate and post had given as good as it had received from that sliding vehicle. He figured it was most likely some city people out playing with their four-wheel drive, which at the time weren't all that common.

Mom and Dad had been able to call his parents in Winslow as well as the Howards at their place in Flagstaff. It turned out that his parents were in from the storm and were safe. However, Dad's parents hadn't heard anything from Aunt Christy and her husband and didn't know for sure if they were safely back at the ranch he worked at in southern New Mexico.

As they were preparing to head back to the P Bar J on the tractor Doc Thorpe had told them that if he heard anything he would have his hired man Teddy drive over in the ranch's Dodge Power Wagon and let them know. Dad had given his parents the Thorpes' phone number.

Chapter 13
Pasturage Cattle

It was just a few days after Mom and Dad's cold tractor ride that Teddy from the R_X Ranch came pulling up to our house in the Thorpes' big Power Wagon. He said later that he had been sure to have a smile on his face when he arrived because he wanted us to know right off that he was carrying good news. Christy had phoned her parents after they had gotten back to the ranch near Las Cruces in southern New Mexico. They had to spend a couple nights in Albuquerque due to the storm but other than that they hadn't had any problems. She hadn't thought to call earlier.

The Howards ended up staying in Flagstaff for several days before chancing the drive back to the ranch. Mr. Howard had gotten chains for the rear tires of his Lincoln and his wife's Ford station wagon. They knew that by the time they left for the ranch, Route 66 would be cleared, but once they turned off onto the ranch roads they would have to stop and chain up the rear wheels on their cars. They decided to drive back in separate cars instead of together in case one should get stuck, but they made it just fine.

The big snow storm in late December had caused the arrival date for the pasturage cattle to be moved back long enough to give the snow a chance to melt in the South Pasture. Dad felt that the bright side of the storm was that all of the moisture that would be going into the soil when the snow started melting would provide a big boost in the production of the spring and summer feed as well as the winter annuals. The annuals would start popping up as soon as bare patches appeared and there were some warm days. The extra growth of the winter annuals and the spring feed would provide even better conditions and available forage for the pasturage cattle, as well as the P Bar J's own livestock, than had originally been calculated by the county agent when Dad had had him out looking at the South Pasture.

Dad had kept in contact with the rancher, who owned the feedlot that he had made the deal with and let him know about when he expected the pasture to be ready. As part of the deal the owner of the cattle had agreed to have them inspected by a veterinarian for any diseases that could be passed on to the P Bar J's cattle. Dad was going to be present during the inspection and had volunteered to help gather the cattle.

The storm that had dumped snow on the higher country where the P Bar J Ranch was located had poured rain on the desert ranges. The rain had already caused a spike in the growth of winter annuals such as red brome and filaree on the desert ranch near Hillside off which the pasturage cattle were to be taken. So suddenly the move wasn't as urgent as it had been.

The big snow was taking its time melting from the rangeland, which was fine with Dad since it meant more moisture would be seeping into the ground rather than running off. But I was sure anxious to see it gone. One day a couple weeks or so into the New Year Mrs. Howard had a chore for Lenny and me, and for once Lynda wasn't upset about not being included.

Mrs. Howard was standing on the front porch watching us as we were walking back from the barn after finishing our morning chores. She called to us, and then waved us over. She said, "Boys, I have a job for you two. There's a regular ice flow out behind the house on the north side that's covering the walk. I want to get rid of it before someone slips on it and has a bad fall." There was another reason to want to get all of the accumulated ice and snow away from the house. All of the moisture from it as it melted if left against the house could seep in and damage its foundation.

Glancing over to one side to where some hand tools where leaning up against the house on the front porch she continued, "I had Clay bring up the necessary tools that you boys will need." Looking them over I saw a pick, an ax, a sledgehammer, a sharp-pointed shovel, and a flat-ended scoop shovel. It looked like Clay had thought of everything, including as I found out later an excuse as to why he wouldn't have time to do the ice-clearing job himself that morning. Cowboys tended to shy away from any work that they couldn't do from horseback, especially if it involved picks and shovels.

Well, I thought, we had been caught fair and square and had no way of ducking out of the work. I resigned myself to the task Mrs. Howard had given us and grabbed roughly half of the hand tools that she had had Clay assemble. Lenny took the remainder of the tools and we started around to the north side of the house.

Soon we were laboring away and it didn't seem at all cold out any longer. In fact we had both taken off our jackets and had even rolled up our shirt sleeves ... we were sweating so much.

Years later as an adult whenever I worked up a sweat like that and there was someone around to hear I would usually exclaim something like, "Damn, I am sweating like a game and fish employee at an ethics hearing." That saying also works with unethical pieces of shit like land commissioners, politicians, lawyers, judges, etc. Whenever I think of judges I always think about the conversation overheard at the café in Seligman that Dad and Johnny had shared and that's most likely why I, too think of them as nothing but pieces of dog shit wrapped in robes. They are just lawyers after all. I had also heard an old man at a hardware store in Kingman describe them as such in the summer of '52 and it had stuck with me. As an adult I have always thought that should be their official title ... but I guess it might be just a tad long to fit on a name plate or the door to their chambers. That's the only reason that I can think of.

After a while I became aware of Jay standing out on the back porch having a smoke and watching us work. He was leaning against one of the posts that supported the portion of the house's roof that extended out over the porch. Mrs. Howard didn't allow anyone to smoke in her house, but if anybody could have gotten away with it Jay might have. However, he was well aware of her rule and wouldn't have dreamed of breaking it even if he had felt he was dying from the lack of a smoke. I was using the sledgehammer to break up a thick ice flow that had formed near the outlet of the gutter's downspout. Jay had moved over a little closer to where we were working and eased down in one of the wooden porch rockers. He laid his crutches next to the chair where they would be easy to reach when he needed them.

I looked over at him and said, "Mornin', Jay, how are you doing? Is your leg knitting up okay?"

At my greeting to the old cowboy, Lenny looked up from using the flat-bladed shovel to scoop up the chunks of ice as I broke it up and added his own. "Howdy, Jay, how are you getting along?" he asked.

Jay nodded and returned our greetings. He started to say something to us when Mrs. Howard came out with a cup of coffee and some fresh doughnuts. She set them on the little table next to Jay's chair and said, "Jay, I knew you were out here having a smoke and thought you might like some hot coffee and a snack. If you get cold just give a shout and I will bring you out a blanket. I added a few extra doughnuts for the boys."

"Thank you kindly ma'am, coffee and some of your doughnuts sure does sound good," Jay said.

Jay, grinning from ear to ear, waited until Mrs. Howard had returned to the kitchen before answering our questions. He said, "Well, boys, at my age the old bones sure do take a good spell ahealin', but I am trying to bear up and do my best to put up with all this laying around that is being forced upon me. It sure would plumb tickle me to be able to toss these crutches aside and pitch right in helping you two with your chore of breaking up that ice." With that he reached for a doughnut, took a sip of coffee, sat back in the chair, and sighed.

Without waiting for an invitation Lenny and I had laid down our tools and slipped our work gloves off as we stepped up onto the porch and grabbed a couple of the donuts. We ate them as we listened to Jay telling us more about the "hardships" of his recuperation.

After he had finished one of the doughnuts Jay, looking at the sledgehammer that I had been using and was at the time leaned against one of the rear porch support posts, asked, "Did I ever tell you boys about the best sledgehammer I ever owned?"

We both smiled, knowing a story was coming and shook our heads no. Before he began he took another bite of a doughnut that I was thinking was his third and washed it down with the coffee.

Jay then started in talking about this sledgehammer that he had owned years before and all of the work that he had done with it. He ended with, "I had to replace the handle twice and the head once … but it was the best gall danged sledgehammer I ever had." Then he gave us some time for his punch line to sink in.

Within a short time the plate that had held the doughnuts was cleaned off except for a few tiny crumbs and Jay was heading back into the house … probably to see what other goodies Mrs. Howard was baking I figured. Dad had been right back at Christmas when he told Jay that he was getting spoiled by Abby waiting on him. It looked like he had been putting on more than a little extra weight.

It took Lenny and me a couple of hours to get all the ice and snow cleared away from that side of the house. We knew if we left the snow it would melt and create more ice for us to break up. We carried all of the tools back down to the tool shed, dried them off with a couple of rags, and put them away.

Shortly after we had finished in the tool shed I heard Dad's pickup coming into the headquarters from the north. It looked like he had been to town. The surface of the road had just recently dried out but it had some pretty bad ruts. Still after being snowed in it was nice being able to get to town when it was necessary. Dad saw us and drove down to where we were standing in front of the tool shed.

Getting out of his truck Dad said, "I ran into Seligman to call the man I made the pasturage agreement with. It's all set. He wants the cattle gathered off the desert range he has been leasing and moved up here as soon as possible. Jeff, I am going to need you to go with Clay and me to help do the gather and I have been thinking I might have the two of you ride the train back with the cattle so that we can be sure they get watered properly at the stops along the way."

He then explained to Lenny that he and Johnny were going to have to look after things at the P Bar J while we were gone after the cattle. Lenny wasn't happy about being left behind but he realized that on a ranch some hands had to stay and see to the day-to-day chores and the needs of the livestock.

The man who owned the cattle that Dad had made the deal with was named Vincent Wentworth. The desert ranch, called Many Canyons, was west of a little town named Hillside where there was a railroad. There had been arrangements made to have large stock trucks out at the Many Canyons Ranch to transport the gathered cattle to the rail yard's shipping corrals at Hillside.

Later I found out that the ranch had been named for a battle between the army and Indians that had occurred on what would one day be the ranch in the early 1870s. It had been called "the Battle of Mucho Canones", but the ranch owner, Leonard Elkins, had Americanized the name when hanging it on his outfit.

Dad said that he wanted to give the snow another week or so to melt off the range so we would be leaving for Many Canyons Ranch right after he felt the ground was dry enough. It was several days later at supper when Dad told me to be all packed and ready to go the next morning. He had gone into Seligman again a couple days before and made calls to both Elkins and Wentworth so everything on their end would be ready. He figured that we wouldn't be gone longer than four days or so.

Mr. Elkins had cow hands that worked for him and Wentworth had hired some extra cowboys and they had already begun rounding up the cattle and moving them to a small pasture on the east side of the leased rangeland. Dad was happy about that since gathering cattle in that rough desert country with countless canyons and hills would be a sizeable piece of work in itself.

We were up by 4:30 a.m. the next day and were on the road by 6:00 a.m. In Seligman we made a stop at a diner along Route 66 and picked up a box of fresh doughnuts. Dad and Clay each got a cup of coffee in paper cups and I got a small carton of chocolate milk.

Mom and Mrs. Howard usually had us kids do our school work in the mornings after chores and in the early afternoons after lunch. Since I was going to be gone for a few days they had put together some lessons for me to do along with some reading assignments so I wouldn't get behind. I worked on the lessons and reading during the drive.

In Prescott Dad needed to make a quick stop at an auto parts salvage yard. As he pulled up and parked he turned to Clay and me and said, "I need to take a look out in the yard to see if I can find a mirror to replace that broken one on the passenger door. Not having one over there makes it mighty tricky sometimes when I am backing up with a trailer."

The mirror had gotten busted off back in December when Dad was rushing out to where Jay had been injured. At the time Dad hadn't given the mirror being knocked off the truck any thought at all. He had been totally focused on getting to Jay.

Dad, with Clay and me helping him look for a truck like his Chevy with the same type of mirrors, soon found a suitable replacement. After checking with the owner of the junkyard as to the price, Dad paid him and then walked back to his pickup to grab some tools. Within a few minutes the mirror was removed from the junked truck. Another few minutes and Dad had the "new" mirror installed on his truck. He had to remove the base of the broken-off mirror before attaching the "new" one to the passenger door of the Chevy.

As we started to get back into the pickup to be on our way Dad paused as if he had suddenly remembered something. "Oh, hell, I plumb near forgot about that damned old Ford of your Ma's," he muttered looking at me.

Getting back out of the truck he added, "And I best never hear you say anything to her as to how I refer to that piece of junk, Jeff."

Sometimes when we were out together Dad would make jokes about Fords and always remind me not to repeat them to Mom. He told me that Ford stood for "Fix or Repair Daily." Some years later during the period when I wouldn't think of driving anything but a Chevy I heard an even better one: From Old Russian Dump.

It seemed that the starter on the '36 Ford had started going out just recently and Mom had asked Dad to see about getting a replacement for her beloved old Ford convertible.

"Well, I reckon we might as well go back in and see the yardman and ask if he has a starter on any of the junked

Fords I can take off," Dad said. He hated having to keep that old car in running condition. Plus, he worried about it breaking down sometime and leaving Mom stranded out in the middle of nowhere. As it turned out there were a number of old Fords that could serve as suitable donors to choose from ... something Dad joked about. He looked for one that showed the fewest miles on its odometer in order to get a starter that hopefully didn't have a lot of wear on it. He found one wrecked Ford, which had the same engine as Mom's car, that looked like it had been rolled a few times. It had less than 25,000 miles showing on the odometer.

As Dad got out his tools and went to work removing the starter from the wrecked Ford, he looked to Clay and me and said, "Sure hope that's not 125,000 miles."

Soon the starter was nestled in a sturdy cardboard box Dad had gotten from the yardman and was tucked in a corner of the Chevy's bed. We were back on the road but only for a short distance before our next stop.

On the outskirts of Prescott we stopped again for an early lunch at a cafe before continuing on to the Many Canyons Ranch. After lunch we headed out of town on Iron Springs Road. We passed through Skull Valley and Kirkland Valley. The ranch's headquarters was located in a valley next to the Santa Maria River where it was joined by a good sized creek that came in from the east. I learned during our visit that it was named Kirkland Creek.

The surrounding mountains and foothills were covered with Sonoran Desert vegetation which included saguaros, barrel cactus, ocotillos, paloverdes, and patches of teddy bear chollas among other types of plants. The hillsides were already greening up from the growth of winter annuals that was blanketing the ground between the trees, cacti, and shrubs.

Mr. Wentworth and Mr. Elkins were waiting for us at the main house as was arranged the last time Dad had spoken with them. Elkins gave him the bad news that there had been a problem getting the cattle trucks out to the ranch, and it looked like there would be a delay of several days.

The ranch owner was in a hurry to get rid of Wentworth's cattle since he had made a deal with someone else to pasture a large number of steers to eat the abundant winter annuals that had come up in response to the big rain that had fallen on the desert country in late December. If the annual forbs and grasses weren't eaten soon they would just dry up later in the spring. Elkins knew he only had a short window of opportunity to make some money on the extra feed. The steers were coming in as soon as the other cattle were off the ranch.

Getting an idea, Dad looked at the men and asked, "How many miles is it to Hillside? It doesn't seem to be all that far. At least it didn't seem like it when we drove in today."

"Roy, I don't believe it's any more than fifteen miles ... maybe closer to twelve as the crow flies," Mr. Elkins answered.

Rubbing his chin and looking off in the direction we had just driven in from, my dad said, "Hell, I am thinking that we could just drive the damn cattle over to the shipping pens at the railroad." We had passed Hillside that morning on the way out to the ranch and had stopped off to take a quick look at the pens.

The other men were thinking on it since they both wanted the cattle moved as soon as possible. After giving them a few minutes to chew on the idea, Dad added, "To my thinking that's doable in a partial day's drive in this country, so damn it, let's just go ahead and do it. We will head them out bright and early tomorrow morning. We should be able to eat a late lunch in Hillside after finishing moving the cattle."

The other men nodded in agreement. They were all sure that with my dad, Clay, and me as well as the cowboys that

Mr. Wentworth had working for him the herd could be at the rail road's shipping pens sometime in the mid-afternoon at the latest. Elkins would also provide a few of his cowboys.

Mr. Wentworth said that he would make arrangements to have a large enough load of hay brought in to feed the cattle once they were in the pens in Hillside. They would be hungry after being moved that far. He told my dad that there was a ranch south of Hillside along Date Creek that produced hay in fields along their bottomlands. They sold what they didn't need for their own cattle. It wouldn't take long to get a good-sized load delivered to Hillside.

The rest of the afternoon was spent having a veterinarian check the cattle that had been gathered for any diseases or injuries. A final count was made and agreed upon by my dad and Mr. Wentworth. After that was done Wentworth left to drive to the ranch on Date Creek to make the deal for the hay.

That evening there was a cookout at the Many Canyons Ranch and we were put up for the night in their bunkhouse. The ranch cook had breakfast ready before sunup the next morning. It was good and there was plenty of it. I especially liked the pancakes and thick slices of bacon. I also managed to take care of a pile of scrambled eggs.

Elkins provided us with saddled horses and one of his cowboys had them ready for us by the time we had finished breakfast. The men he was sending along on the drive would see to getting the loaned horses back to the ranch from Hillside. Mr. Elkins was also going to have one of his employees drive Dad's pickup to Hillside and have it waiting for him at the rail yard that afternoon.

Dad took the trail boss position out in front, picking the best route. In order to cover ground faster he had decided to try and stick fairly close to the dirt road that we had come in on the day before.

It turned out that there were a couple of cows that quickly assumed the lead positions, which helped keep the herd moving at a steady pace and in the desired direction. Clay and one of Wentworth's men took the point positions to the left and right of the lead cows to keep them following my dad's selected route. The other cowboys scattered to where they were needed. Some would work the perimeters to insure the herd kept moving together and in our chosen direction instead of theirs.

I was assigned to the rear of the herd in the drag position to keep stragglers from dropping very far behind and to go after the occasional bunch quitters. Before we started Dad rode up to me and handed me his bandana. As I took it he said, "Jeff, if it gets dusty, wet this with your canteen and tie it around your head so that it covers your nose and mouth." When Elkins's ranch hands had saddled our horses they had also attached full canteens to the rigs.

A couple of the other cowboys were also riding drag. Every once in a while a cow would take a notion to break off and head out on its own. I would kick my horse in the ribs just enough to get his attention and it would know what was expected of it. The ranch horses we were using were pretty well trained on cutting off straying cows and pushing them back to the herd ... just like the horses on the P Bar J.

I wasn't wearing chaps and the thorns on the desert brush, such as mesquite and catclaw scratched the hell out of my legs and tore holes in my blue jeans before the drive was over. The cattle that tried to quit the drive usually seemed to do so when there would be a dense patch of brush which we would have to go tearing through in order to catch up to them and get them turned back.

I had broken off a young limber branch from a desert willow to use like a quirt to swat the rears of stragglers and bunch quitters. The cowboys used the ends of their lariats in the same manner to encourage the slow pokes to step up the pace.

Even though it was a fairly warm day on the desert it was early enough in the year not to have to worry much about rattlesnakes. During periods of the year when the buzz tails were active they could cause stampedes during cattle drives. If one cow or a few got spooked by a snake and took off running they could wind up causing a panic in the whole herd. Aside from that the rattlers could cause a horse to start bucking and throw its rider. So all in all I was happy that it wasn't prime rattlesnake season on the desert.

However, it's not just dangerous animals such as rattlesnakes that can cause stampedes by suddenly startling cows that are just ambling along. A jackrabbit, for example, that thunders out from the cover of a bush just as a cow is passing it can also do the trick.

I had noticed several jackrabbits, cottontails, Gambel's quail, a coyote or two, and other smaller animals that the herd managed to flush out ahead of it as we drove them through the country between the Many Canyons Ranch and Hillside. Thankfully none of these caused any disruptions in the herd. Before we had started out that morning Dad had encouraged all of his riders to keep up conversations, or even do a little singing to help keep the cattle calmer during the drive. If the cattle become used to noises around them they were far less likely to get spooked by any other sudden sounds.

There were a number of birds that were perched in the trees and shrubs and they would take flight when the cows and accompanying people on horseback got too close. One of the kinds of birds that I had noticed that day on the desert was black with a crown. I would usually spot them perched in mesquites or catclaws that had mistletoe in their mostly leafless canopies. When they took flight I would see flashes of white on their wings. They were really distinctive-looking birds and seeing them that day sort of stuck with me. It wasn't until several years later when I was taking an ornithology class in college in Las Cruces that I found out what they were. They had the rather odd name of phainopeplas and one of their primary foods was mistletoe berries.

We were carrying food in our saddle bags and stopped for lunch in the late morning near a large stock tank. While we were stopped Dad helped replace a shoe on one of the horses. Luckily he had a pair of needle-nosed pliers in his jeans pocket and enough nails in one of the rolled-up cuffs of his jeans. He used a rock to drive the nails that he held in place with the pliers.

The food we were carrying was intended to just be a snack to tide us over until we were able to eat in Hillside. Our trail food had been prepared for us that morning by the cook at the Many Canyons Ranch. We washed the food down with the water in our canteens. My canteen was about half empty at the time. As Dad had suggested I had used my canteen several times during the ride to wet the bandana that he had loaned me. A wet bandana over my nose and mouth did indeed make it easier to breathe when riding drag.

The owners of the ranches we were passing through had been contacted the day before after the decision had been made to drive the cattle and everyone had given their permission. This included the use of any waters along the way. However, we had to be careful not to pick up any cattle from those ranches while we moved our herd across the country.

The Many Canyons Ranch was mostly in the Sonoran Desert, but as we moved the herd toward Hillside we passed through some areas covered by dense stands of chaparral. The vegetation changed dramatically as we approached Hillside. It opened into a broad desert grassland that stretched eastward toward the Weaver Mountains. I could see railroad tracks cutting across what was known as Grand View. That was a very appropriate name.

Just as my dad had figured, the mid-afternoon found us at the railroad's shipping pens in Hillside. We noticed a load of baled hay stacked near the pens as we rode up to them, pushing the cattle ahead of us. Mr. Wentworth had followed through.

Soon the cattle were in the pens and we were breaking apart the bales and tossing the flakes into the pens. As expected we weren't the only ones hungry after the drive. The cattle had also worked up an appetite.

The cattle drive had gotten us pretty dusty and dirty. Busting apart the hay bales added to our coating of grime. Stopping at a water trough we washed our faces and hands. The sun was hot enough that the cold water felt good. Instead of just splashing water on his face I noticed my dad dunked his head into the trough. I followed suit.

Not having any towels handy we used our sleeves to dry off the best we could. It wouldn't take long for what we missed to evaporate in the dry desert air.

Refreshed by the mini-baths we then headed over to a little café for a meal. As promised Dad's pickup had been left parked near the corrals. He had motioned toward the truck to Clay and me but then changed his mind.

He told us, "I don't know about you two but I am thinking a little walk might feel good after that ride. Let's just leave the truck where it's at for the time being and use foot power." Clay nodded his agreement.

My knees and rear were sore from the ride so I also agreed that it would be good to take a little walk. It probably wasn't more than the equivalent of a few blocks to the café. However, as mentioned before, most cowboys generally frowned on walking when there was a horse or pickup available.

There was a hitching post next to the building for working cowboys from nearby ranches to leave their horses tied to while grabbing a burger or a drink or two ... or three. I wondered how many of them wound up operating a horse under the influence.

A large cottonwood tree towered over the area where the hitching post was located. It was, of course, leafless at the time but during the hot summer weather it would be fully leafed out and would provide welcome shade for the horses. I noticed that any branches or twigs that would have been in reach of the horses had been browsed off. Several horses, including one palomino, were tied at the post by their reins that day. I always noticed palominos.

This was the only place to eat in Hillside and it was a combination café, general store, and bar all under one roof. But the food was good and there was a lot of it. The hamburgers we ordered where huge. They were served with a good-sized pile of fries on the plates. Dad bought me an ice-cold Pepsi to wash it all down. The men had beers with their meals.

The bar was in a separate room off to one side of the building. I managed to take a look inside it once or twice while coming and going from the restroom. The floor of the bar room was covered with sawdust and a scattering of peanut shells.

Like the café portion there were ceiling fans in the bar. The smells in the café were dominated by the beef patties sizzling on the big grill in the kitchen that was off to one side, separated by just a low wall with a counter on top for placing orders and dirty dishes.

On the other hand the smells coming out of the bar were a mixture of spilled beer, sweat, and cigarette smoke. Several of the customers were also smoking in the café side but the smoke didn't seem to be as strong a presence. It looked like everyone in the bar was smoking, making the air look hazy. It seemed like from that time on whenever I would walk past a bar or saloon with an open doorway, and smell the odors coming out of it they would take me back to that day in Hillside with Dad and Clay.

The bar had some interesting looking patrons. There were a few old men that were obviously miners bellied up to the bar. Half a dozen cowboys were sitting at some small tables working on their drinks while catching up on the local news. Their attention was occasionally diverted to the young woman in a low cut blouse and tight Levi's who kept them supplied with fresh drinks and bowls full of salted peanuts.

The doorway separating the café from the barroom only had a set of short swinging doors attached to the middle section and they were pushed open. On one trip back from the restroom I stood next to the doorway and listened to some of the conversations for a few minutes. One of the younger cowboys leaned over to another cowboy that I supposed was a friend of his who was sitting at a nearby table and told him what he would like from Sally but he hadn't seen it on the menu when he had passed through the café. I gathered that Sally was the waitress in the low-cut blouse who was serving drinks in the bar. I wasn't sure what exactly he meant with what he said but I made a note to try and remember it so I could tell it to Lenny. Maybe he would know.

It was about then that Dad looked up from his hamburger and saw me loitering by the doorway to the bar. He yelled, "Jeff, get the hell back here and finish your meal. You don' need to be listening, or watching for that matter, to what's going on in there. Damn it all, if your ma heard that I was letting you hang around saloons we would both get skinned."

I hurried away from the doorway and back to our table. I sure didn't want to be responsible for us getting skinned. I thought of my little detour at the entrance to the bar as just working on my education.

Dad and Clay had finished their burgers and were working on a second round of beers. I quickly finished off my burger and gulped down the rest of my Pepsi. The waitress had left a bowl full of peanuts on our table. Before we left I took a handful and put them in a shirt pocket for later.

I was looking forward to the train ride north. After the cattle were loaded into four or five cars, Dad headed back to the ranch in his pickup. My Grandpa Johnny had made arrangements through railroad friends of his for Clay and me to ride in the caboose on the way back. It would be our job to see that every eight to twelve hours when the train would be stopped to pick up other cattle or freight, to unload, water, and feed our cattle and then get them reloaded. The law said that cattle being shipped had to be watered and fed every 28 hours, but Dad felt that was too long to make them go.

The train passed through Grand View just out of Hillside and then headed through Bells Canyon with the Weaver Mountains off to the south. We then passed through Kirkland Valley, Skull Valley, around Granite Mountain near Prescott, and then on to the north. The train had made brief stops in Kirkland and Skull Valley.

While we were stopped at Del Rio Springs just to the north of Chino Valley Clay and I watered and fed the cattle. We also kept an eye on the cattle in the cars to make sure that any that slipped and fell weren't trampled by the others. If one fell Clay would pull it up by the tail. Pulling the cow up like that helped it get up by its hind legs and then it would be able to get its front legs up. Cows get up by their hind legs first and then their front legs.

Once the cows were up Clay would keep hold of the tails for a few minutes to make sure they didn't collapse again. Just lifting up on their tails helped steady them. Of course that's not a position you wanted to be in if they started peeing or crapping. All in all it was hard work but I enjoyed it since it was a new experience.

One of the things I enjoyed about the trip was listening to Clay's stories about his experiences on various ranches.

He wasn't exactly an old cowboy, but at the time he had over twenty years in as a working cowboy and was full of stories. Some were funny while others told of the cowboy way of doing things. And it was clear that the way of doing things on particular ranches had a lot to do with who was running things and how they expected the job to be done.

Clay told me about the foreman on the ranch he had worked on near Cheyenne. The foreman's name was Elton and he wanted there to never be any doubt as to who was in charge. One day an older cowboy named Larry, who had worked on the ranch before Clay had been hired on, ran into him at a bar.

When Larry found out Clay worked for his previous boss, he asked, "Does old Elton still ride a long trot?" Clay, knowing all too well what he was talking about, replied "Yeah, he sure as hell does." A long trot was a fast, steady mile-eating pace on a horse.

Larry then related a story to Clay about how after a long day branding over three hundred calves they had started out back to camp with Elton in the lead at his customary long trot. Larry, exhausted from the day's work, eventually slowed his horse to a walk and fell way behind. He knew his horse was tired too from chasing after calves all day. When he eventually arrived at camp there was Elton waiting for him where he would have to stop to unsaddle.

First Elton asked if there had been any problems ..."Did your horse go lame?' ... are you feeling poorly?"

After Larry answered each of the foreman's questions with a short "No", Elton told him, "Damn it all, when I ride into camp at the end of the day's work my men ride in with me, not following way the hell back!"

Larry, tired and pretty well beat up from the long day, got mad and responded that where he came from cowboys walked their horses when they were tired. At that point Elton simply said, "Well, goddamn it old son, you ain't where you came from."

From then on while he was looking around for a job on another ranch Larry would always be sure to ride in right behind Elton. Clay told me that the cowboy rule was that the foreman would always be ahead of the men and they would follow him single file. He then added that he was sure happy that Roy wasn't a stickler for piddling things like that.

Dad cared too much for his hired hands and the horses to run either of them hard after a long day. I knew from watching my dad riding with his hired hands that he didn't care much about who was out front. He sure didn't think that he always needed to be. Sometimes he would even race one of his cowboys to a gate just to be the one to open it ... especially if the cowboy was older than he.

Dad would never have dreamed of making an old cowboy like Jay get down and open a gate for him as he sat on his ass in the saddle just because he was the boss man. When Dad and I would be out riding on the ranch with Jay we would always pretty much split the gate opening duties between the two of us. We figured Jay had opened more than his share during the years he had been a working cowboy. Of course when he was out by himself he had to handle the gates ... but not while my dad, me, Lenny, Clay, or Johnny were with him.

As I had learned last summer from Jay it was a point of honor for the younger men to open the gates for their elders. Of course sometimes this led to good-natured ribbing, with the men arguing about who was the "old man" of the group.

The cattle were to be unloaded at a siding called Yampa west of Seligman and to the north of the P Bar J Ranch. We then would have to drive the cattle south several miles to the north boundary of the P Bar J. But even once we reached our ranch we would still need to push them all the way to the South Pasture. I was watching out a window of the caboose when we started slowing down as the train approached the siding.

Dad, along with Johnny, Lenny, and Lynda, was waiting for us when the train pulled to a stop. Dad had checked the train schedule at the depot in Seligman when he had driven back from Hillside and knew about when we would be reaching the siding. They had brought along extra horses for Clay and me.

After we had the cattle unloaded Dad rode up to me and said, "Jeff, why don't you and Lynda take the points and I will be out ahead scouting a good path for the herd to follow. The two of you just need to keep them heading the way I am riding."

I couldn't help keep from grinning. Lynda and I would be guiding the cattle while my dad led the way. Being a point rider was an important position on a drive and Lynda and I were both feeling pretty proud at being selected for it. But I couldn't help but wonder, however, if Dad had done it knowing that I would want to work with Lynda.

I was also smiling when I rode up to Lenny and said, "Looks like you are riding drag. Don't be eating too much dust ... you wouldn't want to go and spoil your appetite for supper. " He didn't think I was very funny.

I didn't know it at the time but Dad had talked to Clay and Johnny before giving Lynda and me the point positions which they really should have had. But neither one of them was a stickler for things like that and told him that they would be riding behind the point riders a ways making sure they did good. They were both more than happy to take part in the education of a couple of young cowhands.

It didn't take very long to reach the P Bar J Ranch's north boundary gate. The gates on the main roads always had a cattle guard on them just so that in case someone left the gate open the cattle still wouldn't be able to get through. When there was a cattle guard there was always an extra gate down the fence line just a little ways that was kept secured with a chain and padlock. These gates were used when we had to move cattle through or go through on horseback.

Dad reached the gate well ahead of us and had it open waiting for Lynda and me to guide the herd leaders through. Clay, Johnny, and Lenny made sure the rest of the herd followed. Lenny told me later that he had to go after a couple of bunch quitters and turn them back. No doubt Clay and Johnny also had to do that more than once during the course of the drive.

By the time we got the herd settled into the South Pasture and had ridden back to the headquarters I was starting to feel like a real cowboy. After all I now had a few cattle drives under my belt. On the ride back to the headquarters Clay had ridden up to Linda and me and told us what a good job we had done riding point.

There's an old cowboy saying about how to properly adjust your stirrups. If your knees hurt, the stirrups are too short. If your butt hurts, the stirrups are too long. And if both your knees and butt hurt, then they are just right.

Later that evening I was sure feeling all those miles spent in the saddle in my rear end and in my knees. So I guess I had my stirrups adjusted just right. That was little consolation as I put a pillow on the wooden kitchen chair before I sat down to eat my supper.

Chapter 14
Shootout on Broken Wheel Mesa

Johnny was handling more than his share of the cowboying on the ranch and Dad had been pleasantly surprised to find that unlike most cowboys he didn't shy away from doing the necessary ranch work that couldn't be accomplished from the back of a horse. He was adept at working on pump motors, generators, and even stringing fence. Clay was working as hard as possible. He probably didn't want to be outdone by the new, younger hand.

Dad found that he was able to catch up on a few things around the headquarters since Clay and Johnny were taking care of so much of the day-to-day work out on the ranch. He had made up his mind that even when Jay was well enough to resume all of his cowboy duties he would keep Johnny on. He knew that there were a limited number of years that Jay would be physically able to keep working and he fully expected Clay to move on sooner or later to a better job if one happened along.

Jay was on the mend and had long since moved back down to the bunkhouse. According to Dad he'd had a time of it convincing Abby that he would be fine down there with the boys, as he always referred to Clay and Johnny. Jay had felt he was a burden staying at the Howards' house and having Abby fussing over him. Of course Clay and Johnny as well as my dad rode him a lot about how spoiled and soft he was getting with Abby's cooking. And Jay, for a fact, had packed on more than a few extra pounds from the good eating, especially the pies, cakes, and other sweets that Abby knew he was partial to. But even though he wouldn't be eating as high on the hog he was mighty happy being back on his own among the other two hired hands.

To keep busy Jay had even been doing some work around the barn and in the work shop. He had found a number of bridles that could use some mending and had been doing some repair work and preventative maintenance on the saddles. Jay went through a lot of saddle soap getting the tack in good shape from the drying effects of the Arizona climate. He had made horsehair hat bands for Lenny and me. I was pretty proud of the one he gave me and I kept it through three or four hats before it started falling apart.

On this late winter morning we were sitting at the kitchen table finishing a big breakfast of steak and eggs when we heard a horn honking. Dad looked out to see a sheriff's department car coming into the headquarters. Dad had at first thought that it was Parker stopping by for a visit but looking out he saw that the vehicle was marked as a Yavapai County sheriff's car instead of the Mohave County markings on Parker's rig. As we watched out the kitchen window it skidded to a stop in front of the house next to where Dad usually left his Chevy ranch truck parked when he was at the house.

"Oh, hell, something must be up ... that's a deputy I haven't seen before," Dad said as he headed for the door to meet the deputy just as he walked up to our door and started to knock.

Opening the door Dad reached out to shake hands with the deputy as he asked, "Damn deputy, something all mighty important must have happened to get you out of a nice cozy cafe and out into the sticks this early." The deputy, still shaking hands, gave my dad a grim smile and replied, "It sure as hell wasn't my choice to take a drive in the country this morning, Mr. Dean."

The deputy, after the forced smile had faded, introduced himself as Joey Rankling and then asked my dad to just call him Joey. Dad replied that he should call him Roy, instead of the Mr. Dean that he had been using.

Deputy Rankling was a heavyset man with gray hair, a pot belly, and a handlebar mustache. I remember wondering how he got the ends of the mustache to stay up. They seemed to be defying gravity.

After introductions and handshakes, the deputy said, "Roy, we have gotten a report that all hell broke out yesterday evening down on the Broken W Ranch south of here. It sounds like there are at least a couple people dead and maybe a few wounded. I have been told to get out there as soon as I can. The county coroner and a couple of his assistants, along with a doctor and a nurse are already on their way but they have been told to stay back and not to do a damn thing other than treat the wounded until I can get out there and take a look. I will need to figure out what exactly happened before any of the bodies are moved or any evidence that might be there gets messed with." But the deputy hadn't yet said why he was on our doorstep rather than on his way to the Broken W.

Dad knew something had brought him out to the P Bar J and he invited Rankling in and they sat at the kitchen table while the deputy quickly filled my dad in on what was known and slowly got around to what he needed in the way of help. Mom had cleared away the breakfast dishes and had made a fresh pot of coffee for the men to drink while they talked.

I had already been interested about what had happened to bring this deputy from Prescott out to the P Bar J, but my interest level shot up several notches when the deputy told Dad that a shootout involving several people had taken place on the Broken W Ranch. That was the ranch Lenny and I had visited with Jay during the previous summer. It was owned and run by an old friend of Jay's named Lester Doggett. We had taken a mean old bull that had been causing problems on the P Bar J out to Lester's ranch. I still wished that we had gotten rid of the damn thing before it had killed one of our dogs.

We had crossed Broken Wheel Mesa on that summer of '52 trip and had waited at the corral at the end of the mesa that overlooks CF Canyon for Lester to meet us with horses. I figured it was the same corral that the deputy was talking about. I hadn't seen any others up there.

A man who had been out on Broken Wheel Mesa hunting coyotes had heard several gun shots and had gone to check it out. He had driven up near the corral, and seeing bodies on the ground had started to get out and see if there were any that were wounded that he might be able to help. About the time he opened his door he heard a shot as a bullet slammed into the hood of his truck. He then decided that he needed to high tail it out of there as fast as his old truck could take him. About the time he got turned around another bullet hit the tailgate of his truck and another came through the back window on the passenger side of the truck's cab and out the windshield.

The hunter drove into Seligman and found a phone and called it in to the sheriff's office in Prescott. The deputy stationed in Seligman, Orv Milliken, had headed out to the mesa that evening. Radio contact had been lost and the deputy hadn't been heard from since a garbled radio transmission close to mid-night when he reported that he had arrived on the scene and could see bodies on the ground with his spotlight. The last thing he said was that he was "going to check it out."

Rankling had been near Seligman delivering some papers that morning to the local justice of the peace. After making the delivery he had stopped at a local café for breakfast. He was there when he got the call to go and see if he could track down the local deputy. And he needed to make sure it was safe for the coroner and others to go in. Not being familiar with the area he asked some of the locals who were also eating at the café for directions to Broken Wheel Mesa.

"Well, Roy, I reckon I best get myself moving and head out there to see what's up. But I had heard tell that one of your hired hands is personal friends with the rancher out there. I was thinking that if it turns out that he is the one that done all the shooting it might be helpful to bring him along, if he's agreeable. Just maybe, your hired hand can talk him into laying down his gun and talking to us," Joey said, finally revealing the reason he had come out to the P Bar J Ranch that morning.

One old cowboy at the café in Seligman who told him how to go about finding his way out there had added how that mesa was on Lester Doggett's place. From there someone else had mentioned how Jay Kirby on the P Bar J was a good friend of Doggett's. That last bit of information had brought the deputy out to the P Bar J.

Dad had already reached the conclusion that Rankling had spent most of his time in the office and wasn't looking forward to getting into a situation where someone might be shooting at him, especially by himself. He had mentioned that he had heard about my dad's involvement in chasing after the Owsley gang and more than likely was hoping that he would volunteer to accompany him, especially if one of his employees would be going.

I told Dad that it sounded like what had happened had occurred at the corral where Jay, Lenny, and I had waited for Jay's friend when we had taken the old wild bull out to the Broken W. I proceeded to tell Dad and the Deputy all I could remember about the country out there, but after six or seven months my memory was a little fuzzy. Besides I had only been eleven years old at the time.

After listening to me, Dad turned to the deputy and said, "Okay, I think Jay will want to do what he can especially if it might help his old friend. But he is recovering from a busted leg and isn't much good over any distance. But I will walk over to the bunkhouse and see if he feels like taking a ride out to the Broken W."

Dad had already made up his mind that he was going to accompany the deputy out to the Broken W Ranch and he was figuring, like the deputy, that if Jay's friend was involved in the shooting it might be handy to have Jay with them. Jay might be able to talk old Lester into giving himself up. At least the old rancher might be more willing to talk to them if he saw Jay there. There was another reason to bring Jay along. If it came to more shooting, especially if the shooter turned out not be Lester, Jay even hobbling on crutches near the vehicle could still handle a shotgun better than most. Dad didn't know the deputy and he had his doubts about how effective the pudgy officer would be if it came to a shootout at that isolated corral overlooking CF Canyon. He didn't have any doubts at all about Jay backing him.

Dad went over to the bunkhouse and talked to Jay. Jay jumped up from the table in the kitchen area of the bunkhouse where he had been working on a new horsehair bridle when he heard the news.

After Dad had filled the old cowboy in on what had happened on the Broken W and how his friend might be involved, Jay immediately volunteered to accompany him and the deputy out to the ranch. He wanted to leave immediately to help his old friend. Jay told my dad that he would be ready to go in a few minutes and to have the deputy drive up to the bunkhouse when they were ready to pull out.

Mom meanwhile had put together a basket of food, along with a thermos of hot coffee for them to take since there was no way of knowing how long they would have to stay out. She had included enough food for all three men, plus a little extra.

Jay had asked my dad if he should grab a gun as he put his old black cowboy hat on his head. The deputy had earlier told Dad that he carried several weapons in his trunk so he just smiled at Jay's question and told him not to bother with any of his own weapons ... they would most likely have a trunk full courtesy of the sheriff's department. However, that didn't keep Dad from bringing along his .45 caliber pistol that had been his father's. Dad walked back to our house and let the deputy know that both Jay and he were going to be accompanying him.

Hearing that news, Rankling looked relieved and said, "Roy, I sure do appreciate this." They then went out to the deputy's car, got in and drove down to the bunkhouse. Jay was heading out the door by the time the vehicle came to a stop. Dad got out, met his old cowboy and then walked with him to the car.

When they reached the vehicle Dad motioned for Jay to follow him to the rear of it and popped the trunk open. Dad waved a hand over a 30-06 rifle, with a scope mounted on it, two shotguns (one with sawed off twin barrels), and a couple pistols that Jay recognized as Colt .45 caliber automatics. Closing the trunk Dad simply remarked, "Yep, like I said, I think we should be covered."

As Jay was getting in the back seat of the deputy's rig he said, "Roy, I would be surprised if it turned out that Lester was involved in this. I have known that old boy for a hell of a long time and I will tell you flat out that I just don't think it's in him."

After a brief pause Jay added, "Unless of course it was just plain self-defense that he couldn't sidestep around any which way in hell. He sure as hell don't have much backup in him if someone crowds him."

Dad, after climbing back in the front passenger seat, turned his head to face Jay and answered, "Jay, I haven't met the man but I trust your judgment. We have to go see what happened out there, because according to the person who reported it someone sure shot the hell out of some folks ... and whoever the bastard is he just might not be finished with his killing. So the three of us will need to keep that in mind and tread awfully damn carefully once we get out there. I am thinking that more than likely we will be in someone's sights."

With that Rankling slipped the car into gear and they headed out from the P Bar J's headquarters. The three men were headed out to face whatever danger was waiting for them on the Broken W Ranch and Broken Wheel Mesa.

Until we saw Dad and Jay returning two days later it was a tense time at the P Bar J Ranch. We tried to keep busy with the day-to-day chores, plus Dad had left instructions for a few things he wanted taken care of while he was gone.

Just after dark on the second day, Mom, Lenny, Lynda, and I were out on the front porch looking off at the access road when we saw headlights. There were some anxious moments until the vehicle got close enough that we could see Dad and Jay in a sheriff department vehicle … but not the one they had left in.

We also noticed that Deputy Rankling wasn't behind the wheel. Everyone rushed out to where they pulled up next to Dad's battered old Chevy pickup that he simply referred to as his work rig.

Dad, knowing that we all would have been worried during his absence, sported an obviously forced smile as he opened the front passenger door and got out. He had noticed us looking at the car and knew we were wondering why they had returned in a different vehicle than they had left in with a different deputy driving.

He went around and opened the passenger door behind the driver and helped Jay out of the car. He then looked over the roof of the sheriff's car and said "Jeff, give me a hand with Jay … his leg is bothering him."

Before saying anything else to us Dad looked in at the driver and said, "We really appreciate you giving us a lift home, Dan … and Jay and I sure are sorry about Orv and Joey. Rankling was a good man and I am sure Orv Milliken was, also."

We heard the deputy respond with, "You are sure welcome, Mr. Dean, and thanks again for what you did out on that mesa. There's going to be a hell of a lot of people wearing badges wanting to shake your hand." Dad looked a little uncomfortable at that and just nodded and lifted a hand in goodbye.

I noticed that there was a tone in Dad's voice when he talked with the deputy. It sounded like he didn't particularly like the man and was more than ready to be rid of him. The deputy wasn't invited in for even a cup of coffee.

As the deputy backed the car up and then drove off Dad immediately turned to us and said, "Betsy, kids ... I need to say right off that Jay and I are alright. But some mighty bad things happened out in the Broken W country."

We then all started into the house with me helping to steady Jay. Dad continued with what he had started when he had told us that some bad things had happened, "I got some news to tell you and I think we probably should all be sitting down for it. I will sure enough tell you the whole damn sorry story. But Jay and I would really appreciate something to eat while I am telling the tale."

With that we all continued on into the kitchen and sat down with no idea of what we were about to hear. Mom started in preparing a late dinner for the men. The rest of us had already eaten a few hours earlier.

Once we were settled around the kitchen table Dad proceeded to tell us what had happened at the Broken W corral and the surrounding country. Jay added a few details from time to time but for the most part he let my dad tell the story. It wasn't good; Dad's life would never really be the same.

The road out to the edge of the mesa overlooking CF Canyon and the headquarters of the Broken W that sat nestled at the bottom was rough on a car. The heavy snow that had fallen after Christmas had melted and in places the road's surface was boggy with deep ruts in places that were filled with water and mud. In those spots the deputy steered the vehicle off the road in order to avoid getting stuck. During one such off-road excursion the car's police radio antenna was broken off by a low juniper branch. At the time no one had noticed.

Dad and Jay would have quickly lost count of the number of rock strikes against the bottom of the vehicle if either had bothered to try. When they got close enough to get a view of the juniper post corral near the edge of the mesa the deputy, at Dad's request, brought the vehicle to a stop. With the naked eye they could already see bodies on the ground near the corral. Dad was thinking that it was a good thing that the buzzards were still gone for the winter.

A Sheriff's department car was parked off to one side of the corral. It looked like the car's tires were flat. Rankling told them the obvious ... that it was Milliken's patrol vehicle.

Dad and Jay nodded to each other and got out and headed to the rear of their vehicle. When Rankling had joined them Dad said, "Unless you want to play it differently, Deputy, I think it's best if we walk in from here to see what we are facing." He had already seen that the coroners and others who were supposed to be on their way out hadn't yet arrived and he was relieved. Since they might be having to move quickly, Dad told Jay to wait by the vehicle and if the others arrived to hold them at this point until he signaled them to come on up to the corral. Dad knew that walking for any distance was painful for Jay and he sure wouldn't be able to run. The deputy retrieved a pair of binoculars from the car's trunk while they were planning what to do.

"Joey and I will go on up to the corral and try and make contact with the other deputy if he's around and then glass the canyon. If it's clear I will wave to you. But stay back here until the others arrive. Get one of them to drive

Rankling's car up there. With your busted leg I don't think you can handle the clutch," Dad instructed Jay as he handed him the sawed off double barrel shotgun from the trunk. Before closing the trunk lid Dad grabbed the rifle thinking it would come in handy if he had to shoot from any distance and expect to hit something, especially since it had a scope.

Before my dad and the deputy left him however, Jay said, "Roy, I still don't believe Lester is involved in this here mess, no way, no how. You need me to try and talk to him and find out what happened to those poor fellas over by the corral, you give me a yell."

"I understand, Jay, but from what we can see from here those people lying crumbled up on the ground out there are sure enough dead and someone sure as hell pulled the trigger on them," Dad replied.

Dad and Rankling then started making their way toward the corral. Dad was a natural leader and in situations like this took command and others, even a deputy who by his position should have been in the lead, would let him. During World War II Dad had been in plenty of situations leading men while other men were trying to kill them.

As he led the way Dad carefully scanned the corral, the seemingly abandoned patrol car, and surrounding area looking for whoever had shot the people. They were close enough to the corral that Dad and the deputy could see at least two bodies and maybe three. There was a large truck for hauling livestock backed up to the loading chute. The corral was full of cattle.

Although Dad didn't personally know Lester he had heard a bunch of stories about him from Jay over the years but even if he hadn't he sure didn't want to shoot an old cowboy. He had spent his life looking up to them. They were his people. So he had assured Jay that his old pal would be given every chance to explain himself and give himself up if that was what it came to.

Mom, while listening, had gotten the supper meal warmed up and had placed full plates of food in front of Dad and Jay. She had also refilled their coffee cups.

Dad paused briefly in telling the story while Mom was serving them. He wiped his eyes with a shirt sleeve instead of the bandana that he usually always carried in a back pocket, took a deep breath, and then continued. I was wondering why he didn't have his bandana and I was about to find out.

After taking a sip of his fresh coffee he continued, "It was about then that I had turned from looking at Rankling while we discussed the situation and the possible whereabouts of the other deputy and I looked off toward a thick stand of junipers. The trees were beyond the corral at the rim of the mesa. I caught a glimpse of sunlight gleaming off metal and figured it was a gun barrel. I yelled at Joey to get down and I plowed in behind a clump of yuccas which was just about the only cover to be had where we had been standing. Rankling had gotten behind another clump. The dust hadn't settled around us before shots were howling through the air over us. One of the bullets took off a yucca stalk and it landed on my head as I started to look up to see if I could spot the shooter."

I knew that dirt usually was mounded up around clumps of yuccas so they would have provided a fair amount of protection from bullets … as long as Dad and Joey stayed low. Dad paused a moment to study the grounds at the bottom of his now mostly empty coffee cup.

The mesa was covered with malapais rocks and Dad noticed when he started to use the scope on the rifle to zero in on the shooter that it had been smashed when he had dived for cover. Then he thought to check the barrel and discovered it was packed with dirt. Not having time to fool with it he just laid the rifle aside and pulled his pistol from his coat pocket. Dad paused again as he collected his thoughts on what happened next.

Mom took the opportunity to ask Dad and Jay if they wanted anything else to eat. I could tell that Mom was shaken by what she was hearing but because he was there telling about it ... at least she knew he had escaped being harmed.

Dad replied to her question that coffee was all he felt like having some more of right then. He then emptied the little bit left in his cup, grounds and all, before handing it to Mom. She carried it over to the sink and rinsed it out first before she refilled it from the pot on the stove. Jay also just wanted another cup of coffee and she gave him a refill at the same time. As she set the hot cup of coffee down in front of him Mom noted that Jay hadn't eaten much of the meal she had heated up for them.

Picking up his third fresh cup of hot coffee, Dad blew on it and had a sip before continuing, "Looking off toward those junipers I saw part of a yellow checkered shirt and got off a shot with my .45 aiming a little off center hoping for a shoulder hit. I heard what sounded like a hit and it was followed by a curse and then a few more shots were sent in our direction ... but they seemed to be sort of wild.

"While the shooter in the checkered shirt and I were exchanging shots I heard Jay's voice from back at the car yelling out his friends' name a few times and identifying himself and asking if they could talk. As far I could hear he didn't get any response other than more gunfire."

Dad told us that he and the deputy stayed behind the yucca clumps hugging the ground for several minutes after the last shot was fired. Finally Dad told Rankling to stay put and he got up slowly and while keeping an eye on the clump of trees continued on to the corral. It looked like at least a couple of the cows in the corral had been shot. That made my dad even madder.

After looking in the truck and the patrol car to make sure they were empty he carefully checked the bodies on the ground. Two were dead and the third one was unconscious and bleeding from a wound in his side. Unzipping the man's coat Dad tore his shirt open so he could examine the wound. Dad pulled out his bandana and wadded it up and pressed it against the man's wound to try and stem the flow of blood. He slid the man's belt out of its loops and adjusted it so it went around the man's middle high enough to hold the bandana tightly against the wound. That's about all Dad could do to help the man at the time. Before leaving the wounded man's side he zipped up his coat so he would stay warm.

By that point Dad had decided that the shooter must have scrambled on down the slope into CF Canyon. He waved to Joey and told him it was safe. Joey in turn waved to Jay to let him know to come on up to the corral. The coroners and doctors had arrived and had been waiting with Jay. As Dad had requested Jay had one of them drive the deputy's rig up to the corral.

As they pulled up and started getting out of the vehicles Dad waved them over to the wounded man and the doctor and his assistant immediately set about their jobs. Standing looking over their shoulders while they were working Dad told them, "Let me know as soon as he comes around. I really need to talk to him to see what the hell happened out here to cause all of this before I take off down into that canyon to find the man responsible."

Seeing the urgency the doctor used smelling salts to bring the man around. There was fear on his face as he opened his eyes and said, "Oh, god, is he still shooting at us?" He was visibly relieved when he saw the uniformed deputy and my dad standing there beside the doctor. Dad knelt down and asked the man his name and if he could tell them what had happened.

The man said that his name was Tom; he and the others had been shot by a man who claimed he was working for Lester Doggett. The three men had been sent out to pick up a load of cattle that Lester had sold to their boss who had a ranch down on the desert near the town of Congress. The agreement called for them meeting Lester up at the corral and paying him in cash for the cattle after they were loaded.

As the man talked Dad got a pretty good picture of what had happened. The wounded man told the story of how Lester's hired hand had come to be on the Broken W Ranch. The rancher Tom worked for was a good friend of Lester's and had talked with the Broken W owner about his new hired hand when they had made the deal on the cattle. The hired hand, a stranger to everyone in the area, had recently wandered into that country on a motorcycle. After the cycle had broken down on the mesa the man had camped out for a while. Eventually he made his way on foot down into CF Canyon and had hit Lester up for a job while telling him a hard luck story.

Tom said that when they had showed up to get the cattle at the prearranged time he was surprised that Lester was not present to see to the loading and receiving the cash payment as was planned. Instead the hired man, who identified himself as John James, was waiting alone at the corral. James's story was that Lester was feeling poorly and had sent him to take care of the business. Tom said that he and his two helpers were skeptical of the man's name ... it sounded phony to them ... as well as his story about Lester. Tom's boss had made it clear that they were to hand over the payment to Mr. Doggett only and they had also been instructed to get a receipt and a bill of sale.

When Tom had told the man claiming to represent Lester that he would just hike on down to the house at the bottom of the canyon and give Mr. Doggett the money for the cattle in person and get the signed paperwork, James became angry and turned and walked into the stand of trees at the edge of the mesa. He returned a few minutes later with a rifle and started firing at the men. That was the last thing Tom remembered before coming to and seeing the doctor and the others. Then he suddenly must have thought of the whereabouts of the cash he had been entrusted with by his employer to be used to pay for the cattle. Tom asked my dad if he would check the left inside pocket of his coat. The doctor had already unzipped the man's heavy winter coat so he could look at his injury the way my dad had done earlier. Dad lifted the left side of the open coat and looked until he saw a partially hidden inside pocket. He reached in and found a fairly thick envelope and pulled it out. He held it in front of Tom's face and asked, "Is this the money for the cattle?" After the injured man nodded Dad added, "James must not have had time to search you men or else he assumed it had been in your truck somewhere." Dad then tucked the envelope back in the inside pocket and zipped Tom's coat up.

 All this time Deputy Rankling had been standing off to the side and listening. Dad hadn't paid a lot of attention to the deputy with all of the stuff going on since they had been pinned behind the clump of yucca. He was startled when he looked over at the officer and saw blood on his left shirtsleeve. His face was looking mighty pale. Dad quickly went over to Deputy Rankling and asked him if he was okay and if he had been shot.

 Dad told us at first when he saw the blood on the deputy's shirt he thought the man might have just gotten a bad cut on the malapais rock while diving for cover. Rankling told him not to worry. He had gotten nicked, as he put it, by one of the shots when they were on the ground behind the yuccas. He didn't say anything because at the time Dad had plenty on his plate and didn't need to be worried about him.

 About then the doctor's assistant had come over and ripped Joey's shirtsleeve apart so he could see the wound. It did indeed turn out to be a minor flesh wound and had missed hitting a bone. Soon Rankling was patched up but with any gunshot wound, and the resultant blood loss, there was a danger of the person going into shock. Dad insisted that the deputy stay with his work rig and rest up a little. Dad volunteered to go after the shooter and try to find Lester and the other deputy.

Rankling protested saying that it was his job, but Dad insisted. He didn't want to have to worry about the wounded and pretty inexperienced deputy while trying to track down the person who had been shooting at them and was still a threat to them getting off this mesa safely.

"Joey, even though your wound isn't all that serious you have lost blood and you don't need to be climbing in and out of this canyon after someone who is trying his damnedest to kill us," Dad told him.

Before leaving to find the man calling himself John James, Dad turned to Jay and said, "I hate to say it but I figure that your friend is most likely dead. This jasper heard about the money to be paid for the cattle and figured he could take it for himself. And if he's willing to shoot down three men here at the corral, one more wouldn't make a damn bit of difference to the son-of-a-bitch."

"Yeah, Roy, I pretty much done reached the same conclusion listening to that wounded hired man talking," Jay said. With that Jay was quiet for a moment while he watched my dad getting the long barreled shotgun out of the trunk of the deputy's vehicle.

As my dad started off Jay called out, "Roy, if what you said about Lester being dead turns out to be true I would take it as a personal favor if that piece of cow shit you are going after resists arrest." Dad nodded in understanding and then he told both men to arm themselves and stay with the vehicle and if anyone other than he should stick his head up out of that canyon to shoot first and worry about it later.

The coroners and the medical personnel had already headed out with the wounded man and the two bodies. The doctor had tried to get Joey to go with them but the deputy had downplayed his injury and joked that he had lost more blood from a bad shaving cut. He assured them that he would be fine with the doctoring he had received and that his duty was to stay here until the shooter was caught.

Sure that Jay and the deputy would be able to watch each other's backs Dad hadn't worried about leaving them on the mesa while he went into the canyon to see about Lester and the missing deputy as well as trying to stop James. Moving forward cautiously Dad first checked out the stand of trees where the man known as James had been shooting from when they first arrived. He found the man's motorcycle parked between a couple of large alligator junipers. It was a Vincent Black Shadow and even covered in dust with a dented tank and a torn up saddle the big cycle was still a beautiful machine. Dad told us later that he couldn't help but admire it and he figured that it was a late '40s model that most likely had been stolen. Checking the cycle over quickly Dad thought that even though it was pretty beat up it still looked like it might be operable. So on the chance the owner might somehow make his way back to it he pulled out his pocket knife and slashed the tires and then tore out the fuel line. The story about the motorcycle breaking down might have been just that … a story so my dad wasn't taking any chances. He made sure it wouldn't provide the killer with a means of escape.

Dad told us that after taking care of the crook's motorcycle he started down to the bottom of the canyon, carefully moving from cover to cover that was provided by the abundant large bushes, trees, and occasional boulders. He was glad that he had worn his work boots instead of cowboy boots.

Before long he was wading across the clear, deep water in the creek. The creek had been fed by snowmelt and was deeper than it was during summers. Dad said that it was over his waist in places and at one point he jumped between boulders that were sticking out of the water in order to avoid deeper pools.

Looking at the house and outbuildings he scanned the windows and doorways for the shooter. Seeing nothing he continued on to the house. The front door had been left wide open. He eased slowly through the doorway with the .45 cocked and ready in his right hand.

Inside he found Lester, or rather his body, sitting in an easy chair in front of the fireplace. He had been shot in the back of the head and most likely never knew what was happening. Dad told us that upon finding Lester's body he couldn't suppress a "Goddamn it!" He had wanted to save Jay's friend even though he knew before starting down into CF Canyon that there wasn't much of a chance in actually doing so. He looked like he had been dead at least a day.

Dad then checked out the other rooms in the house on the chance that the shooter was hiding somewhere inside it. The last room was the kitchen at the rear of the house and it had a door leading out to a screened in porch. Walking out onto the porch Dad saw a long-barreled ten-gauge shotgun on the floor along with a couple spent shells. Seeing the discarded shotgun had given him a bad feeling in the pit of his stomach. He knew Lester hadn't been shot with a shotgun so the killer must have shot someone else.

About the time he was having these thoughts Dad looked out through the screens and saw a body in a uniform lying behind the house. From the body's position Dad knew that the person was dead but he walked outside and checked to be sure. This was Deputy Milliken and it looked as if James had nailed him with the shotgun as he was approaching the rear door of the house. Dad knew that the poor bastard would have been dead before he hit the ground.

About then Dad heard a shot that sounded like it came from up on the mesa. A second shot that sounded as if it had come from the same gun followed a few seconds later. Dad immediately tore out around the back of the house and headed back across the creek. Dad told us he said aloud to himself, "Jesus Christ, the bastard must have circled back around and is trying to steal Rankling's patrol car."

The climb down the slope had been bad enough and Dad knew that going up it on foot and stopping to catch his breath a few times would take longer than he figured he had. The corral and barn were nearby so he ran over to them in hopes of finding a horse.

From the corral he could see a few horses off on the far side of the pasture. But he knew it would take him too long to go after one of them. Then turning toward the barn Dad was surprised to see a good-sized spotted horse checking out a feed bin attached to the rear of the building. Lester had most likely kept oats or hay in it.

Dad stopped in his story at that point like he almost had to keep himself from laughing and then said, "As soon as I saw the horse I couldn't keep myself from saying, 'Ah, hell did it have to be a damn Appaloosa?' and then I quickly added to myself, 'Well, old boy beggars can't be choosers.''

For some reason Dad didn't care much for Appaloosas. I think that he thought they were too temperamental or stubborn, although they were known for being intelligent, for a horse anyway, and sure-footed in rough or steep country.

Many years later I heard an old cowboy telling a story in a bar about "one of his friends" that made me think of Dad and his feelings about Appaloosas. It was of course just a story.

It seemed that an old rancher was feeling poorly and went to see his doctor. The news wasn't good. "Well, I hate to be the one to tell you, Walt, but you only have six months to live."

Walt was taken aback by the news and said in a pleading voice, "Doc, that's not enough time, you gotta do something!"

The doctor thought on it for a minute and then said, "I tell you what. When you leave my office go on out and buy yourself a Ford pickup and an Appaloosa horse."

The old rancher stared at the doctor like he had lost his mind and asked him, "How in the hell will that made me live longer than six months?"

The doctor replied, "It won't, but it will sure as hell seem like longer."

Just inside the door of the barn Dad found a rope halter and slipped it on the horse. Not bothering with looking for a saddle he grabbed a handful of mane and jumped up onto the Appaloosa's back. He hoped the damn thing wouldn't start bucking since he didn't have time to fool with it. Without giving the horse time to think about the stranger on its back Dad kicked it in the ribs and pointed it toward the creek.

On the hurried climb up the slope out of the canyon Dad told us that he didn't bother with seeking cover or trying not to make any noise. The horse was crashing through brush and sending rocks tumbling down the slope behind it as he kept his boot heels jammed into its ribs. His only concerns were first for Jay and secondly for the deputy.

Dad had left the wounded deputy and his old friend and employee up on the mesa thinking they would be safe. There was no telling what had happened while he had been down in the canyon on what had turned out to be a wild goose chase. He didn't know Rankling very well but since he was mostly an office worker Dad didn't have much confidence in the man's ability to protect himself much less Jay.

Once at the top Dad came out through the cover of the trees and surveyed the scene. He jumped down off the horse and gave it a swat on the rear with his hat to get it to head back down into the canyon where it would be safe from any shooting.

His heart skipped a beat when he saw Joey's body lying face down on the ground in front of his sheriff's department rig. The man in the yellow checked shirt had been standing next to the body looking down at it when Dad left the cover of the trees and continued toward the sheriff's department vehicle.

Seeing the man start toward the driver's side of the car and thinking that inside the car was the only place Jay could be Dad yelled for the man to stop and throw down his weapon. Instead the killer turned his gun toward Dad. As he did he heard Jay yell out from inside the car "Hey, Peckerwood!"

The killer started to turn back toward the car at the sound of Jay's voice. Knowing that Jay was trying to divert the man's attention from him, Dad immediately lifted his .45 and shot him before the man could shoot Jay who had been lying down in the car's backseat sleeping when the shooting had started. The man fell backward and didn't move after hitting the ground. Dad walked up to the vehicle and kicked the rifle James had been carrying away from his body.

Dad then looked down at the man wearing the now blood-soaked yellow-checked shirt. Dad knew that he had hit him just then in the middle of his back but noticed dried blood on the man's left arm. He realized that he must have hit him in the arm earlier when the man was shooting from the stand of trees. Although the damned killer had gotten hit twice it looked to Dad like the man could possibly survive. At least the piece of shit was still breathing and didn't have blood coming out of his mouth.

Looking into the car Dad called out, "Jay, it's me, Roy, are you okay?" His heart was in his throat for the few seconds that lapsed before he heard Jay say, "Yeah, I am okay I reckon ... what about that bastard in the yeller shirt?"

Before Dad answered Jay's question he told him that he would be right back and then walked over to the deputy's body lying in front of the vehicle to check on him even though he was already pretty sure of what he would find. The killer's first shot had hit the hapless deputy in the middle of the back. That one had put Rankling down face-first on the ground. The second shot had been delivered to the back of his head. Dad paused a few moments looking at Rankling's head wound. As he stood there he thought of Lester and the two deputies both being essentially executed.

Then Dad heard the killer moaning. It sounded as if he was coming to. The sound the killer was making took his attention away from the murdered deputy. Glancing over towards the wounded killer Dad saw that the man calling himself John James had one arm under him. The killer had been unconscious earlier when Dad had kicked the rifle away from his hand. Dad wouldn't have known whether or not the man had a pistol stuck down in his waistband at the small of his back. The man's shirttail had hung over the waistband when he had been standing.

That evening when Dad was relating the events on the mesa to us in our kitchen he simply said, "I was forced to shoot the man again at that point." We weren't told the rest of the story about Lester's and Rankling's killer around the kitchen table that day. Instead I heard the details from various people my dad had confided in through the years at one point or another to get things off his chest.

Upon hearing the moans and seeing that the man seemed to be reaching for something behind him ... perhaps a concealed gun or other weapon like a knife, Dad calmly walked back over to the killer.

When the killer saw my dad start toward him with the .45 he froze. With fear in his eyes he screamed "Nooooo! I was just ..."

As Dad raised the pistol he said, "To hell with you" and shot him in the forehead with the .45. The shot cut off the killer's plea in mid-sentence.

He then got around to answering Jay's earlier question. "Turns out that he was damned serious about resisting arrest," Dad replied.

"I am sure as hell glad to hear that, Roy," came the reply from Jay. After a pause Jay added, "It would have been a plum shame if the piece of cow pie had given himself up and had demanded his rights." Dad answered in response, "Yeah, Jay that was pretty much my thinking." That was all the two men said about it right then.

Chapter 15
A Night on the Mesa

Dad then walked back to the patrol car and opened the side door. He looked in at his old friend safe and sound, with relief washing over him. Jay filled him in on what had happened while my dad had been down in the canyon. Not long after Dad had left the two of them he had got to feeling tired and had lain down to rest in the back seat while Rankling was standing guard.

The deputy had turned away from the canyon's rim to light a cigarette when James had snuck up and shot him in the back. Jay had earlier loaded the double-barrel sawed-off shotgun and had laid it on the car's back floorboard so it would be handy if he needed it. He had heard the two shots that had killed the deputy and guessed what had happened without rising up to look. He knew it was too late to help the deputy. Instead he waited for the killer to come to him. Fortunately the shooter had taken his time. When Dad checked the bodies later it looked like James had actually stopped and smoked the cigarette that Rankling had been in the process of lighting before checking out the car. He must have assumed that it was empty.

Lying across the wide backseat with his head toward the car's passenger side he slowly brought the twin barrels of the shotgun up and waited for the shooter to come into view. As Jay had expected him to do he was approaching the vehicle on the driver's side to see if the keys were in the ignition.

But Dad coming into the open, challenging the killer and ordering him to drop his weapons, and then advancing to draw his attention had changed Jay's plans. The old cowboy knew that once my dad left the cover of the trees he would be totally exposed so that was why he had yelled out to the killer ... to give Roy time to shoot first while James was momentarily distracted.

After listening to Jay for a few minutes Dad walked back to the killer's body and rolled him over to see what he had been trying to grab. What he saw surprised him. Even though there was a gun tucked into the waist band of his pants it appeared that the man had actually been trying to remove a softball size rock that he was lying on. His right hand was still wrapped around one side of it. Dad shook his head as he realized that was what the killer had been trying to tell him.

"It doesn't make a rat's ass bit of difference" he said aloud as he grabbed hold of the killer's feet and dragged him off twenty or thirty yards away from the car. He then walked back over to where Jay stood leaning against the patrol car.

He told Jay about there being a pistol stuck in the killer's waist band. Jay asked, "What kind of pistol was it Roy?" When my dad responded, "I didn't take much notice of it ... just saw enough of the grips sticking out of his pants to be able to say it was a big old six-shooter of some sort. Most likely a .45 or a .44."

Upon hearing that Jay said, "I think I need to take me a look at it just to satisfy my curiosity." With that Jay grabbed his crutches that had been leaning against the side of the patrol car and the two men walked over to where my dad had dragged and unceremoniously dumped the killer's body face up.

Dad turned the body over so Jay could take a look at the shooter's gun. He then pulled the dead man's shirt tail up and plucked the gun out of the waist band and showed it to Jay. It was a beat up old .45 Remington. As soon as he saw it Jay's face turned dark and after he had hobbled off a little ways on the crutches he said, "That there is Lester's gun ... he would carry it sometimes for snakes when he was out riding. Sure is a damn shame he didn't get a chance to use it on that one." As Jay finished talking he had nodded back toward where the killer lay on the ground.

Jay handed the old pistol back to my dad and he walked over to the body and stuck it back in the dead killer's waist band. He then turned the body back over on its back.

Dad told us at the kitchen table that the killer's shirt tail being untucked might have saved him from getting shot. He said that it looked like the killer had been lying on it and was having trouble reaching under it and getting to his hidden gun. That delay gave Dad time to see what he was doing and put an end to it without providing any details. He hadn't mentioned to us that the man was "going for a rock." Of course once James had moved the rock most likely the gun would have been the next item he would have grabbed.

After they were back at the patrol car my dad got out a tarp he had found in the vehicle's trunk. He laid it out flat on the ground and placed the deputy's body on it. Then he wrapped him in it and used a piece of rope that he had also found in the truck to secure it. He then carried the body over to the rear of the car and carefully placed it on the ground. Seeing another tarp in the trunk he started to do the same thing to the killer's body but thinking of something he stopped and turned toward Jay. Dad told him, "Well, I reckon I ought to go through that bird's pockets and wallet to see just who the hell he is, err, was." With that Dad partially spread the second tarp out next to the killer's body in order to have a place to lay out anything he found while performing his grim task.

While Dad was telling us the story he paused and reached into a shirt pocket for his tally book that he always carried. He referred to that as he continued, "The first thing I found on him was an old Barlow knife stuck down in one of the front pockets of his jeans. It had two blades and the larger of the two was snapped off near the tip. The same pocket also contained a key ring with a rabbit's foot and three or four keys. A shirt pocket contained a gold pocket watch with Lester Doggett's name engraved on the back of the case. His wallet contained seven dollars in ones, two fives, a ten and a few photos, and a driver's license."

At "driver's license" Dad had paused again and took a long swig of a fourth cup of coffee that had cooled considerably while he had been talking. "That license was the shocker ... there it was ... his name was James Owsley Johnson. That killer was evidently part of the Owsley family, and judging from his name, I am guessing he was probably a cousin to the ones we had the run in with late last summer," Dad said.

He told us later that one of the photos he had found in the guy's wallet was of an older lady that may have been the killer's mother. There was another photo of a pretty, young woman in what looked like a prom dress.

Dad went on to say how he wondered how much of a fit Parker was going to throw when he found out that there were more of these bastards prowling around. He figured that this one had heard that Lester was out there running an isolated ranch on his own and felt it would be a good place to hide while looking for something to steal or someone to harm. The man probably got scared out of the towns after Parker had stumbled upon the other members of the Owsley family in the stolen Hudson north of the P Bar J.

Dad had found out later that this one along with another unidentified man (it would be almost five years before we found out who that one had probably been) and the three Parker had encountered had been frequenting the bars in Seligman and Ash Fork before Christmas and had been asking not only about the on-going search for the bank money but also about him, Parker, Jay, and the P Bar J. In addition to the bank money it seemed that the Owsleys were also looking for revenge.

There was a small empty canvas bag in the back of the deputy's car and my dad dumped the stuff he had taken from Johnston's pockets into it from the tarp. Jay had identified the knife as also belonging to Lester.

Dad then unfolded the tarp completely and covered the killer's body with it. It was then that he happened to remember something.

Earlier, while he was moving Rankling's body, Dad had happened to look down in front of the car and had noticed oil on the ground under the engine. After covering Jame's body he got down and looked under the car and saw that oil was dripping at a steady pace from a hole in the oil pan. One of the many rock strikes on the drive over the mesa must have punctured it. Dad wasn't happy with that discovery. He had been thinking that the two of them could take the patrol car into Seligman and make the necessary calls to the sheriff's department and then catch a ride back to the P Bar J by the late evening. Well, hell, so much for that idea he thought.

Getting back on his feet Dad told Jay, "Well, looks like we won't be going anywhere until someone comes looking for us. The car has a busted oil pan." Jay had been watching Dad crawl under the vehicle and had heard the muttered "Oh, shit ... goddamn it" so he had already figured out that whatever had happened to the patrol car wasn't good.

Then Dad thought about calling for help on the car's radio. When all he could get on the two-way was static he started checking to see if any connections had shaken loose on the rough drive back here. It was then that he discovered the missing antennae.

Dad remembered the juniper branches scraping against the roof of the car occasionally but hadn't thought about the police antennae being ripped off. Oh, well he thought Milliken's patrol car should have a working radio or at least an antennae he could borrow. Walking over to the car and checking it Dad discovered that the shooter had not only torn out the police radio from the dash he had also broken the antennae into several pieces. Checking under the hood he saw that the carburetor had been smashed by a large rock. The stock truck had been similarly disabled.

So that settled it ... they were stuck out there at least for the night. Once Rankling didn't show up back in Seligman or make radio contact someone else would be sent out, but no one would probably show up until the next morning at the earliest.

Dad figured that if they got a fire throwing up enough smoke into the air someone would see it and report it. That might serve to speed up a rescue party being sent out. With Jay helping as much as he could they started gathering dead wood to build a fire. They broke off several live branches from the junipers over past the corral once they had the fire going good and tossed them in. The green wood and needles produced a lot of smoke as they were consumed in the fire.

Of course there was another reason for the fire. It was late winter and while the sun had been out all day and it was shirtsleeve weather, both Dad and Jay knew that as soon as the sun dipped behind the mountains off to the west it would be getting mighty chilly out on the open mesa. Luckily both Rankling and Milliken had carried blankets in the trunks of their patrol cars. Dad figured they were kept in the cars for accident victims at crash sites but he sure was glad to find them. They would make the night a lot more comfortable.

Once they had the fire going and a good supply of wood piled near it my dad became aware of his stomach doing a little growling. He realized that it had been quite awhile since breakfast. He then dug out the food that my mom had packed, along with the thermos of coffee. He pulled a couple of the larger logs he had collected for the fire off a ways so he and Jay could use them to sit on.

Then as they watched the sun disappearing behind the mountains off to the west they ate roast beef sandwiches and drank lukewarm coffee and thought about the day.

Neither man felt much like talking for a time while they processed their thoughts on the events of the day. Jay had lost a longtime friend. Dad had had to kill a man. It was the first time outside of the war that he had ever killed anyone.

However, the fact that Dad knew with certainty, that if ever a man needed killing, this one certainly did, made it a hell of a lot easier to deal with. After an hour or two of staring into the fire and not finding any answers both men felt the need to talk about something that would get their minds off the mesa and on to other places and times.

The men were not in any hurry to go to sleep and have the dreams come. They stayed out by the fire until close to mid-night just talking. They mostly stayed away from the events of that day. Like me Dad enjoyed listening to Jay tell stories about his early cowboy days before and after his service in World War I. Neither of them much liked talking about their wartime experiences.

Jay and my dad did eventually discuss the fate of the killer ... him reaching for what turned out to be a rock and my dad dispensing his own justice to the killer of Jay's friend and the deputies. Around the campfire on the mesa that evening Jay said, taking a sip of coffee that my dad had poured for him from the thermos, "Roy, between you and me, and that is how it is gonna stay, what happened out here was pure justice. Ifn' that old boy had gotten the chance to be hauled into town and patched up, some lyin' little reptilian bastard of a lawyer would have tried his damnedest to get him out of a one-way ticket to death row."

My dad was listening and staring into the fire. He would nod once in a while at the appropriate pauses while Jay did the talking. He knew that the old cowboy, who had lost a good friend, needed to do a lot of talking. Both men knew that my dad could have easily stopped the wounded man from reaching for whatever had been behind his back without shooting him. The plain fact was that he had simply had enough of the bastard who had tried to kill them.

"And, Roy," Jay continued, "once that murdering little shit had landed in prison he would eventually get out and be worse for the experience." I knew what Jay had probably been referring to.

I remembered once while at a general store with my Dad he was talking with some old-timers who had a folding table set up and were playing dominos and discussing and solving the ills of the country ... if not the world. One old cowboy had said how prisons just taught a crook to be a worse crook.

After that got his audience's attention he followed it with, "You know there was a gunman named John Wesley Hardin who was probably one of the worst killers in the old Wild West. He was a murderer, robber, horse thief ... you name it and he had done it. He had probably even forced his amorous attentions on a few pigs and other barnyard animals. Well, he got sent to prison for a pretty long stretch and got his-self an education. Then when he finally got released into society he was a hell of a lot worse ... and lower... he was a goddamn lawyer! Boys, I offer that as concrete proof that prisons just destroy any fragment of character that a murderer or horse thief might have had going in."

Like the conversation Dad and Johnny had overheard at the café in Seligman about lawyers and judges that one about prisons making criminals worse by sometimes turning them into lawyers had stuck with him ... and me. Dad had told Jay and several others about both of the conversations. Whenever he repeated them everyone listening would always laugh and agree to the assessment of lawyers and judges. It wasn't uncommon for someone to add a story about a negative experience they had or a friend or relative had with one or more of the dog turds.

After Jay had gotten it off his chest about how he was glad that the killer had died on the mesa, Dad and he sat staring at the fire a little while longer. Occasionally my dad would get up and toss more wood on it.

It was around 2:00 a.m. before they decided to turn in. Then they had spent the rest of their forced night out on the mesa sleeping in Rankling's patrol car. The large four-door sedan had wide bench seats and while Dad said he couldn't exactly stretch out to his full length, as he put it, he managed to sleep alright for the most part. Occasionally during the night when Dad would wake up he would get out and feed wood to the fire just in case someone was out looking for them.

They awoke about the time the sun started rising above the eastern edge of the mesa and Dad immediately got the signal fire going again. In the mid-morning the deputy who had ended up bringing them back to the P Bar J Ranch had showed up to check on the whereabouts of Milliken and Rankling since they hadn't called in or returned to Seligman or Prescott.

Once the deputy had arrived Dad at first asked him to radio in and have his department call the coroner's office to request that they come back out for the bodies of the two deputies and the killer's, as well as for Lester's. They would also have to send deputies and investigators out to document the scene of the crimes, both on the mesa and at Lester's house. However, the radio transmissions were breaking up and they had so much static it was difficult to get a coherent message through. So Dad asked him to drive into Seligman and make the necessary phone calls.

While the deputy was gone to make the calls Dad left Jay to watch over the bodies so no varmints got to them and for the second time in two days started hiking back down to Lester's headquarters. He was thinking that he was doing a lot more hiking than any self-respecting cowboy would want to do. By the time he reached the creek his toes were feeling like they were rubbed raw from being pushed up against the inside of the fronts of his boots. It would have been worse if he had been wearing his cowboy boots, but even his work boots sure weren't designed for this downhill travel. Back in those days no one we knew had ever heard of hiking boots.

Reaching Lester's headquarters after crossing the creek Dad went to the barn and got a bait of oats and then went out to the horse pasture and caught and saddled three horses, including the Appaloosa that he had ridden bareback the day before. It had returned to the corral after he had set it loose like he figured it would.

Looking around the barn Dad found an old tarp and used his pocket knife to cut it in half. Then he used the two pieces to wrap around Lester's and Milliken's bodies. Before moving the deputy's body he had taken a stick and drew an outline around it in the dirt so anyone checking later would be able to tell the position of the body.

Dad then tied the bodies over the saddles of two of the horses, a roan and a dun. He had decided that he would ride the Appaloosa again since it hadn't given him any problems the day before. Neither of the other two horses liked having dead bodies on them but they settled down after a few minutes and Dad was able to lead them up out of the canyon to the corral on the mesa where the first shootings had occurred.

After the coroner arrived with three deputies in two other cars Dad gave a statement as to what had happened and how Lester's and Orv Milliken's bodies were located and positioned when he had found them in or near the old cowboy's house.

The three deputies, including the one that had come out earlier, had seen the bodies of their colleagues and they had also looked at the killer's body. They took special notice of the bullet hole in his forehead. Then they all made a point of shaking Dad's hand and slapping him on the back for the job he had done dealing with the killer.

The coroner examined Rankling's body first. Dad and Jay sat at the remains of their campfire. The day had warmed up to the point where neither were bothering to feed it anymore wood and were just letting it die down.

Dad noticed that the three deputies were huddled next to the open trunk of one of their cars. After a few minutes a deputy came over to the campfire and squatted on his heels next to my dad.

In a low voice, so as not to be overheard by the coroner he said, "Mr. Dean, the boys and I were wondering if the fucker over there under the tarp needs a handgun just so there's no questions later on. Most of us keep a few off the record guns stashed in our trunks and other places for cases like this. It seems that once in a while some dumb shit forgets to bring his own gun to a shootout and we have to provide him with one afterwards." The deputy laughed at the last bit, but my dad didn't see anything funny in it.

The deputy had essentially asked my dad if they needed to provide the killer with a hidden gun ... so there wouldn't be any question that the shooting of him had been justified. It amounted to planting evidence and the deputy thought it was funny.

Immediately following the offer Dad shook his head and walked over to Johnson's body. He rolled it over so that the deputies as well as the coroner could see the pistol stuck in his waistband. He didn't say anything but looked at the deputy who had asked and just shook his head again to indicate the disgust he felt toward him.

My dad mentioned the deputy's offer to others later and told them that he sure didn't care much for it. He maintained that he didn't need a crooked deputy's help to justify what he had done ... even if Johnson hadn't had the hidden pistol. After the shootout on the mesa Dad never had much use for sheriff departments ... especially Yavapai

County's. In his experience anyway the deputies were mostly untrained and unethical and the sheriffs were mostly just political hacks and sometimes were even drunks on top of that.

We found out later that when the county sheriff learned of what had happened he had offered Dad a job any time he wanted it. He also extended his thanks for the way that Dad had "taken care of things" out on that isolated mesa where his deputy had been killed while lying wounded and helpless on the ground.

Dad had just told him that he wasn't interested. Later I heard him telling Jay and Clay about the sheriff's job offer. He told Jay what he thought of the sheriff and his inept deputies and that he, "... sure as hell didn't want to join up with the pieces of shit."

At the time Dad had shot the killer in the head he wasn't sure that he actually was going for a weapon. He was however, at his limit of seeing the violence this person had inflicted on several good men, all of whom he had pretty much murdered in cold blood. The men that had been gunned downed around the corral had been unarmed. At the kitchen table that evening Dad had simply told us that the shooter had died of his wounds before he could get medical help. It was sort of the truth.

I remember how shocked I was when I first heard the whole story of what happened out on that mesa. It had mostly come to me in bits and pieces. I had overheard part of what had happened from conversations between Dad and Mom when they thought I was out of earshot or wasn't paying attention. Through the years as I got older I would occasionally ask dad questions about it. Some of the details I picked up from hired hands, or from Dad's friends that he had confided in.

I had wondered for a long time how he could have calmly shot James Owsley Johnson in the head. Then years later when I was living with Aunt Christy and her husband on a ranch in the foothills of the Organ Mountains just east of Las Cruces, New Mexico I happened to meet a man who had served with my dad during World War II.

At the time I was attending the New Mexico College of Agriculture and Mechanic Arts. At least that was its name when I started school there in the fall of 1959. A year later it became New Mexico State University.

The man provided feed for a small herd of cattle that the college maintained for grazing research on experimental pastures. He had heard that one of the students was named Dean and was from Arizona. One day he looked me up and asked if by chance I knew a Roy Dean. He was quite surprised when I told him that was my father's name.

After a few more back and forth questions and answers this man, named Fred Myers, told me that he had served in a squad led by my dad on a mission deep into Nazi occupied France.

At the time of that first meeting we had talked a while about what my dad had been doing since the war and he caught me up on what he had been doing and had told me to say hello for him when I went back home. After that initial meeting we would stop and talk usually whenever we happened to run into each other. It was a few months later that he told me about what had happened on that mission. It was after I had told him about the shootout on the mesa.

The squad had stumbled upon three German soldiers in what had appeared to be an abandoned house. The Americans had gone into it to get out of a miserable driving, cold rain for a short break before they pushed on to their objective. The Germans evidently had the same idea a little earlier and had made the mistake of falling sleep without having someone stand guard.

After the Germans had been captured, relieved of weapons and tied up, the Americans realized that they now had an unexpected problem to deal with. They were running late to reach their objective and sure couldn't achieve it successfully while dragging along three prisoners cross country. Turning them loose to sound an alarm was out of the question.

The American soldiers discussed the problem for a few minutes. The mission was critical and would save the lives of a lot of American and British soldiers if it was successfully completed. A few options had been discussed and rejected as impractical before Dad abruptly turned back toward the prisoners as he told his men, "Well, I guess I have something to do."

He then walked over to the opposite side of the room where the Germans were sitting on the floor, and with only a, "Sorry fellas, but this is war and we just ain't got the goddamn time ...," which they probably didn't even understand, he pulled a small automatic pistol from a shoulder holster and made three quick kill shots to their heads. Slipping the still smoking gun back in its holster he looked out through a window to see that the worst part of the storm had passed.

Picking up his rucksack he started toward the door. Without slowing down he said over a shoulder to his shocked, surprised men, "Come on, boys, Ike has given us a job that needs to be done ... and as it is we are going to be pushing like hell to get it done in time." They were going to set explosives and they needed to be detonated by a deadline that had been handed down to them by their commander. It was understood, however, that this had come from Eisenhower. Myers said that the men all knew that my dad didn't really have a choice and it said a lot about him that he hadn't ordered his men to do it.

Dad had seen what this man had done to Lester, and the deputies as well as the others whose bodies were lying in the dirt out by the corral. He figured that it was his job to put an end to the bastard so he wouldn't have a chance to harm anyone else, so that's what he did.

Chapter 16
The Buzzards Return

Although Dad was sure that he had dispensed justice out on the Broken W Ranch looking back on the aftermath of the shooting I know it changed him at least for a while. He wasn't as quick to laugh and seemed to be lost in his thoughts a lot.

Lester hadn't been his friend and he had never even seen him while he was alive, but discovering the murdered old cowboy's body had been disturbing. It was difficult for Dad to get the picture of Lester out of his thoughts, sitting in his chair with a bullet hole in the back of his head and most of his forehead blown off by the exit wound.

Just as he had done when Michael T had gotten himself killed, Dad spent time thinking of "what ifs" about Lester as well as Rankling. He wondered if he could have done something different out on the mesa that would have prevented Deputy Rankling from being killed. If only he hadn't hiked down into the canyon after the killer he thought. Maybe he should have stayed with Jay and the deputy and let the killer try and get through them. Several more scenarios ran through his head.

At least he didn't have to blame himself for Deputy Milliken's death. He had most likely already run into the business end of that ten-gauge shotgun before Rankling had arrived at the P Bar J looking for help.

One other thing didn't bother Dad ... the killing of James Owsley Johnson out on the mesa. However, he was troubled by the fact that the killer had turned out to be an Owsley. But only because he found himself wondering just how many more members of that damn family would come around looking for the stolen money and revenge.

He even started drinking for a short time. However, he usually didn't start until late at night. I think it helped him get to sleep. But eventually he let go of any guilt and came to realize he had done the right things out there on the mesa based on what he knew at the time. And, hell, if the Owsleys wanted to cause more trouble then let the bastards come ... he would greet them with his .45 or a twelve-gauge shotgun goddamn it!

Deputy Parker had made a trip out to the P Bar J one afternoon to deliver some news that he thought would help cheer up my dad. He came into the headquarters and pulled up in front of the barn where Lenny and I were helping my dad unload a load of hay from a flatbed trailer. We were carrying the bales into the barn and stacking them in a corner.

I think that I was the first one to notice that the deputy's usual dead-pan look wasn't on his face. He was actually smiling.

"Well Parker, what brings you out this way? Isn't there a bench in some burger joint in Kingman that you could be keeping warm? From appearances I am guessing at least whatever it is it's good news," Dad said walking up and shaking hands with the deputy who had become a friend, of sorts, over the past year. I think in reality Parker thought of my dad as a friend, but Dad didn't in return. He just didn't think much of sheriff's departments and the deputies that worked for them in general.

"Yeah, I sort of think that it is good news. But, Roy you be the judge once you have heard it. You know how Garland Owsley had been sentenced to death and there was talk that some god damn do-gooder group was trying to get him a new trial?" Parker responded and then stopped to wait for a response. He was clearly enjoying his role as a bearer of glad tidings and was definitely drawing it out.

Dad picked up on something he had already said, however. "Wait a minute, Parker, what's this damn 'had been sentenced to death' shit? That bastard had best still be sitting in Florence awaiting his date with the gas chamber!" Dad exclaimed.

"Now don't you worry none at all about that, Roy. No, what I came out to tell you is that last night it seems that old Garland got ahold of some shoelaces and went and hung himself in his cell. Now ain't that just a goddamn shame?" the deputy said with a big grin.

That news sort of stopped my dad right in his tracks. I guess the word for what he was for a moment was flabbergasted. Dad looked at me and Lenny. We had both been listening intently to the deputy. He told us to get back to work stacking hay bales and that he needed to talk with the deputy for a few minutes alone.

As they started to walk out away from the barn I heard my dad say, "Shit, Parker, those boys don't need to be hearing about no jailhouse suicide, goddamn it."

A short while later I heard a car door close and then the deputy's car started up. When Dad came back into the barn he seemed to have had a load lifted off him.

Of course I didn't know the reason then. It turned out that Dad had been worried that if there was a new trial for Garland then he might be asked about his role in killing a member of his family out on the mesa. Now that wouldn't ever be a problem. Garland had done everyone a favor.

It wouldn't be until later that Dad would begin to suspect that Parker had had a role in Garland's death. But nothing was ever proved. In any case Dad never held it against the deputy. They both had come to share a firm belief that there were way too many Owsleys in the world. And that the bastards were just wasting air.

We had other visitors out at the ranch during the late winter and early spring. The sheriffs of both Mohave and Yavapai Counties stopped by to talk to my dad. They thanked him for what he had done out on the mesa and told him that he had a job with them if he ever wanted it. But it was another surprise visitor that held the most interest for me.

We were once again working down at the barn when we heard the sound of a vehicle rattling down our road. Dad recognized the government trapper's pickup when he saw it coming into the headquarters. Looking out the open doors of the barn he said, "Now what the hell does he want? I thought I had made it pretty damn clear even for a government man that I didn't want him doing his work on the P Bar J!" With that he stormed out to meet the interloper.

What happened next was completely different from what my dad or I had expected. Bringing his truck to an easy stop before my dad had reached him, the driver hopped out and met him with his right arm extended and said, "Howdy, I am Preston Denton and I am guessing that you are Mr. Dean. I have sure been wanting to meet you and," glancing down at his hand continued with, "shake your hand."

Dad wasn't quite sure what to make of the greeting, but took the outstretched hand and while he was shaking it he said, "Yeah, I am Roy Dean, and I know who you are and what you do and we don't need your services on this ranch as long I am the man running it."

"Oh, I understand that, Mr. Dean, and I can appreciate your stand on the whole matter of predator control. But that's not why I am here today. As a matter of fact, my plate is kept pretty much full to overflowing just working with the ranchers who want me out on their places. No, what I am out here for is more of a personal matter, and I would sure appreciate an hour or so of your time to tell you about it," the government trapper replied.

Dad then invited Mr. Denton up to our house. It was getting close to noon and Dad told him that if he wanted to have a talk they might as well do it over lunch. At our house Dad introduced him to Mom and asked her to set another place for lunch.

First he told us that his real last name wasn't Denton, but rather Denham. Dad immediately recognized that name and asked, "So are you any kin to that family that was killed south of here back in the '30s?"

Our guest answered, "Yes, I am, and that's what I want to talk to you about." With that he began to tell his story as we ate lunch. He certainly had an interesting story to tell.

He had been ten years old when he had watched and heard his family being slaughtered by the Owsleys. His mother, Ora, had heard what was happening out in her front yard that day and knew right off that the Owsleys were after their money and figured that her husband Crompton had blabbed and bragged too much over the jugs as they passed them around. Crompton Denham had made a sizeable amount of money selling his moonshine. It was a fact that hadn't gone unnoticed by the Owsleys.

The heads of the two families had become drinking buddies. Crompton had a still down next to the creek in Jacks Canyon. Orton Owsley and his no-account family, which included his wife and four sons, would frequently make the trip down to buy or trade for the moonshine. The girlfriend of the oldest son was with them on this particular trip. One of Orton's brothers was also with them.

Preston didn't know if Orton had any daughters. If he did they never accompanied their parents and brothers on their moonshine buying trips. Most of the time Crompton would offer the Owsleys drinks before and after they had made a purchase. He always made a point of having a few jugs around for sampling as he put it. Orton's wife always joined the men in drinking rather than socializing with Mrs. Denham.

This particular day they had gotten an early start on their drinking. But Preston told us that he figured later that the Owsleys weren't really drinking near as much as they pretended they were. They must have waited to make a move against the Denham family until Crompton along with his three older sons and the oldest son's wife were all falling down drunk. The only member of the Denham family who didn't join in with the drinking besides Preston, of course, was his mother. She had her youngest boy in the house with her while she tended to some housework and cooking. Preston said that his mother never wanted him to be around the adults when they were drinking.

As they were drinking the people outside got louder and louder. It sounded to Ora like her husband was arguing with old man Owsley, as Orton was usually called. Then she had heard someone shouting or yelling and then there were some gun shots and screams. Looking out the open front door of the little cabin she was horrified to see one of the Owsleys standing over the body of her daughter-in-law. He was calmly wiping blood off a long knife while smiling and looking at the cabin. Stepping out on the porch and glancing quickly around the front yard she saw other bodies on the ground. None of her kinfolk were still standing. There was nothing she could do but retreat and try to save her youngest child.

Back inside she closed the door and propped a chair in front of it. However, she really had no illusions about a door hung on leather hinges being an effective barrier for more than a few seconds. But maybe those few seconds would be enough time to let her baby escape. With a death grip on the little boy's hand she ran across the cabin's floor, grabbing a cast-iron skillet as they passed the cook stove. She quickly used the heavy skillet to bust out the window frame from the sill and scraped away any fragments of glass remaining.

As I was listening I thought about how I had noticed that the window in the rear of the cabin had been pushed or rather knocked out from the inside. Now I knew it had been done so a terrified mother could save her little boy's life.

Once she had the broken glass scraped, away Preston's mother then sent him out through the window and told him not to stop running until he couldn't run no more. The scared little boy did as his mother told him.

As he was running he could hear the cabin's door being kicked down and then his mother's screams. She most likely had used the skillet as a weapon to try and delay her attackers as long as possible to provide Preston with more time to disappear amid the brush, boulders, and the thick stand of junipers that lay beyond the rear of the cabin.

The frightened youngster had spent his first night up on a ridge west of what had been his home. Luckily the boy had spent the previous two years roaming around this country pretty much on his own and as a result knew the easier climbing routes and even the game trails. He had watched the sun set and had remembered his parents talking about a town to the west. So he looked to where the sun disappeared and knew that was west. He studied the hills in that direction until he memorized one particular peak. Come the morning he would set out toward that land mark and repeat the process every day until he reached a city.

He would stop once in a while and scoop up a handful of berries beneath one of the abundant juniper trees and chew on them. He drank out of creeks that didn't have much more than a trickle. Sometimes all he could find was a stagnant pot hole along an otherwise dried-up stream.

The little boy was due for some luck and on the morning of the third day he got it. He stumbled into a woodcutter's camp in the foothills of the Hualapai Mountains. The wife of one of them took the boy into Kingman and left him at the police station. Not having any reports of a missing child and not being able to get any useful information from him they in turn deposited the little boy at the local orphanage. They figured that he would be claimed by his family before long. However, with his family dead he had stayed there until he was eighteen years old.

He hadn't talked much when he was first placed in the orphanage and he had known enough not to say what his last name was. If the killers knew about him they might try to kill him, too. The orphanage gave him the last name of Denton after he had started to say his name and then stopped after the first part ... "Den." The person taking it down finished it with "ton" and then asked if that was right and he nodded that it was. The people running the orphanage knew only that he had come from Oklahoma.

When he turned eighteen he was turned out of the orphanage. He hopped a freight train out of town and ended up spending a few years just riding the rails and doing day labor whenever he could find any to earn money for food and tobacco. He eventually got on as a trapper with the government and had moved around the West in that job.

Preston told my dad that soon after getting transferred back to Kingman he had made a point of talking to the man who had been the deputy sheriff that had been sent out to investigate the killing of his family. The man was by then retired and running a bar on Route 66 in Kingman. The former deputy had told him about burying the family. Through some casual questions Preston had learned which grave contained the older lady, as the man referred to her. That was Preston's mother.

After his talk with the old lawman, Preston had driven in as far as he could on the Holden Ranch and then hiked back to his family's old cabin. Since that first trip he had been out there a number of times to visit and to leave flowers on his mother's grave. He had checked around beforehand and learned that there wasn't much chance of running into anyone that might ask questions on the Holden Ranch.

The Owsleys had frequently visited his family prior to the murders and Preston had heard their names mentioned enough that he knew which members of the Owsley family had taken part in the robbery and murders. Preston wanted to see justice meted out. The killers were the parents, Orton and Wanda, three of their sons, a young girl named Sissy, and a brother of Orton's named Buddy. Preston didn't know the girl's last name and admitted that "Sissy" was most likely just a nickname. The sons were Garland and Harland who had been involved in the robberies and murders the previous summer, and an older brother named Leland.

"Sissy was Leland's girlfriend and hadn't been no more than fifteen or sixteen years old at the time they killed my family. I am not sure if she helped them that day but she was there and sure didn't do anything to stop it," Preston told us.

Looking over at me and then back at my dad, Preston said, "The way I remember, it Garland and Harland must have been not much older than your boy's age at the time. Members of that family must have been born killers. They sure knew how to rob and shoot people."

Mom who was also listening asked, "But I thought you said the Owsleys had four sons that were there that day?"

Preston answered, "Yes, there were four there, Mrs. Dean. However, their youngest boy, and I forget his name, must have only been around four or five years old then and was most likely napping, perhaps in the Owsleys' old car. He probably didn't know what his family was doing. Of course if he took after the others he is most likely guilty of other killings by now."

Preston went on and told my dad how he had been working for his agency for close to ten years and his job of hunting and trapping predators that preyed on livestock had allowed him to roam over much of Arizona and the neighboring states. He had been trying to get back to Kingman or Seligman so he could visit the graves of his family on a regular basis and see to their upkeep, plus he thought he might be able to learn something about the whereabouts of the rest of the Owsleys. He had been transferred to Kingman just a few months earlier after the man who had been there retired. Previously he had lived in western Nevada.

His new co-workers told him about the big excitement as they called it of the previous summer when the bank in Kingman had been robbed by the Owsley gang. He had heard about the posse my dad had gone on and how Jay had accounted for one of the gang who had made the mistake of trying to invade the ranch headquarters.

Preston said, "Roy, it's difficult to express just how pleased I was to hear how Harland had ended up at the bottom of Devil's Hole with a horse on top of him. Then hearing that Garland hung himself, damn that was even better news."

Since he had been back he had done a little checking but hadn't been able to find any information on Orton, Wanda, Leland, and Sissy, as well as the youngest boy whose name he couldn't remember. While he didn't hold the youngest son accountable for the killings due to his youth at the time he would sure be interested in finding him and see if he had witnessed the attack or later heard family members talking about it.

"Of course, Orton and Wanda might be dead by now," Preston said, and then added, "They weren't what you would call spring chickens back in '34." The mention of that year made me think of the calendar I had seen in the Denham's old cabin.

Preston asked my dad if he would ask Parker to check for information on the Owsleys. Perhaps the deputy would be able to contact other sheriff departments and police departments in other states.

"I will ask him the next time he's out here to do some checking, but I would be surprised if he hadn't already tried finding out all he could about the Owsleys," my dad told him.

Finishing his story Preston told my dad, mom and me that it was important for us not to tell anyone about him being a member of the Denham family. He said that he wanted someone he could trust to know the truth about what had happened to his family and his real name. It was especially important if something should happen to him. He figured that my dad was that person.

So it turned out that I had been right when I thought that the Owsleys might have been involved when I had first heard the story about the Denham family being killed from my dad. However, knowing that the Owsleys were capable of something like that sure didn't make me sleep better at nights.

They had most likely abandoned their homestead and fled the area after robbing and murdering the Denhams since they would have been aware that one member of the family had escaped and could identify them. But now they seemed to be drifting back. Some members of that no-good family had come back to the area the previous summer, others had been caught prowling around near the P Bar J's north boundary before Christmas, and another had killed a good old cowboy for the price of some cattle and an old pistol.

Even though Dad didn't change his mind about predator control, Preston became a regular visitor to the ranch. Whenever he was out working on an adjacent ranch he would come by to say hi and to have a cup of coffee and a piece of pie while he and my dad talked about stuff in general. Preston would also let him know if he had seen a spot on a boundary fence or gate that needed attention or if he had seen anyone suspicious on the ranch roads. It was tough for me not to share what he had told us with Lenny and Lynda, but I kept his identity a secret since I realized the danger to him if the wrong people should find out who he really was.

When the cows started dropping their calves in late February and early March we did have some losses from coyotes and an occasional mountain lion. However, Dad didn't get too excited about it. The losses were relatively minor. He didn't even mention them to Preston.

Dad was in the habit of scanning the sky whenever he was outside during the summers for buzzards circling a dead or dying animal. Occasionally it would turn out to be a calf or cow that was still alive and could be saved with a little medical attention. Or sometimes the buzzard would inadvertently lead him to a cow stuck in the mud of a drying stock tank. So whenever Dad saw them circling he would usually ride out to investigate or else send one of his cowboys to check.

Although, I never heard them referred to as anything except "buzzards" while I was growing up, these big scavengers were actually turkey vultures. They would leave in the fall and return usually in the early spring. As a result any animal that happened to get into a bad situation or die during the time that the buzzards were gone usually wouldn't be discovered except by chance.

One cold morning in late March of 1953 after the long, hard winter was finally winding down, I was headed toward the barn when I happened to glance off toward Heckler Canyon. It was small as southwest canyons go but there were a few good-sized cottonwoods along it. I could see that a few of the large, leafless trees were being used as roosts for buzzards. I noticed that they had spread their wings on their perches while facing east towards the rising sun trying to soak up the warmth of the rays.

Down at the barn Dad and Clay were busy removing the snow-plow from the front of the Massey-Harris Challenger tractor so they could put the road-grading blade back on it. The main road that connected the ranch to Route 66 had gotten badly rutted over the winter as had most of the other ranch roads. All of them would need to be graded.

I reported to Dad that the buzzards had returned. He was surprised and told me that he hadn't noticed yet that they had come back. Dad and Clay both said that the buzzards must have just recently made it back to our country. They both complimented me on my observation.

Later that day I made another observation concerning the buzzards. Since we had started using water buckets to trap and kill the numerous pack rats around the headquarters late the previous summer we had been dumping the drowned rats in a small wash out behind the barn. It hadn't taken the coyotes long to discover them. I noticed that the buzzards had also found the dead rats. A few of the buzzards were on the ground there at the wash helping themselves. It seemed that the coyotes now had competition for the easy meals that the drowned pack rats provided.

Jay had suggested the method of killing the pack rats the previous summer after they had built a nest under the hood of Mom's car while she was visiting the ranch. That was when she was still living in Winslow. Jay's friend, Lester Doggett on the Broken W Ranch, had told us how he was using five-gallon buckets to control pack rats as well as other rodents around his headquarters when we went out to his outfit last summer.

Lester had filled the buckets about halfway up with water and then placed them around places where rats and ground squirrels had taken up uninvited residence, like his barn. After they were in place he leaned a board or tree branch against the top lip of the bucket on roughly a 45-degree angle. The pieces of wood served as ladders for the little varmints to climb up on once they picked up the scent of the water. At the top the rodents would fall into the water and since it was only filled halfway up they wouldn't be able to escape and would drown.

It was pretty simple, didn't involve any poisons or expense other than the cost of the buckets, and it was pretty damn effective in getting rid of the destructive pack rats. They would chew into a vehicle's wiring if it was left parked for very long where they were abundant. In was an all too common problem around ranch headquarters and this method of control had mostly solved it for us.

The only downside was that seeing the half-filled buckets now served to remind Jay of his murdered friend. I had only met Lester that one time but he had left a lasting impression on me as a good cowboy. He was certainly missed by Jay.

A day of two after I had noticed the buzzards my dad had Lenny and me help him roll up some old barbed wire at the headquarters. As we were working he happened to look up and saw several buzzards circling off to the northwest of the headquarters. Of course he was curious about what the big scavengers were so interested in.

"Jeff," he said pointing off towards the northwest, "See those buzzards over there? Why don't you and Lenny saddle up a couple horses and go check it out for me? I would like to know what those birds have found out there."

With the warming weather the past few weeks we hadn't had to go out in the mornings to break ice on the stock tanks and troughs at all so we hadn't been spending much time in the saddle. This sounded like it would be a nice leisurely outing for Lenny and me. Truthfully, rolling up old rusted barbed wire wasn't much fun. I had gotten several scratches and small cuts on my arms and I had even managed to rip a few small holes in the leather gloves that Lynda had given me for Christmas.

Likewise, Lenny was ready for something else to do besides rolling wire. "Sure thing, Dad! We will ride out and take a look," I had quickly answered for both of us

We then laid down the ends of the old wire and started off toward the corral to saddle up. Down at the barn we each grabbed small buckets and dipped them in a bin of oats. As usual we used the oats as lures or bait to get the horses to come to us rather than having to chase after them. Once the half dozen or so horses that were in the corral had gathered around us we picked out a couple to ride and slipped halters on them and led them back to the barn where the tack was kept.

We set the buckets on the ground in front of them while Lenny and I went to get the saddles and blankets and set them out in the sun for a few minutes. Since the horses would be carrying us several miles back and forth a meal of oats would be good for them before they started working. It was similar to filling a vehicle's gas tank before starting out on a trip.

While the horses were eating and the blankets and saddles warmed up a little in the sun on a corral rail, I went up to my house and made a couple sandwiches for us to take along on the ride. Before long Lenny and I were heading out of the headquarters towards the northwest while taking little verbal jabs at each other.

Lenny was still kidding me about how I had fallen into the stock tank while we were breaking ice before Christmas and we had to go back to my house so I could change into dry socks and boots. Every once in a while he would even bring up the big crash back in August when I had damaged Bucky and had required a trip to the doctor in Seligman for my injuries.

Being kidded about either of those incidents was sort of wearing thin. I was lucky that Lenny hadn't been with me when I fell off my bike while riding the pipeline or else he probably would have been calling me "clumsy", or worse. I didn't need to give him any additional ammunition, that was for sure. For my part, I had started referring to Lenny as either a "city boy" or "city slicker" depending on my mood, since the Howards had been spending more and more time in Flagstaff since New Year's.

We headed south on a ranch road before taking another two-tracker west that led past Catfish Tank. Travelling on the roads wasn't as much fun as striking out cross country on horseback but it was faster, as well as safer. The horses were less likely to stumble, fall, or step into a hole left by the plentiful burrowing animals. Among other things, badgers and rock squirrels were fairly common on the ranch.

I had been really pleased earlier that morning that even though it had been cold, the sky was clear. I didn't want to have to deal with anymore damn snow storms. The cottonwoods that the buzzards were using for roost trees were covered with green buds ... another sign besides the return of the buzzards that spring had arrived.

As it got on towards late morning, even with a slight breeze it was shirt-sleeve weather. The sun was shining in a mostly clear sky. I had been happy to hang up my winter coat in the closet a few days before. For today Lenny and I just had light denim jackets tied behind our saddles on the outside chance that the wind might pick up later in the afternoon. But we hadn't travelled very far past Catfish Tank when threatening-looking clouds started moving in and we started thinking we might have made a mistake not bringing along our heavy coats. That time of year the weather could change mighty fast.

And it seemed to do exactly that after we had travelled far enough that it wasn't feasible to return to the headquarters for warmer duds. While there had been warm sunshine that morning, by noon the sun was mostly staying behind the clouds that had seemed to form or move in pretty damn quick. The clouds, coupled with temperatures no warmer than the upper 40s, and a cold wind that seemed to come out of nowhere also around noon and was getting progressively stronger all came together to make it mighty uncomfortable being out most of that day perched on a saddle.

We both reached behind our saddles about the same time and untied the rawhide strings that were holding our jackets. Doing it fairly slowly so as not to spook our horses we slipped them on while riding. The denim didn't provide a lot of warmth but at least it cut the wind a little. I sure wished that I had my winter coat that I had been way too anxious to hang up in the closet for the season.

As we were rding along we kept glancing off towards the buzzards and angling the horses accordingly. Having left the ranch road west of Catfish Tank we weaved through a fairly thick stand of junipers on a flat that seemed to be getting rockier the farther north we rode.

Finally it got to the point that it was too rocky to safely continue on with the horses. I didn't want to have a crash in those rocks with a horse, and I sure didn't want to have to tell my dad that my horse was lying out there with a broken leg.

Turning to Lenny who was also looking out over the rocks covering the ground toward the north I said, "I guess we best tie the horses to a juniper and continue on foot."

"Yeah, I was thinking pretty much the same thing, Jeff," he replied.

In that country we didn't have to go out of our way to find a juniper. You could say that they were usually pretty handy. Soon the reins of our horses were looped around a couple of low branches of an old alligator juniper and we were scrambling over rocks while keeping track of the buzzards that were circling over something on the ground. Before leaving the horses I had grabbed a pair of binoculars from my saddlebags. I figured once we reached a high point in the rocks we could scan the country with them.

It was nice to be out of the saddle and walking around. Nothing is colder on a windy day than sitting up in a saddle atop a horse. It's especially true if you aren't properly dressed or prepared for it like the two of us that day.

We had both gotten cold during our ride, and climbing around on the rocks served to warm us up a little. Plus, the wind didn't seem quite as bad among the big rocks and boulders. However, we both still felt cold.

The previous summer we hadn't gotten out to this rocky area to look around so it was new to us. Normally we would both be happy to be out doing some exploring. But Lenny didn't like being cold any better than I did. Our conversation as we were climbing around and over the rocks and boulders pretty much centered on wishing we had bought along something heavier than the light-weight denim jackets.

"Lenny let's try to find out what those buzzards have found to eat as fast as possible so we can get on back to the headquarters ... and out of this damn wind," I said.

"Sounds good to me, Jeff," Lenny quickly replied as he buttoned the top button on his jacket. I had already done that on mine. Seemed we were both thinking along the same lines.

Although scrambling around on and between the boulders as we continued heading north warmed us up a little more we were both ready to head back to the barn. So the stage was set for us to miss making a grisly discovery that day as twelve-year-olds.

Standing at the top of a particularly large granite boulder I looked off about a hundred feet farther north and saw several buzzards on the ground picking at what appeared to be a couple of dead coyotes. Other buzzards were in the sky circling. Taking the binoculars out of their battered leather case I took a look through them. It appeared that the buzzards had found two dead animals that I now recognized to be dogs rather than coyotes. From what was left of them one looked like a beagle and the other might have been a German Sheppard.

Lowering the binoculars before handing them to Lenny so he could take a look I was wondering what in the hell was a beagle doing out in this country. Clearly neither of the dogs belonged on the P Bar J or even any of the neighboring ranches as far as I knew and must have wandered in from the north. They could have gotten separated from folks out looking for the Owsleys' bank loot, or simply been dumped out on the rangeland by city people who got tired of taking care of them.

Stray dogs were a continuous problem on ranches since city folks seemed to think that ranches would be good homes for their unwanted pets. They must not have realized that the dogs wouldn't be able to survive on their own and would be considered food by animals such as coyotes, mountain lions, and bears. A relatively small dog like a beagle wouldn't have much of a chance at all. Untrained city dogs weren't any use to a rancher and some of the bigger breeds had even been known to kill calves ... until the rancher could catch up to them when he had a .30-06 within reach.

As Lenny surveyed the scene with the binoculars we discussed what might have happened and decided that something, either a mountain lion or a pack of coyotes, had attacked the beagle and the big German Sheppard had tried to help it.

Neither of us was too interested in getting any closer to the dead dogs. We could smell a pretty foul odor from our perch up in the rocks and assumed it was coming from the unlucky dogs. It would be years before we found out that we had been wrong about the source of that awful smell. At the time we had no idea what a dead human body smelled like.

Although we didn't know it at the time, in a low area another twenty or so feet beyond the dead dogs, and shielded from our view by a couple of large rocks, lay what at the time would have been the partially decomposed body of a man. We also couldn't see the buzzards that were undoubtedly paying him a visit.

Next to the body was a high-powered rifle, equipped with a scope. A booted foot was wedged tightly in a crack or rather, a crevice, between a couple of rocks. As the man was hurriedly trying to make his way through the rocks, during a cold December night, he had stepped into the opening. The bones in the trapped foot had snapped as he fell. Most likely he froze to death that first night.

Since it was cold and windy that day and Lenny and I were in a hurry to get back to the headquarters the body would lie out on the rocks for almost five years before it was discovered. I would be the one who found it while trying to figure out if I had really heard a shot when Jay's horse fell and if it was connected to what at the time was just thought of as just another ranching accident. We were to find out differently.

We would also find out that the Owsley clan and their gang hadn't forgotten about their member who had been shot by Jay at the P Bar J's headquarters, or Dad's role in the posse that had chased the gang. The nighttime chase had resulted in the death of another family member, and the capture of two others. Dad's later killing of James Owsley Johnston on the mesa out on the Broken W would have undoubtedly been known to them later on too.

They also held a grudge against Deputy Parker for the Owsley that he had arrested near their old homestead and for the one he shot and killed. Hell, most likely they even blamed the deputy for the uncle that was killed by the exploding shotgun. The Owsleys sure hadn't forgotten about the missing money from their relatives' crime spree either.

***

It turned out that I got lucky concerning that stolen bull. Less than a week after I had reported it stolen the rustlers tried moving it through a livestock auction near Prescott along with several other head of cattle that they had obtained in the same manner. While checking over the lot a livestock inspector recognized that the brands on the cattle had been altered and that it had been done recently. The brands were still fresh. The bills of sale the thieves had were equally questionable in the inspector's opinion.

I was notified that the bull had been recovered and I made arrangements to have it transported back to the ranch. I had taken a truck and trailer down to pick it up. While the bull was being loaded the manager of the stockyard and I got to talking about the price of cattle. It wasn't particularly good at the time, plus the cost of everything else was going up such as fuel, supplemental feed … and the list goes on and on.

Trying to end the conversation on a happier note he repeated an old joke … that unfortunately sure seemed to have more truth in it every time I told it or heard it from someone else.

He said, "These old boys were rustling cattle and would even break into the rancher's storerooms and steal loads of feed … and damn, don't you know that by the time the bastards managed to sell those cows they wound up losing money on the deal."

Soon I had the bull back and that episode was behind me. However, I did often think back to the day I had spent out driving around and checking waters looking for it. The smells of the garlic-seasoned turkey leg that day had brought back a lot of pleasant memories of that first holiday season and winter that I had spent on the P Bar J Ranch.

A few days after I had returned with my rustled bull a blizzard packing cold temperatures and strong winds hit the ranch. I had been following the weather reports with a sense of growing concern. They were predicting anywhere from a foot to two of snow, and possibly even more. I was thinking about that forecast snowfall and knew that with the strong winds to go with it the drifts would be much deeper.

The snow started falling that night before I went to bed. I awoke a few times during the night to the sound of howling winds and thought about my livestock out in the storm.

In the morning a few hours before dawn I was brought out of my troubled sleep by a loud crashing noise. Jumping out of bed I tried switching on a nearby wall switch. Nothing happened and the room was still pitch black. A year or so earlier I had had a solar-powered set-up installed to provide electricity for the houses and other buildings at the headquarters. I had gotten to an age where I just didn't want to have to fool around with the diesel generators to provide the power any longer. I had gotten plumb tired of working on that old diesel motor. And up to right then the solar unit had been dependable and trouble free.

Plus, the added benefit of going solar was not having to hear that diesel running, even though it wasn't much compared to the god awful noise that a hit and miss engine gave off. Such were my thoughts as I made my way through the house in total darkness, being careful not to stub a toe, to the kitchen where I kept a flashlight and a couple of Coleman lanterns.

I opened drawers as I came to them and felt around in each one for a flashlight. I found one in the third drawer that I searched. Switching the light on I was relieved to see a reasonably strong beam of light coming from it. The thought occurred to me that they were making batteries better nowadays then back when I was using them in a Roy Rogers lantern or in the headlight of my Black Phantom.

Using the flashlight I rechecked the drawers for matches. Finding a package, I next went to the pantry off the rear of the kitchen and got a Coleman lantern down from a top shelf. I checked the fuel reservoir and found it almost full. The mantles appeared to be intact. I thought so far so good.

Back in the kitchen I set the lantern on the table and pumped it several times to build up pressure and then lit the mantles. Soon the kitchen was lit by the strong light given off by the white gas-fueled lantern.

I am not sure why the thought hit me at the time but I couldn't help thinking that a Coleman lantern was sure a hell of a lot more efficient than a shadowgee. Then that got me thinking about the old shadowgee that we found in Lost Cabin Canyon and how Lenny and I had made our own shadowgee in the summer of '52. We had used it to provide light on a campout.

Those thoughts of that long ago summer made me smile as I slipped on a heavy coat and stuck the flashlight into one of its big front pockets. Next I grabbed a pair of lace-up work boots and sat down on a chair next to the kitchen table and put them on. Near the rear door I found a pair of old rubber overshoes to put on over my boots. Then by lantern light I headed out to see what had caused the failure of my solar-powered generator.

The sight that greeted me was almost otherworldly. Snow was drifted up in places several feet high just as I had dreaded might happen and it was still falling and being blown around by the strong winds. Neither the snow nor the winds showed any sign of slowing down anytime soon. But the most eerie sight illuminated by the lantern's light were the bare, gray branches rising from the huge prone trunk of a hundred or so year-old cottonwood tree that had been brought down probably by a combination of a buildup of snow on its branches and the winds.

It had come crashing down in the space between the solar unit and the house, taking out all of the power lines with it. I had thought about the old tree falling before and had been thinking of having it removed, but the storm had done it before I could get around to it. At least it had missed the house. That sure was something to be grateful for. As big as that tree was it could have pretty much flattened the house.

Getting the power back on would be the first thing to do after it got light enough to work outside. Luckily I had a good supply of extra electrical wire down at the tool shed. I then trudged down to the bunkhouse and woke up my hired hands and told them what had happened with the power lines and about the other work that lay ahead of them that day due to the storm. I thought of Dad all those years ago telling Clay and Johnny pretty much the same thing. From what I had seen between the house and the bunkhouse this storm was worse than the one in late '52 had been ... and this son-of-a-bitch wasn't over yet.

The cattle and horses out on the range would not be able to reach forage through the thick blanket of snow. We would have to get feed out to them, clear away snow, and chop holes in the ice on troughs and tanks so they could get water.

Winter blizzards of this magnitude were not real frequent in Arizona but they happened often enough that it was a good idea to keep a supply of hay on hand for emergency feeding. The hay also came in handy during the frequent droughts.

I had laid in a good supply of native hay and had it stored in a barn that had been added just for that purpose down below the main barn and corrals. Hay had to be kept out of the weather before it was used to keep it from getting wet and then moldy. Hay left out in the open would also get eaten by the goddamn elk long before it could be used for cattle feed.

I even had a snow plow attachment that could be bolted to one of the four-wheel-drive ranch pickups to help in getting through this kind of snow accumulation. The trucks could also easily pull a trailer full of hay. Even though that kind of rig would move a lot faster than the old Massey-Harris Challenger that my dad had used, our day would still be long and hard before feed had been taken out to all of the livestock and the power lines had been repaired and all the other work that needed doing was done. The other work that would be necessary would include working on getting the main ranch roads cleared. But that could wait a day or two.

Just like the big snow at the tail end of 1952 had brought all of that good spring feed for the pasturage cattle Dad had put on the ranch for some extra income I knew this one would also be beneficial for the forage. It would sure provide a good start to the spring growth. However, that knowledge didn't make the snow I was shoveling off the walks that morning any lighter or the wind any warmer. Also, I still needed to get out the chainsaw and start in on the old cottonwood that had fallen. And there was the snow on the roofs that had to be dealt with before they started collapsing.

Dammed, if it wasn't going to be a long winter day ... and the way it was shaping up I would be out in the damn snow all day. I found myself wondering if there was any more turkey left in the freezer. I could almost smell the garlic.

The Author

Patrick H. Boles was born in Owosso, Michigan and grew up in the nearby small town of Corunna. He arrived in the Southwest courtesy of the U.S. Air Force when he was assigned to a base in Albuquerque, New Mexico. He received a B.S. degree in biology from Eastern New Mexico University and an M.S. degree, also in biology, from New Mexico State University. He has worked as an environmental specialist, biologist, ecologist, and rangeland manager for government agencies in Wyoming, New Mexico, and Arizona.

The author has spent over 20 years working with longtime ranchers in Arizona and listening to their stories of ranch life and "the old days." He has spent many days out roaming over ranches and backcountry afoot, in four-wheel-drive vehicles, and on horseback. He filled several journals with notes on the field work and the conversations with ranchers/old-timers as well as on his own experiences out on the ranches. This firsthand experience was drawn upon when writing the P Bar J books in order to give a realistic feeling to the setting (based on a real cattle ranch with the name changed), events, and characters.

He lives in the Southwest with his wife where he is working on other book projects (both fiction and non-fiction), including the third, and final, P Bar J Ranch book, and a Southwestern Field Journal. They have two grown children.

Author's email: muchocanones72@yahoo.com

Made in United States
North Haven, CT
13 September 2022

24091887R00143